hope

in the Rain

Sandy Sinnett

5 Prince Publishing, LLC

This is a fictional work. The names, characters, incidents, places, and locations are solely the concepts and products of the author's imagination or are used to create a fictitious story and should not be construed as real.

5 PRINCE PUBLISHING AND BOOKS, LLC
PO Box 16507
Denver, CO 80216
www.5PrinceBooks.com

ISBN 13: 978-1-63112-195-1 ISBN 10: 1-63112-195-2
HOPE IN THE RAIN
SANDY SINNETT
Copyright Sandy Sinnett 2017
Published by 5 Prince Publishing

Photo Credit: Front Cover Viola Estrella

Any opinions expressed by the author in this work are not necessarily the opinions of 5 Prince Publishing, LLC

Second Edition/Second Printing MAY 2017 Printed U.S.A.
5 PRINCE PUBLISHING AND BOOKS, LLC

Dedication

To Mrs. Laura Tinnin-Lewis, my soul-sister in Christ, one of my dearest girlfriends in life, and a strong, beautiful, breast cancer survivor. Thank you for blessing me with your friendship and your life. I love you, sister!

Acknowledgments

To Jesse, my oldest—thank you for designing my first book cover ever. It will always be my favorite. I love you!

To my parents—for having me, loving me, and instilling in me a love of reading from a very young age.

To Kelle—thank you for your friendship, girl. And thank you for the many coffee chats and movie nights, and for listening to me go on and on about this book and all the drama that came with it. You are a very special blessing to me! Love ya!

To my fellow Oly Fedders, and especially to Abby who jok-ingly told me to write my stories down for fun—thank you for your unfailing support and encouragement. I appreciate you all more than you know.

In Memory of Gregg J. Haugland, fellow author and a dear friend. Gregg mentored me and pushed me to be a better writer every day. He shared his knowledge with me, and his novels, which kept me inspired. I will remember him always.

hope

in the Rain

going home

Gulley washer. That's what most Midwesterners refer to as a torrential downpour of rain coming down in thick, white sheets. It falls so hard that it's nearly impossible to see your hand in front of your face. Yet there I was standing right in the middle of one like a little girl, drenched from head to toe and breathing in the sweet smell of the warm, summer rain.

Thunderstorms were one of my favorite things about visiting my Illinois hometown. When I was much smaller, I used to think the thunder was God moving his furniture or bowling a few sets. Now it's just a reminder that God is always present, and it makes me realize that my life is in his capable hands.

The rain also smelled better there than it did in Seattle. Instead of oil on asphalt, it smelled like freshly mowed grass and sunshine stirring around together. I remember the first gulley washer I experienced was during a family vacation; I couldn't have been more than four years old. The rain came down so hard it stung the surface of my skin. Water started rising, forming puddles in the grass all around our camper, and then my dad picked me up, put me in a cardboard box, and pushed me around under the awning. The rain was cold and blew sideways but I didn't care. In that moment, that little box took me to a place far, far away; I could go anywhere in the world.

Since then, I've always found a sense of hope in the rain, how it washes away the old and makes everything fresh and new again. Maybe that's why I love living in the Pacific Northwest so much. "You'd better get in here, Laci. It's almost time to go!" My mom yelled from the front porch. She was inside canning strawberry preserves—the smell alone made me gain ten pounds!

Growing up there wasn't all that bad. We definitely enjoyed eating from our garden all summer. My favorite meal was home-grown sliced tomatoes, green beans with baby new potatoes, cucumbers and vinegar, and sweet corn on the cob. It didn't get any better than that. Although I was terribly bored there as a teenager and we had no neighbors except an adventurous girl that lived next door, I have always considered it home.

After losing my husband a few years ago, going back there gave me more joy than I ever thought possible.

All good things would come to an end however. My ten days of vacation were up and I was heading back to Seattle. The kids were staying another week. They didn't get much time with their grandparents, and I thought it would be nice for them to have one more week together. With Andrew gone, finding time to visit was difficult to say the least. My new position at the bank took up most of my time and anything left over got sucked up with carting the kids to their activities, keeping up with laundry, cooking the same boring meals over and over, and staring at the dirty dishes as they piled up in the sink. Such a glamorous life I led!

I tried my best to plan fun outings for us, but eventually we were pulled in a hundred different directions. Todd, sixteen, had his youth group, and that was the only place he wanted to be. Emma was my ten-year-old drama diva going on twenty. Between Girl Scouts and violin, she spent her time learning new crafts from YouTube and making colorful messes at my kitchen table. Travis was seven and lived to play baseball, so naturally we were constantly running to his games or practice. And Evan had his own life now. He would be twenty-two in a few months and with college and his reserve duty, I hardly saw him anymore. He stopped in from time to time to do laundry and borrow the big screen TV, but never stayed long enough for me. I was glad he could spend some time with us before he headed back to school, but I already missed him. Our crazy routine felt endless at times.

After a quick change of clothes, I packed my bags and loaded them in the car, then said my goodbyes.

"Come over here and give me my hugs, kids! Be good for your grandparents and have fun okay?" I said as they tackled me with hugs and kisses.

Evan held on pretty tight with his bear hug and whispered in my ear, "Go on a date while you're home, Mom. It's been almost three years. It's okay and you deserve to find someone again."

I smiled as the tears well up in my eyes, but I quickly wiped them away. "I have all the men I need in my life with you three boys, trust me. Thanks for looking out for me though."

I climbed into the van, my emotions raw, and Dad and I headed for the airport. We shared small talk for a few miles but mostly, we rode on in silence while listening to his favorite country music stations. My dad had had a hard time knowing what to say since Andrew died. I guessed his heart was so heavy for me and the kids that he'd rather not say anything. I didn't mind though. It was just as hard for me, and it usually ended up with mascara running down my face.

Andrew and I would have celebrated twenty-five years this coming October. We met in college and married young, only in our early twenties. It seemed like yesterday. The fog in Seattle that morning he died was unusually thick and dense, making the roads quite slick. Andrew was on one of his routes for work when a semi-truck driver lost control of his rig, and it skidded across the highway, hitting Andrew's truck head on. I got the call at work, and my world had never been the same since then. The kids and I had been in and out of counseling, and I even moved them into a private school for more one-on-one attention, but nothing helped. For a time, we stayed in the same house where Andrew and I loved each other and our family lived and laughed together, but that made things worse. I thought we would want to be where he walked and talked, where we opened gifts at Christmas, and where he played his guitar on the back porch. But his memory was everywhere—in every blooming flower we planted, every stain we couldn't remove, and the never-quite-right yellow paint on the kitchen walls. Oddly enough, these memories were part of the problem. None of us could move forward. So I made one of the hardest decisions of my life, and we moved to a small town about an hour south of Seattle. Eventually, the kids settled into new schools, made new friends, and got more involved with the distractions of youth. I found a great job, and we joined an amazing church. We started laughing again, and it felt good.

Going back home for the summer was good medicine though. We swam, relaxed, joked, and laughed with our family and friends. It was wonderful not to be looked at as the "family who lost their dad" for once. I was looking forward to my week alone without the kids in some ways and dreading it in others—worried that the quietness of the house would cause my sadness to return. But I had some wonderful gal pals at work who had promised to keep me busy and get me out of the house for a girls' night or a day at the beach.

We entered the St. Louis International Airport and made our way to the departure area to unload. Rain continued to pour down, along with my tears that spilled onto dad's shirt as I hugged his neck tight.

"It's okay to have fun this week, sweetie. You know we'll take good care of the kids."

"I know, Dad." Despite his faults, my dad had always been my rock, although I didn't realize it or appreciate it until the last few years.

I gathered my bags, checked in for my flight, and then headed to the nearest Starbucks for a much needed mocha fix. Boarding time came pretty fast, and I stepped into my designated line. I love to people-watch at the airport—so many interesting faces, tattoos, hair styles, and outfits. I looked through the boarding lines at my fellow travelers. They were fairly normal folks for the most part, but there were also a few I prayed to God wouldn't end up anywhere near me on that flight. Secretly, I hoped for an empty row. *Ugh*. If only I could *be* that lucky! But from the looks of it, that wasn't a good probability. While I scanned the crowds however, I noticed a man walk up to my boarding area. He stopped and rested against the handle of his carry-on bag, probably waiting to board his flight. Now he was someone I would *definitely* enjoy sitting next to on my flight! He casually looked around and didn't seem to be in any real hurry. I was glad because I couldn't take my eyes off him.

He stood rather tall with a rugged, stocky build, sandy-brown hair, brown eyes and a kind, tan face; very handsome indeed. But my favorite part by far, was his neatly cut goatee. He looked to be about my age, or so I hoped. To put it mildly, I'd have to say he was downright *yummy*! He gave off an air of strength and confidence, and looked quite nice in his stylish clothes: long khaki shorts and a dark blue polo shirt that made his brown eyes stand out. If I had to guess, I'd say he was a business man of some sort—probably executive management, financially sound, and most likely had a love for golf. He appeared genuine and personable as he smiled at the older woman who stood next to him. I imagined he also smelled as good as he looked, which was one of my biggest weaknesses–a man wearing nice cologne!

I felt guilty for even thinking about him that way, despite the fact that my parents, my pastor, my kids, and even my in-laws were all encouraging me to move forward and not be afraid to look for love again. Somehow, it just felt wrong. Surely there was some specific amount of time that I was required to mourn before

I was allowed to be happy again; I just wish I knew when that was. Still, I looked back at him, and a smile spread across my face. My row was called and I headed down the walkway onto the plane. My seat was located in the middle, naturally. The passenger next to the window was already seated; she seemed like a quiet person and I was happy about that. The seat to my left stayed empty for quite some time, so I started to get my hopes up that it would remain that way.

That was when I looked up and saw him. *Him!* He was on my plane! He walked down the aisle looking for his seat, and I just stared at him—mentally willing him to look at me. It was one of those moments when that Jedi-mind-trick would've come in real handy. On the inside, I screamed "Sit by me, sit by me," but I knew I wouldn't get that lucky. I always got stuck sitting next to the big, hairy, sweaty guy or the sweet, antique, chatty lady.

Then he stopped at my aisle, looked down at the empty seat, and smiled at me and said, "This one must be mine." And then he sat down next to me.

I was his alright; no doubt about that!

seat 16d

I tucked my Zune into my hot pink carry-on bag, settled into my seat, and put on my seatbelt to prepare for takeoff. As he did the same, his shoulder brushed against mine. In that moment, I was close enough to breathe him in, and I was right. He did smell as good as he looked! Better than I imagined!

"Hi," he whispered and smiled. My cheeks were burning hot, no doubt glowing the darkest shade of red in the color wheel.

"Hi," I replied, returning his smile. I prayed he wouldn't notice my obvious blushing. His deep brown eyes had me mesmerized, and I didn't know what to say next. I felt like a teenager on a first date. He pulled an iPad out of his bag and turned it off. I was a little disappointed that he might use it on the entire flight since I had hoped to get to know him. The plane careened toward the sky, and my rapidly accelerating heart rate followed suit. It pounded so hard I thought it would leap out of my chest. I was sure he could hear it over the roaring engines. I closed my eyes and tried to lower it before I went into cardiac arrest right there next to him. Once we were in the air, the seatbelt light went off, and I turned on my device to find some music.

Then out of my peripheral vision, I saw his handsome face turn towards me. "Is Phoenix home for you?" he said.

I was so excited that he spoke to me that it took me a

second to snap back to reality and respond. I smiled and said, "No,

um, I'm from Washington, outside of Seattle. I'm just passing through on a layover. What about you?"

The only words that came to mind were '*holy cow*'! He was not only extremely good-looking, but his deep voice and rich southern accent dripped with notes of sweet tea and honey in the summer. I knew in a hot second that he was probably from one of the Carolinas. He sounded like my dear friend and neighbor Sheryl; she was from South Carolina, and I always loved listening to her talk.

"I'm from a little town outside of Raleigh-Durham, North Carolina. I'm traveling on business. My brother and I just closed on the purchase of our very own winery last week. Now I'm out visiting some other wineries around the country to learn more about the business and help get ours up and running."

My mouth dropped open a little as he mentioned his new winery. He was so far out of my league! I knew nothing about wine or grapes and was certain I would crash and burn if I even tried to pretend like I did. I stuttered in my reply. "Wow, that's impressive. Congratulations! What's the name of your winery?"

"Well, we haven't actually named it yet. That's on the preverbal 'to-do' list of things we need to accomplish pretty soon. It's kind of hard to pick a name; I want it to mean something. Wineries are usually named after their owner, the land that surrounds it, or sometimes even the town. There is a lot to learn and we're both a little overwhelmed with the work ahead of us. I'm excited to get started, though." His gorgeous brown eyes twinkled in the light coming through the window. It was like watching a kid talking about his shiny new toy. "I've always wanted to visit the Seattle area but haven't had an opportunity to get up that way yet. I've been reading about all the award-winning vineyards and wineries up there. Y'all have hundreds of 'em! It must be a perfect climate up there for growing grapes," he said.

My immediate goal was to keep this conversation going for as long as possible. The more I could listen to his sweet voice the

better! I couldn't help but laugh when we got to talking about the weather.

"Well, I'm not sure about that. The climate where I live is mostly wet, but it's worth it to experience one of our summers. We have the most beautiful, clear blue skies you've ever seen and the best part is that there's no humidity." And I would *love* to be his reason to visit Washington and see one of those summers.

"Does it really rain as much as everyone says?"

"I suppose so, but honestly, I don't mind. I think the rain brings in good things, plus you get used to it after a while. I had no idea there were so many wineries nearby. Looks like you'll just have to come up and visit one sometime." I smiled and blushed the second I said the words.

Nodding his head up and down, he replied, "I just might do that." A sweet smile appeared on his face. "So, what do you do?" "Oh, something far less glamorous than winemaking, I assure you. I'm a marketing coordinator for a local bank in Olympia. I plan events, work with charitable organizations, keep our website up to date, things like that. I'm one of the fortunate few who actually love my job. Actually, if you've ever seen the movie *It's a Wonderful Life*, you've basically seen a glimpse of the bank where I work. We even call our customers by their first name, believe it or not," I said with enthusiasm, then realized how *fast* I had been talking–he probably thought I was crazy!

"I watch that movie every Christmas with my mom. It's her favorite. And I can definitely tell you enjoy your job," he said with a soft laugh.

"Yeah, sorry. I get a little passionate when I talk about it." "It's quite all right; that kind of passion is refreshing. Besides,

you're a little walking advertisement; I'm sure they love that." He simply smiled at me, and in that moment, I realized I was completely hooked.

"So, tell me about Raleigh, or is it Raleigh-Durham? What's it like?"

"It's Raleigh and Durham, two separate cities, but where I'm from we like to merge the two as one. Not sure why. I think it's a nice place, though. I get up there a couple times a week. It's your typical big city, full of history, amazing museums, great restaurants, and of course, we have the best wine in the country, but I'm a little biased."

"That sounds like Seattle. I love to visit the city, but I don't get up there as often as I'd like. I'm not really sure about their wine selection though. I don't know that much about wine in general. The only wine I drink is a late harvest Riesling, mostly because it's sweet and I just like sweet things." That sounded really lame so I quickly changed the subject. "I suppose being from North Carolina you're a Dukes fan too?" I asked. I tried to show off my limited sports knowledge in an effort to impress him. At that point I realized I was officially flirting and thought I'd better draw it back a few notches.

"Uh-oh, now that's hittin' below the belt," he said in the sweetest southern drawl. "I'm just kidding," he laughed then continued. "Actually, I don't really follow basketball much. I'm more of a minor league baseball fan myself. My favorite team is the Hickory Crawdads. Ever heard of them?" he asked. I couldn't help but laugh. The name cracked me up!

"Um, no, I don't believe I have. Are they really named after crawdads? Seriously?"

"Hey now, don't go diggin' on my Crawdads," he said. "Don't y'all have a team named after reindeer or something?"

I laughed, but I was impressed that he'd heard of them. It felt really good to laugh again. He earned big points for being funny! "That's kind of close. They're actually called the Rainiers. I think they were named after Mount Rainier or Rainier cherries or both. I'm not really sure to be honest." I was actually curious now, so I made a mental note to Google it later.

"Oh okay. Well, that's not much better." And he laughed along with me.

My mind was filled with questions that I wanted to ask, but I was afraid I might bother him. I wanted to learn more about his new winery. It was exciting to know someone about to embark on such an incredible adventure. I decided to use what little wine knowledge I had from my past and hoped that would be enough to keep him talking.

"I used to work for the food and beverage director at the Adam's Mark hotel years ago. One of his jobs was to help the chef pick out the wines to serve in our restaurant each night. They let me help taste a few once. Mostly I thought they were all bitter, and as I recall, I didn't like any of them," I said, embarrassed at my confession of being so illiterate when it came to his field of expertise.

"I'm sorry they did that. That's probably the worst way to experience wine for the first time! Did they even have you taste different foods with each one?" He sounded somewhat miffed on my behalf.

"Not that I remember. I just sipped one glass after another.

But where would I go if I wanted to learn more about wine?"

To my delight, we talked for the next few hours, discussing everything from different wines to pairing wine with food. That led to other things like where we grew up and even what our favorite foods and board games were. We learned that we both loved Christmas. At one point, he hinted to a recent family tragedy which caused him to rethink his life and ultimately buy the winery. I could tell it was something quite personal, so I refrained from asking anything more. We went back and forth with questions and small talk, laughing at this and that. The time flew by, at least for me. For the most part, our conversation was kept to simple, random things. I couldn't help but notice though how comfortable he was talking to me. I liked that. I hung on to every word, nearly swooning every time he said "ya'll." He talked about his son Caleb who loved to surf, and I bragged about my daughter Emma, the aspiring artist and potentially the next Food Network star. And then I told him about my wonderful boys— all three of them. In retrospect, I probably should have thought more carefully about sharing the whole "I have four kids" thing. He was sure to lose interest in me now, if there was any to begin with! But he didn't seem to care. Now I was the one growing more comfortable with him.

"I was actually in Phoenix once. I remember eating at an amazing Mexican restaurant with a gorgeous outdoor patio. There were strings of white lights hanging all around. It was so beautiful, and the food was great too!"

His face lit up. "Well, if I see it I'll be sure to give it a try. I like to visit a new restaurant every time I travel so I can go back home and try to recreate the recipes. I enjoy cooking almost as much as much as winemaking."

Why did he have to say that? Images of him cooking in a big gourmet kitchen now drifted through my mind, and it was all I could do to stay focused on the conversation at hand. That wasn't good. I felt myself being drawn to him more and more with each passing minute and the chances of him ever remembering me after our flight were not in my favor! What was I doing?

"I enjoy it too. I cook a lot with my daughter Emma. She is constantly watching the food channel and then wants to make everything she's seen." The memory of Emma standing on her little wooden stool trying to see above the counter made me smile. "That's great you can share that with her. It sounds like you're

a good mom." It felt so natural talking with him. At this rate, we could've talked all night. He was truly genuine and so kind; I could see his true personality shine through the longer we talked and I longed for more. He had me completely charmed! During our conversation, he never mentioned a wife or girlfriend, so I was optimistic that there wasn't one. I supposed he could be with- holding that little tidbit of information just to be nice. Naturally, I never mentioned my marital status, or lack thereof. It's just not normal bringing that up to a total stranger. As far as a conversation starter though, it would certainly be memorable, *'Oh by the way, I'm a widow. Want a piece of gum?'*

After thinking about gum, it sounded good, so I took a package out of my bag and pulled out a piece. Without missing a beat, I held the package out and offered him a piece like it was something I had always done—a natural impulse. It felt surreal, like we were *together*. He took the gum and said, "Thank you." I laid my head back to rest; my long day had caught up with me, and I wanted to sleep. I sensed that he wanted to relax too, so I stopped asking questions and remained quiet for a while. He opened his tablet and found a solitaire game to play, so I put my ear buds in and scanned for a Lady Antebellum song. Finally I found my favorite, *Just a Kiss*. I closed my eyes, but all I could see was him. *Ugh*!

While I listened, my imagination ran away at a full sprint so I decided it was best to just turn the music off and read my book instead. At least this way I would appear more available in case he wanted to talk again, because I was positively *available*! I didn't want to miss out on one word. And to my good fortune, about fifteen minutes later, he did.

"I noticed you were listening to Lady A earlier. They're good," he commented.

"Yeah, they're one of my favorites. I love all types of music though—country, jazz, rock, even pop now and then. Music takes me away from the stresses in life. I guess that's why I get lost in it sometimes. Not that you wanted to know all that. Sorry." I laughed it off, but I wanted to choke myself with a sock. Why I rambled on and on I would never know!

The pilot's voice came over the speaker. "Ladies and gentlemen, please take your seats and make sure your seatbelts are fastened as we prepare for landing at Phoenix International Airport. Our arrival time will be about fifteen minutes from now. Temperature is a warm ninety-eight degrees and the skies are clear. Thank you for flying with us, and we hope you enjoy your stay."

My heart sank at the thought of never seeing this man again, and then it hit me, I didn't even know his name! Not once did either of us introduce ourselves. That made it even worse. But then he reached down to put away his tablet and pulled out some papers and that's when I saw it!

His boarding pass was in plain sight and his name was printed in bold across the top: Mitchell Young. I paused and thanked God for showing me the way! I kept saying his name over and over in my head so I wouldn't forget, like that would ever happen. Our time was almost up though as I felt the plane start to make its descent.

"It was really nice visiting with you today. It made the flight more enjoyable. I can't remember the last time I talked that much with a fellow passenger. I hope you have a nice stay here in Phoenix." My voice held a sad tone, and I was nervous about how he would reply. I extended my hand toward him slowly and said, "My name is Laci by the way, with an *i*. I'm sorry I never introduced myself earlier."

He held his hand out to meet mine and smiled. "Hi Laci, it was very nice to meet you. I'm Mitch. I enjoyed talking with you too. It's too bad we have to land." He looked down and smiled. As I shook his soft, strong hand, I felt chills go up and down my spine. Did he just say "it's too bad we had to land"? This was nuts! How could I feel this way about a guy I just met a few hours ago? Somehow, I couldn't help think that he might feel the same way after his comment. Knowing me though, I was probably reading way too much into it.

I didn't want to let go of his hand, but we had in fact landed, and it was time to move on. We gathered our carry-on bags, stood up, and waited for the passengers to move. Another hint of his cologne stirred in the air as he stood up. If I could keep that scent on my clothes forever, I would be happy! The air conditioning had been turned down, and the cabin was heating up quickly, much like my insides. It felt like a lava lamp in there; huge bubbles of anticipation, excitement, nervousness, and even sadness floated around knowing that our time was about over. Hopefully it wouldn't erupt anytime soon.

He cleared his throat and said, "Do you have a long layover before your next flight?"

"No, not that long. About three hours, I guess. That gives me plenty of time to eat, grab coffee, and find a new book. I'll be done with this one before my next flight." My stomach was in knots as we walked off the plane and out to the gate area. He was ahead of me, and the distance between us started to grow. I wanted to yell out for him, but what would I say? 'Hey, I think I've fallen in love with you after four hours…let's have dinner!'

Before he was completely out of range, I said, "Have a nice evening, Mitch. Take care."

He looked back toward me and smiled. "You too. Goodbye, Laci," he stammered. For a brief second, he looked like he was about to say something else, but he kept going instead.

I stood there for a moment, or two, or three—and watched him walk away. Finally, I turned and headed in the opposite direction. My wild fantasy of him turning around and running back to me was obviously *not* going to happen. He was simply the passenger in seat 16D, nothing more, and that completely sucked. My chest was heavy, like there was an elephant sitting on top of me, and it was more than I could stand. I wanted to bury my head in a pillow and scream or cry. It had only been a few hours since we'd met, but I haven't had feelings like that in a long time. I couldn't explain it, but there were moments while we talked that he seemed to fill all the empty places inside of me. I never thought anyone would do that again. I resolved myself to the fact that I had gone completely mental—the beginning stages of a breakdown that I had long been expecting.

I made my way to the restroom to freshen up and got ready to face the next three hours alone. My instincts told me to grab a big latte to help me maintain some sense of dignity, so I thought it wise to follow them. I searched out the nearest coffee shop, and along the way, I passed by several windows that opened up to the Phoenix horizon. The sun was about to set, so I stopped to take in the view. It was breathtaking. Amazing sandy mountains, prickly cacti, a few tumbleweeds, and the most beautiful and unusual flowers I had ever seen. The sky was ablaze with orange and pink streaks and I longed to be outside in the warm air and feel the heat from the sun on my skin, with him right beside me.

take the plunge

Mitch walked away from her and on toward the baggage claim area. His heart was heavy and filled with regret because he hadn't said something more—waited with her, asked her to dinner, something! He decided to stop at a nearby bistro café to call his son and check in.

"Hey, dad," Caleb shouted excitedly into the phone.

"Hey Caleb, how is everything?" Mitch replied, his words sad and heavy, and his spirit weighed down with regret.

"It's all good here. You just landing?"

"Yeah, I'm just heading over to the baggage area. How is Grams doing?"

"She's great, a little tired today but spunky as ever. She's making us chicken and dumplings for dinner tonight." Caleb loved his grandma and her cooking. He was twenty years old now and didn't really need to stay with her when his dad traveled, but he enjoyed spending time with her so she wouldn't be as lonely.

"Yeah, she never lacks in the spunk department despite everything." Mitch's melancholy tone was transparent in his voice, and Caleb could sense something wasn't right. "Is everything okay, dad? You sound a little down or something."

"Caleb"—he paused and let out a long breath—"this is going to sound a little crazy so bear with me for a minute. I sort of met someone on the plane today and—"

Caleb cut him off mid-sentence and yelled into the phone, "A woman! You met a woman, didn't you?"

Mitch laughed and said, "Calm down, son. Yes, I met a woman on the plane today. I just said goodbye to her a few minutes ago. She has another flight in about three hours to Seattle. She's pretty, funny, easy to talk to, and real. We laughed about the craziest things today. She rambles too, but in a cute way. It was nice. I haven't felt that comfortable with another woman since… well, in a long time."

"Wow. So you kind of like her?" Caleb smiled through the phone at his dad's news. Caleb had been waiting a long time for something like this to happen, but he wasn't sure it ever would. "She must really be something for you to call me about her after just one four-hour flight. That or she's a real babe!" he added, laughing.

"Well, she's definitely easy on the eyes. Blonde, a radiant smile and nice tan—" Mitch rambled on but Caleb cut him off.

"I get the point, dad. TMI! What are you going to do now? You said she left for her next flight, so did you get her number? Are you going to see her again?"

Mitch drew in a deep breath and growled. "Ugh…no! That's just it, I didn't do anything. I just walked away. But what was I supposed to do? I just met her four hours ago. The last thing I want her to think is that I have a habit of picking up women on a regular basis when I travel. If I hunt her down now, then I'm bordering on creepy-stalker guy." Mitch dropped his head and knew he could have done things differently. Caleb was right.

"Dad, have you left the gate area yet?"

"No, I'm not far from our arrival gate. I couldn't seem to walk any farther." Mitch said and looked back at where he last saw her.

Caleb laughed at his dad's comment then asked, "And you know where she's headed right?"

"Well, yeah I suppose I do." Suddenly Mitch's heart jumped as he realized the possibility in what his son had just suggested.

"Then you have three hours until she leaves, so go find her!" Caleb said with a loud and encouraging voice.

Apprehensive as a school boy with his first crush, Mitch replied, "I haven't done this in a long time, son. What if I screw it up? What if she's married or engaged? I don't think she had a ring on that I remember, but that doesn't mean anything these days." He rubbed his forehead and struggled to make a decision, wondering if this was the right thing to do.

Caleb said quietly, "Dad, I love you and I know you better than anyone. If you feel this way about her after just four hours, and you think there could be *any* chance she feels the same about you, then you are wasting precious time talking to me. Hang up and go take her to dinner!"

Mitch was so proud of his son and of the man he was becoming despite the agony of losing his mother a few years ago to breast cancer. He was smart beyond his years.

"You know, for a twenty-year-old, you have the wisdom of Job at times."

"Yeah, me and Job go way back. Gotta run though, dad. Now go find her and call me with the 'deets' later. But not all of them because it might gross me out." He laughed.

"And now we're back to the old Caleb I know and love. See you soon, son, and thanks," Mitch said and laughed as he hung up. He got up and walked directly to a flight status board.

"Departures…Seattle flight in three hours…Where is the gate? Ah there it is…Gate C5. Just down a little farther than where we arrived," he mumbled to himself.

He picked up the pace and walked directly to her departure gate, intently searching through the people as they passed and anxious to see Laci's sweet face which he had committed to memory. He arrived at the entrance to the gate and panned the awaiting passengers that were sitting and standing, but she was nowhere in sight. *She could by anywhere right now*, he thought. He walked back out to the main hall and made a 360-degree scan of the area, and as he looked over toward the windows, his eyes were drawn to a hot pink carry-on bag sitting on the floor next to a pair of lovely, tan, toned legs. His heart sped up when he looked up and saw her face, staring out the window. The light from the sunset cast a soft pink glow on her face, and Mitch stood frozen and stared at this beautiful, funny woman who he had only laid eyes on a few hours earlier. He wondered if he was making the biggest mistake of his life, but he countered with the thought that if he didn't at least try and talk to her again, he would regret it forever, and that would be the biggest mistake of all.

He watched Laci as she picked up her bag and walked away. His heart raced as the thought of losing her for the second time swept over him. Unwilling to let that happen, he pushed his way through the crowd and shouted her name out over the din of the crowd.

back to reality

Home sweet home at last. It was such an odd feeling to be there without my kids running around. I tried not to dwell on the emptiness around me and unpacked my car. It's late but there was no way I would be able to sleep yet, so I headed straight for the fridge instead. I was pleased to find that my sweet friend Lena had left a bottle of my favorite Riesling chilling inside. I laughed and immediately thought of Mitch, the wine expert, and wondered if he would approve of my selection. I sat down at the breakfast bar and started going through mail. This was the worst part about going on vacation—coming home to a stack of bills and junk mail. After a few sips, I couldn't concentrate on anything. My head was filled with sweet memories of the day and I was exhausted. I finished my wine and called it a night. Work would start tomorrow and it would be a welcome distraction.

The next morning came much too early and I was already dragging. My first stop was one of my favorite coffee shops, Cutters Point. I pulled into the drive-through and saw my favorite baristas in the window. Katie and Sarah both greeted me with big smiles and asked me how my vacation went, and if I wanted my usual. While I waited, I visited with Kathleen about nursing school and wished her the best. All the girls were so nice and I loved that they knew me and my drink. She handed me my coffee, and I waved goodbye and made my way downtown.

Traffic was pretty light and the sun was shining, so I cranked up the music and opened the sunroof—my favorite way to start the day. At a stoplight, I sent a text to my friend Teri and asked her to stop by my office in a few minutes. I wanted her to hear the news when I told the others.

I walked in and the girls greeted me with big hugs and "welcome backs." I had missed them. We gathered together to recap our weekends, then I gave them the basic highlights of my vacation, purposely leaving out any mention of 16D. I wanted to wait until Sandy arrived so I could tell them all at once. Sandy is the marketing director and my boss, the *best* boss I've ever had. I couldn't wait to tell her about my Airplane Man. After Andrew died, I became a borderline workaholic, and she and I developed a strong bond in many ways. While I waited for her to arrive, I decided to catch up on the hundred plus emails sitting in my inbox. You would think after people receive an "out-of-office" message that they wouldn't email you anymore, but they do anyway.

My best friend, Laura, had sent me a couple of daily quotes, so I decided to send her an email from my phone and fill her in on all the details about my creepy stalker guy, as well as remind her about my upcoming big event.

SUBJECT: Catching up!

Hey girl! I miss you. I hope you are still coming up for my sandcastle beach party on the 24th, I have *so* much to tell you and it has to be done in person! Don't be late! This is the biggest event I've ever planned, so I'll need you there for moral support. I'm going to be a nervous wreck. Call me later tonight so I can fill you in on my flight to Phoenix and the pleasant surprise I encountered in seat 16D!

Love you, Sis.

Laci

I continued to filter through messages when I saw Sandy walk in. Casually, I got up and walked into her office to say good morning, motioning to the other girls to come into her office.

She looked up and laughed. "Uh oh, this looks like trouble!

What is going on?"

I proceeded to share a few details about my vacation with the family and then I dropped the bomb. "So, basically it was a relaxing, very uneventful vacation up until my flight back. That's when I was lucky enough to sit next to a very handsome man who owns his own winery and asked me to dinner on my layover," I said, casually. Sandy choked on her sip of water after I shared my news.

Gail, another dear friend and coworker, let out a huge squeal, clapping her hands and jumping up and down. "You met a man on the plane yesterday? A man who owns his own winery? And you had dinner with him? Oh good grief, how romantic. I can't believe it!" Gail exclaimed.

Sandy chimed in too. "Romantic? Are you crazy? He could have been a sicko or a serial killer, or worse!"

"And what's worse than a serial killer exactly?" Lena asked then laughed at Sandy's overreaction to my adventures with Airplane Man.

"It's okay, really. He was a perfect gentleman, complete with all the southern charm I could stand. He was actually too much of a gentleman. He kissed my hand when we said goodbye. I didn't even get a hug and I was really hoping to get one before I left. Man, did he smell good. I gave him my business card and he put his contact info in my cell phone. Look."

I took out my phone and showed them the entry for Creepy Stalker Guy. Sandy gave me the "what the heck" look. I paused for a minute and then told them the bigger news.

"There's one more thing. It's a small thing really, but it's a big coincidence. He lost his wife the same year and month that I lost Andrew. I know it sounds crazy you guys, but I think we met for a reason." The girls were quiet and I could see the goose bumps on Lena's arms. I proceeded to share all the details of our day together, smiling from ear to ear as I talked. Gail and Lena were thrilled at my news. Teri, Sue, and Sandy were still in a state of shock, but they seemed happy for me.

"Well, he seems to have you all worked up, that's for sure. I haven't seen you this giddy in forever. You're not going to be worth anything today, are you?" Sandy asked as she laughed and threw her hands up in defeat. She gave me a big hug and I knew she was thrilled for me, even if she thought I was totally crazy for getting involved with a complete stranger. "Okay, party's over for now. Get to work sister! You have a big event coming up, and we have lots of details to finalize, not to mention the other deadlines coming up."

"I'm on it boss," I said happily and headed to my office.

Aside from my kids and my job, these women have been my lifeline these past few years. When I lost Andrew, Sandy, Gail, Lena, Teri, and Sue rallied to my corner to show their support, offer advice, and hold me while I cried all those tears when it became too hard to cope. They rooted me on to look for new possibilities in life. Words can't even begin to express what their friendship has meant and I don't think I'd be the same person today had it not been for their support. They are my extended family and helped me through the worst time of my life. It's only right that they share in my newfound excitement and happiness.

I cleaned out the rest of my emails and remembered that I had sent Laura a message, so I checked my phone for a reply. But there was nothing yet. There was a reply to the message I sent, but it wasn't from Laura's email address. Suddenly my mouth went dry and my palms started to sweat as I realized what I had done. I was so used to typing *LM* when sending Laura an email that I forgot I have a new address in my phone that begins with *LM* too. Oh no! I had accidentally sent my message to *him*. And he replied!

FROM: LMYoung@zmail.com

SUBJECT: RE: Catching up!

I'd be open to catching up with you myself. And for the record, I wouldn't consider us total strangers anymore seeing as how we just shared dinner together, a dinner that I thoroughly enjoyed by the way. I'm guessing however that this email was probably meant for someone else since you started it with "hey girl," but I'm glad it didn't make it to her.

I almost deleted it, but then I saw your name at the end, and somehow I had a feeling it was you to begin with. So tell me more about this beach party you're helping plan. Can anyone attend?

Was I the "pleasant surprise" you mentioned to your friend? I hope so; you were to me as well. I've been thinking about you constantly since we said goodbye. My winery tour in Phoenix was nice, but my flight home was unbearably boring compared to the flight out there, sitting next to you. At the risk of sounding like the creepy stalker guy that I am, I miss you. Is that weird for me to say this soon?

Have a good day, Ms. Laci. Thank you for the mistaken email; it made my day.

Looking forward to your reply,

16D

He missed me! I was ecstatic to read his words, but frustrated at how careless I was with my email. It had never been an issue before. He must have thought I was a complete idiot, or that I had sent it on purpose to get his attention. I would never do that. How would I respond? Should I respond at all? Granted, I'd hoped we would talk again soon, but I wasn't exactly prepared for it just yet, mentally or emotionally. I didn't want to rush this. And why did he ask if anyone can come to my event?

I forced myself through the rest of my day as if I hadn't received his email, but by four o'clock that afternoon, it was all I could think about. Gail poked her head in my office knowing that I was perplexed about something.

"Okay, I know that look. What's up? Too many projects for your first day back?" she said.

I laughed. "I wish it were that. It's him, Gail. Read this!" I showed her the email on my phone and explained how I had sent it to him by mistake. Naturally, she cracked up and did the happy dance thinking about all the possibilities my email blunder had just created.

"Have you answered him yet?"

"No. I don't know how to reply. The last thing I want is for him to think I'm desperate."

"He's been thinking about you constantly," she sang jokingly in her quirky little voice. I couldn't help but laugh at her antics. It was exactly the break I needed from my mental stress.

"I can't stop thinking about him either, Gail. It's crazy right? We spent what, seven hours together? That's tip-of-the-iceberg stuff. How can this possibly become anything?" I flopped my head down on my desk out of exasperation, and it made a dull, thud- type noise and caused a slight ache afterward. It only masked the ache in my chest though.

Everything in me wanted to reply, but I knew I had to think it through first.

"Well, I know this, Laci. You haven't stopped smiling all day, and I've spent too many days working with the old "gloomy Laci" to go back now. I like this new, fun, happy Laci and would like her to stick around. If emailing this guy is what it takes to make that happen, then get typing girlfriend! If you don't, I will, and you *know* I would do it." Gail laughed and went back to her desk. She was right. He was the reason that everything was better today. My coffee tasted better, the music sounded sweeter, and the sun shined brighter. Picturing his handsome, goateed face *still* made me blush. And with that thought, I pulled my head up.

It's more than his nice features though – something about him just resonated inside of me, and woke a part of me that I had long forgotten was there. I felt at home with 16D…and I wanted that feeling to stay.

After work, I stopped by my favorite Mexican restaurant to pick up some dinner. It would be my first real evening alone without the kids; I could relax and do nothing. After I ate and had a glass of wine, I sent Teri a text to let her know the latest with Airplane Man. I continued to procrastinate sending my inevitable reply to his email by cleaning the kitchen, washing some clothes, and flipping through channels on the TV. Finally, a little after ten or so, I went up to my room, pulled out my laptop and decided it was time to reply. There was a three-hour time difference between us, so hopefully he was asleep and unable to reply. I opened his email and read through it again. Reading his words made me smile. Heat flooded my cheeks and flipped on that little red switch. I hit reply and began typing.

SUBJECT: RE: Catching up! Dear 16D,

You probably thought I was a bit spacey for sending that email and not realizing I had used your address, but in my defense, my best friend's email has the exact same initials as you. What a strange coincidence. So, you see, I'm so used to typing *LM* to get her email to pop up that I didn't realize your email now appears before hers. Anyway, I'm sorry for the mix-up. But I must admit that I was also glad it accidentally went to you. I'm not sure I would have had the guts to initiate an email on my own just yet. Not that I didn't want to, because I did. Just nervous I guess. Sorry, I tend to ramble in email form as well. It's a bad habit.

To answer your questions, yes, you were a very pleasant surprise on the flight; that is a good thing! As far as it being weird that you miss me, I would have to say no; it's not weird at all. I'm very flattered to hear that I'm missed.

I'm still trying to wrap my head around the sad yet similar circumstances we share. I believe someone in the universe thought we should meet and I'm glad we did.

The beach event I'm helping plan is a major fundraiser/auction for a local children's museum. They have fun, hands-on activities that teach kids everything from water conservation to expressing their inner actor. It's quite amazing actually. I help with decorations and catering for the event. Our bank sponsors it. I'm a bit nervous, but it's a lot of fun and I really enjoying being a part of the planning. Anyone can go for a price, but it's a bit out of the way for you, I'm afraid.

I'm glad your winery tour went well. You'll have to tell me what you learned. I'm anxious to know more about what you do. I'm sorry the return flight wasn't what you'd hoped. Next time I'll have to stick around and keep you company.

Well, I'd better go. Sorry this is so long. I hope you and Caleb are doing well. Did you tell him "thank you" for me?

Missing 16D,

Laci

P.S. How 'bout those Crawdads?

After two restarts, several changes, and the tenth review, I finally clicked send. Even though I knew his reply wouldn't come until tomorrow, my adrenaline was pumping, so I walked around for a bit. I went down the hall and checked my clothes in the dryer, walked through the kids' rooms and said goodnight to each of them, as if they were there. I went back to my room, changed my clothes, and washed my face, hoping to make myself tired in the process. And I waited...

a changed man

Mitch finished his reply to an email he had mistakenly received from Laci earlier that day, and then he and Caleb hopped in the car and headed over to his mom's house for dinner. Ever since he had returned home from his trip, he'd been anxious to tell his mom about Laci. For so long, the weekly family dinner at her house was a constant reminder of how much he missed his wife. He always went home feeling a little worse than when he arrived. Each week he'd hoped it would improve, but it always ended the same. Tonight however, with the excitement of buying the winery and his recent trip, he knew things would be different.

Caleb felt it too, and he knew why. Laci had changed every- thing in a matter of hours. For the first time in years, his dad had a smile on his face that wouldn't go away. Caleb saw it the minute he had walked in the door the day before, even more than when he had signed the papers for the winery. Mitch had no sooner dropped his luggage on the floor when he started telling Caleb all the details about his dinner with Laci. He was a changed man, and Caleb looked forward to the day when he would be able to thank Laci for bringing his dad back to life.

"Are you nervous about telling Grams tonight?" Caleb asked as they drove.

"A little I guess, but I think she'll be relieved. The part she'll have the most trouble with is that I feel this strongly after only knowing her for seven hours. That will take some time for her to absorb." Mitch knew his mom when it came to affairs of the heart and she was pretty set in her ways, definitely the old-fashioned type.

They arrived at her house and went inside. Caleb was barely in the door when his fingers were already taste-testing the sauce his Grandma had simmering on the stove. She slapped his hand, "Caleb Lee, get out of my kitchen before I turn you on my knee!" she shouted, laughing at the same time, and then tapped the side of her cheek. Caleb knew that was his cue to give Grams her weekly peck on the cheek. He obliged, and then ran off to watch TV until dinner.

Mitch stood by the counter, watching his mom cook. After taking one look at him, she smiled and said, "Luke Mitchell Young, what is that I see on your sweet face?" It was obvious to her that he had a renewed sense about him. Something big had happened.

"Hey, Mama." Mitch's smile grew and he gave her a big bear hug, and then whispered in her ear, "I found her."

She looked up at him with a smile on her face and tears in her eyes. "Well then, I want to hear all about her."

All through dinner and dessert, he shared every detail—how they met, their dinner together, and their similar past that seemed to draw them together. He barely touched his food; he was too excited to eat. His mother simply listened and watched his eyes light up as he talked about the woman who had already stolen his heart. Seeing him so happy brought her joy, yet she was worried at the same time.

"She sounds lovely, Mitch. I can see how much you care for her. When will you see her again?"

But there was an obvious edge to her voice, and Mitch sensed it right away. "Well, there are some outstanding wineries around Washington and Oregon that I would love to visit and are located fairly close to her. I thought I'd try to go up next week and visit one—maybe visit her too and ask her out on a real date. But you obviously have some concerns, so what is it, Mama? Let me hear it." He smiled in anticipation of her wise, motherly advice.

"It just seems a bit fast doesn't it? First you buy this run-down winery and now you are ready to fly across the country to date a woman. I guess I worry about you getting hurt, that's all. That's what moms do best you know. Just promise me you'll be careful. Do you even know if she feels the same way about you?"

"Yes, I think she does. It's hard to explain, but everything felt right when I was with her. Better than right, it was like we were meant to find each other, Mama." Mitch's eyes lit up and his mom shed a tear.

"Come on Mama, don't cry. This is a good thing, you'll see." Mitch gave his mom another hug. They got up and cleared the dishes from the table.

"Well, I hope she at least shares the same values as you." "Actually, she reminds me a lot of you."

Mitch knew what his mom meant though. She had very traditional, southern values. Ever since Mitch was old enough to date, she'd always encouraged him to date girls who shared those values. But, when he was in college, he purposely dated girls who didn't fit her mold out of sheer spite. Somehow, those relationships always ended in disaster, except for Karin, his late wife. She broke the mold and he fell hard. And when he lost her, all the life in him and his veracious spirit died right along with her. He got better of course, especially when he found the winery, but even that didn't seem fill the huge void inside—until he met Laci. She had changed everything. He wasn't sure how, and it seemed impossible that he could feel this way, but within just a few hours, she had brought him back to life. That was exactly what he needed.

As he washed the dishes, he thought about how funny life was, how everything could suddenly change in an instant. He wasn't even supposed to be on her flight. His original flight was

cancelled due to a mechanical failure, and they had rebooked him on Laci's flight. They gave him the only aisle seat left—the one next to her. He hadn't shared that little detail with her, but he kept it to himself, knowing that it didn't matter how they met. He just knew it was meant to happen.

"We'd better head home, Mama. Dinner was delicious, as usual," Mitch said as he gave her a hug goodbye.

"Anytime darlin' you know that. And Mitch, I'm very happy that you met Laci, I really am. Your dad would be happy too, you know?"

"I know he would. I love you, mom."

Caleb barreled through the kitchen, kissed his Grams on the cheek, and took off out the door. Mitch and his mom laughed as he flew by.

"I wish I had his energy!" she said, laughing, and waved goodbye as Mitch followed him out.

The car ride home was short. They only lived a few miles away from his mom. Caleb couldn't contain his enthusiasm any longer. "So, spill! What did Grams say?"

Mitch smiled. "She's happy for me. I could see it in her eyes. She's just worried that it's happening too fast, like I knew she would."

"Yeah I can see that. I mean it was just one day and she's pretty far away. Do you think it can work?"

"It sounds crazy, but I think it can. I know in my heart that Laci and I met for a reason, Caleb. I haven't figured out all the logistics just yet, but I know this: if God brought her to me, then I need to trust that he's worked out all the other details too."

After Mitch and Caleb arrived back home, Caleb decided to go out and meet his friends for a late night movie, and Mitch spent the next couple of hours catching up on work. At around 1 a.m., his eyes started to hurt and he was wrapping things up when an email notice popped up on his desktop. And there it was—the one message he'd been anticipating all day. *Finally, she answered,* he thought to himself. He opened her message and pictured her saying the words in her reply, laughing out loud at her mention of the Crawdads. Ironically the team was having their best season in years, so he was excited to reply back and brag about their success. As he finished reading, Caleb had returned and poked his head in the office to say goodnight.

"Hey, Dad, still working I see."

Mitch was still smiling from having just read Laci's email. "Well, I'm done with work for tonight. I was just about to send Laci an email."

"Sweet. Well, I'm off to bed. See you in the morning!"

"Hey, before you go, Laci wanted me to tell you thanks for encouraging me to go find her and ask her to dinner during her layover."

Caleb smiled. "That's cool. Tell her "hey" and "you're welcome." So when do you think I'll get to meet her?"

Mitch hadn't thought that far ahead yet, but he should have known Caleb would be anxious to meet her. "Honestly son, I'm not sure. Hopefully soon if things go well. I'm headed up there next week to see a few more wineries and pay her a visit."

Caleb gave him a thumbs-up and yawned, and then he headed up to bed. Mitch smiled and said goodnight. He was so proud of Caleb for being open to his potential relationship. All he could hope was that Laci felt as strongly as he did. He had already researched some wineries and vineyards to visit in her area, and even found one he wanted to sign as a supplier. So, he decided to tell Laci about his upcoming visit in his reply. He reread her message and his heart swelled when he noticed the "Missing 16D" salutation. He smiled as he finished typing his message, clicked send, and then sat back in his chair. *If only I could hear her voice. That would be a nice way to end my day.*

Mitch looked at his watch to determine the current Pacific time; it was ten fifteen there. It was too late to call, but he didn't care. One thing he had learned over the last few years was that

life was short, and he was tired of putting off things that mattered most.

He pulled out her business card and dialed her number.

arrivals

Early Sunday morning, I woke to the sound of birds chirping and my coffee pot brewing. I could already feel the warmth of the sun as it seared through my windows. Anxious to get the day started, I got up, fixed myself a cup of coffee, and then took a few quiet moments out on the back porch. I wasn't alone however. A baby deer was stirring around by my flowers, looking for something good to eat. He found my apple tree, but was quickly discouraged after he realized there was no fruit there whatsoever. My cell phone rang and startled me. It was too early for anyone to be calling. I picked up the phone and my heart immediately picked up pace when I saw that it was Mitch—the only person who could turn my insides to mush in mere seconds!

I smiled, then answered, "Why good morning, Mr. Young.

How did you know I would be up this early?"

"I...oh, Laci, I'm so sorry! I completely forgot about the time difference. I'm so used to calling you later in the day. You were up right? Not just humoring me?" He sounded embarrassed.

"Yes, I was really up, honest. I'm just hanging out on the back porch, taking in the sunrise and visiting with my new little friend."

"A new friend, huh? Should I be jealous?" he asked with a hint of sarcasm.

I laughed. "W-e-l-l, he is quite cute...for a baby deer. Overall though, I'd say you're definitely ahead of the competition."

"I see. It's pretty hard to compete with cute and adorable four legged creatures, but I'm glad I'm still ahead of the 'game.'" And he laughed at himself. "'Game.' Get it?"

But even I had to laugh at his terrible pun. "Oh that's bad. Really bad. Why don't you just tell me why you called, silly? Is everything okay?"

"Yeah, I know it's not like me to call this early, but I know you have an exciting day ahead of you with your kids coming home, and I wanted my first conversation of the day to be with you. Plus, I figured you would spend the rest of your day getting reacquainted with them and we may not get a chance to talk later tonight. I didn't want to go a whole day without hearing your voice. Anyway, have a safe trip to the airport and enjoy your day, okay?" Sincere warmth radiated from his voice.

"I will, and I'll enjoy it even more now that I've talked to you. You do realize that you've become my new addiction, right? Starting and ending my day with your calls. Of course, I would rather start and end my days with seeing you in person." I bit my lip and blushed after I realized what I'd said. But it was true! The thought of him being close enough to hold sent a fever straight through to my core. No longer was my head in control –my heart now led the way. Hearts were best known for impulsive and irrational decisions, but I didn't care. I believed that mine would lead me straight into Mitch's arms, and there was nowhere else I'd rather be.

He laughed, "Soon enough, darlin'. I admit...seeing you again is all I think about too. But until then, I'll wish for the time to fly by. I'll talk to you tomorrow. Be safe, Laci," he said in a quiet, sweet voice.

I said goodbye and hung up wearing a smile. His sweet words were the perfect beginning to my day, even though my heart ached a little knowing that I wouldn't talk to him tonight. He

was right, though. Today *would* be an exciting day and I was too happy to play hostess at a pity party. Plus, it was almost time to go!

Several hours later, I was waiting at the airport, another hour yet until the kids' plane due to arrive. Thanks to my early morning call, I was more motivated than usual and a little ahead of schedule. Luckily, I brought Mitch's book to read and pass the time. I never thought I would enjoy reading it as much as I have. The writing is so rich and heavy, but intoxicating at the same time–much like Mitch is to me. I can't seem to concentrate on reading though – I keep drifting off to think about him. I looked down at my phone and contemplated calling or sending him a text.

Typically, we don't text each other. It's more personal when we actually talk to one another. Besides, I would miss hearing the little inflections in his voice, his laugh, and especially his accent… none of which I would get from a text. But, at that particular moment, the noise and bustle of the airport roared, so I was more inclined to send one…

<Hey! Sitting at airport reading 'The Count'…thinking of you.

Thanks again for your call this am – Laci J>

I didn't expect him to reply, but hopefully it made him smile nonetheless. Surprisingly though, only a few seconds went by and my phone buzzed. I smiled at his reply.

<Ah I see! Are you sure it's not the dashing Edmond that fills your thoughts?>

I laughed and typed my response.

<Certainly not…besides, his heart is spoken for.>

Another few seconds passed and his reply appeared.

<As is mine…>

His reply made my heart leap inside my chest. My fun, light- hearted text was supposed to be fun, but now he's gone and turned it into, well…much more. *Ugh!* I missed even more now. The achy feeling from this morning has returned in spite of the joyous reunion ahead of me. I should have stuck to my own rule—no texting!

The kids' plane finally arrived, and I was instantly distracted by the anticipation of seeing them again. I stood at the gate entrance and saw them barrel through the tunnel and walk up to the gate. Emma and Travis yelled "Mom" so loud that everyone turned to watch our reunion. They nearly knocked me to the floor with their open arms and hugs. It was a wonderful feeling— I've missed them so!

I signed their travel release paperwork, and we went off to baggage claim. Stories about their vacation came out, and they asked lots of questions about what I did without them all week. They couldn't talk fast enough. Travis clung to my leg; I could tell the separation was hard on him.

"I missed you so much, Mom! Did you miss us?" Travis asked. I knelt down and looked him in his eyes. "Travis, Mommy missed you more than I ever thought possible. All of you. I never want you to be gone for that long again, okay?" Travis's smile lit up the room, and he wrapped his little arms around my neck, nearly cutting off my airflow. I didn't care though; my kids were home and I felt whole again. During the drive, Emma and Todd shared funny highlights of their adventures with Grandma and Grandpa. Travis fell asleep.

After we arrived home, we unpacked the bags and spent the rest of the day getting caught up. Mainly we goofed off, snuggled on the couch, watched our favorite movies, and ate way too much junk food. Their voices and laughter filled the house, and I

realized how much I loved hearing that sound. We took a break between movies when my mom called to check in and make sure they arrived safely. She really just wanted to know how much they missed *her*. I hesitated, but I figured I should fill her in on my new friend. She was thrilled and wanted to hear all about him. I was more than happy to provide the details of course, but I gave her the cliff notes version to save time, and we were off the phone in less than twenty minutes—a miracle in itself.

Movie number three started, and not long after, the little ones fell asleep on my lap. Todd was back in his favorite spot— his room—watching movies, and my early morning had finally caught up with me. I was ready for bed. It was the first night that Mitch and I hadn't spent at least an hour or more talking on the phone before going to sleep. I had grown quite fond of our evening chats; it felt strange not having one. I carried the kids to bed and went to my room. Before I turned out the lights, my phone beeped. It was a text from Mitch!

<Goodnight, Ms. Laci. Sweet dreams... J>

I read the words and shook my head, smiling and wondered what I had done to deserve this man. He was so much more than I'd ever hoped. I replied.

<They will be now!>

I supposed that this 'texting thing' wasn't so bad after all. My head fell to the pillow, and the second my eyes closed, Mitch was there.

Sue was covering the phones at the receptionist desk during lunch when a tall, handsome man walked up to the desk.

"Hi, does Laci Kramer work in this office?"

She smiled up at him and said, "Why, yes. Do you have an appointment?"

"Not exactly, I wanted to leave this gift for her. I'm in town a day early and was hoping to surprise her. I could actually use your help, would you mind?" Mitch flashed a smile at her and she melted like hot wax. She remembered Laci's description of her Airplane Man. Based on his unmistakable southern accent, she deducted that the man she was talking to was Airplane Man.

"By any chance, is your name Mitch?"

"Umm, yes...how did you..." He hadn't even finished his question before Sue told him that she worked in the same department as Laci and that Laci had told her and all the other girls about him coming into town this week.

"Well, I suppose that makes this next part a bit easier then, huh?" He smiled and then shared his plan with her. Sue was more than happy to help. Mitch handed her an envelope and said, "There's one more thing. Make sure she reads this *after* she opens the box." Sue nodded in agreement and smiled, then she picked up the phone to call Laci's extension.

Before I could blink, Wednesday was half over and my workday packed with a to-do list the size of Mount Rushmore. For the most part, Sandy and I both felt pretty confident about the event on Friday, but I couldn't relax just yet. As soon as I had, some- thing would have inevitably caught me off guard. It was almost lunch time, and I debated about the cheeseburger and fries that I didn't need but really wanted, and the healthy frozen thing I had brought from home. Before I could decide, the phone rang and gave me more time to ponder my choice.

"Marketing, this is Laci. How may I help you?"

"Hey Laci, this is Sue at the front desk. You have a delivery, sweetie. Can you come down and pick it up?" she said sounding almost giddy, but oddly vague for some reason.

"Umm, sure. I'll be right down. Is it big? Do I need the cart or anything?" I replied, thinking the delivery might be one of my auction purchases or something for the event.

"Nope, I'm sure you can carry it with no trouble." She rushed me off the phone and hung up. I had no idea what was up with her, but I supposed it didn't really matter.

I walked downstairs to the reception desk and saw a long, white box wrapped neatly with a beautiful, hot pink bow tied around the center. I wondered if that was my package, but it looked a little too 'sweet' to be mine—probably meant for another coworker's anniversary, or something mushy like that. I knew better than to get my hopes up. Who would've given me a gift like that anyway?

"Hi Sue, where's my package?"

Sue pointed to the white box, and my eyes lit up like the lights on a Christmas tree.

"What? Are you sure this is for me?"

"Oh, I'm sure. But you have to open it here. I want to see what's inside!" Sue was almost as excited as me, but she was still not acting like her normal self, and she kept peeking over at a man sitting in the lobby with a newspaper in front of his face. I gave up trying to figure her out and focused on my box.

"Okay, okay." I started to pick it up, but it was pretty heavy, so I just slid it over closer to me and decided to open it on the counter. Carefully, I untied the ribbon and opened the lid. Inside, under a thin layer of white tissue paper, I found eleven *gorgeous* long-stemmed, pink roses, the edges tipped with a salmon-orange color. I slapped my hand over my mouth and exclaimed, "Oh my goodness— look! I've never seen roses this beautiful!"

Sue stood up to peek in the box, then she cocked her head sideways a couple of times to remind me about the gentleman in the lobby and told me to keep the noise down. I just laughed. It wasn't exactly easy to hold in my enthusiasm. But as I admired the roses, I realized the box was quite deep and knew it had to

contain something other than roses, so I decided to dig a little deeper. That was when I noticed a second item sitting underneath the roses, wrapped in pink tissue paper. I slid the roses over and lifted it out of the box. It was a bottle of wine! My heart jumped for joy and before I had even read the card, I knew exactly who had sent it. It also explained the odd number of roses. It's been exactly eleven days since we met...but who was counting, right? The funny thing was...we both were. I wanted to scream out loud but couldn't thanks to Newspaper Guy.

"Sue, can you call Teri's extension for me, please? She needs to see this." Sue called her extension, and Teri walked right over from her desk, which was just on the other side of the reception area. I turned toward her then pointed to my box and the wine now sitting out on the counter. She took one look at it and her mouth dropped open. Then she smiled and looked back at me. "Airplane Man?" she squealed.

"Yes!" Teri gave me a hug, and we both jumped up and down, screaming together. We couldn't help it. Sue jumped in again. "Hey ladies, shush! There are customers in the lobby! Will you just read the card already?" She asked in a hasty whisper, although it sounded more like a drill sergeant's order.

"Sorry! Good grief! I *know* who it's from anyway." I slid the card out of the tiny envelope and read it out loud to appease both of them.

Inside this box you'll find,

Eleven roses for each day of time (since we've met) And a bottle of Oregon's finest

Pinot Noir Red wine (for your first tasting lesson tonight)

—Mitch

My mouth fell wide open and nearly hit the floor after I read his words. I couldn't move. I stared at Teri and asked, "What does he mean, 'tonight'? He won't even be here until tomorrow. Maybe I got the package a day early?"

"Psst, Laci," Sue said quietly, and then she handed me an envelope. "Here. This came with your package, dear. You might want to read it next." A mischievous smile now covered her face. I looked at her with confusion as to why she was just now giving it to me, but she didn't say anything more. My heart raced, and I was suddenly a bundle of nerves. I started to open the note, and out of the corner of my eye, I noticed that the gentleman in the lobby had stood up to leave. Now I could finally be happy and loud at the same time! Once he disappeared out of my peripheral vision, I read the note.

It simply said...

Turn Around

My hands trembled, and I dropped the note on the floor. Slowly, I turned around. Standing a short distance behind me was Mitch, staring at me with his beautiful smile. He was so handsome in his jeans; blue-and-white, pin-striped cotton shirt; and casual navy blazer. He was the man reading the paper, and he had been watching me the entire time! My knees were shaking, and I was suddenly unable to speak. I stared at him and smiled. All the joy and anticipation of seeing him again overflowed and my eyes filled with tears.

"Mercy, darlin', if I had known this would be your reaction to a few flowers and wine, I would have done it days ago!" He walked up to me and took my hands, lifting them up to his lips and kissing the back of each one. Pulling me in a little closer, he leaned down next to my ear and whispered, "Surprise."

Darlin'. He called me darlin' – that wasn't fair at all. Hearing him use that word nearly caused me hyperventilate!

My cheeks were wet from the tears that slowly trickled down, and I couldn't resist him anymore. I stepped in closer to him, put my arms around his neck then I took the hug that I had dreamt about since I had left him at the gate. He gave in to my embrace

and lifted me up, squeezing me tighter. I whispered in his ear, "Thank you. I love surprises!"

We held each other for what seemed like forever, and then he put me down and held me by the hand. I couldn't seem to pull my eyes away from him, but the girls were all staring at us and growing ever so impatient for an introduction. Sue had taken the liberty of making a few more calls because there was now a small audience gathered around to watch the show. Taking the hint, I introduced Mitch to each of them, my Airplane Man. Lena, Gail, and Teri were all giggles and smiles, and Sue was already back to work. Mitch started visiting with them and then we decided to take our little party somewhere a little less public. I put the wine back in the box, and he carried it upstairs for me. Once we were in my department, I gave him the fifty-cent tour. Sandy was back in her office, so I brought Mitch in to meet her.

"Sandy, this is Mitch, the man from the airplane."

"Ah, Airplane Man. We've heard a lot about you around here— all good of course," Sandy said with a smile as she extended her hand to greet him. Mitch just smiled, looking a tad embarrassed by her comment. No more than I was though. I couldn't believe she just said that! The last thing I wanted him to think was that I was some sort of Chatty Cathy doll, clambering on and on to everyone about my Airplane Man. I totally did that, of course, but he didn't need to *know*. He remained the perfect gentleman, however. "It's nice to meet you, ma'am." He smiled.

Now that I had completely embarrassed myself and him, we walked into my office. I stood behind my desk, not quite sure what to say after that. I opened my box and looked at the flowers again, then searched around for a vase. Mitch sat down in my chair and started spinning it around like a kid would do. He then reached over, grabbed my arm, and turned me around to face him. I was not only embarrassed, but still in shock from his surprise visit and the fact that he was now sitting in my office, in my chair.

I smiled a halfhearted smile and looked down at the floor away from him. "I'm sorry about that. I haven't really told everyone about you, honest," I said, and looked into his warm eyes. "It's fine, really. I like it. Makes me think you kind of like me," he said, smiling.

"Oh, I definitely like you. No doubt about that. And I still can't believe you're here. What on earth made you come out a day early?" He gave me a sweet look, stood up, and took my hands into his.

"You did. I didn't see the point in putting this off any longer. I needed to see you. The picture of you that I had etched in my mind just wasn't enough anymore." He confessed as he softly rubbed his thumbs over my hands.

His answer took my breath away and made me somewhat dizzy. I could feel my face getting hot and my knees were unsteady once again. It felt like I was in a dream and I prayed that no one would wake me! Hearing his words, I knew that no matter what happened from this moment forward, as crazy as it sounded, my future was with him.

In a hushed voice, I replied, "Wow…I must say, Mr. Young, you're pretty good at this 'courting' thing." The temperature in the room suddenly became quite warm, or maybe that was just my internal thermostat rising…

He laughed and pulled me toward him, wrapped his arms around me gently, and lay his cheek down on my head. "Darlin', you haven't seen anything yet." I closed my eyes and simply enjoyed the moment. It was short-lived though. "Speaking of courting, I was hoping we could have our first date tonight. But if that isn't going to work or if you already have plans, I understand. I know I'm a day early."

I looked down at his hands that were still holding mine, and I realized that there was nothing that could keep me from being with him that night.

"Well, as it turns out, I have this amazing friend. And if I know her, she'll do just about anything to make sure I can go." My heart raced, literally trying to beat its way out of my chest as I realized our first date was now scheduled for later that night. Mitch smiled and we started walking toward the door.

"Yeah, your friends are a hoot, a little on the hyper side maybe, but really nice. I can tell they think the world of you," he said.

"You have no idea. When I told them you were coming up this week, I think I suffered partial hearing loss from Lena's scream." Remembering it made me laugh, and he stared at me with a big smile on his face. "What?" I asked.

"Your laugh, it's even sweeter in person," he said and gave me another quick hug. "Well, I'd better take off. I've got a few things to take care of before tonight. Text me your address and I'll pick you up around six thirty, okay? And you'd better get back to work. You've goofed off enough for one day, don't you think?" He had a big smile on his face and a bounce to his step as we walked out the door and into the hall.

"I suppose you're right. But it was well worth it!" I said, as I waved goodbye.

Before he got too far though, he turned back and said softly, "Until tonight, Ms. Laci."

And I stood there with a smile plastered all over my face and watched him walk away. He was out of sight, so I went back into my office, a bit dazed. All I could do was stare off into space as I thought about his surprise visit, the beautiful flowers, the note, turning around to see him there. It was all swirling around in my head—better than my best dream. Trying to imagine what our evening would hold was impossible. At that moment though, I was perfectly content just reliving the day. My airplane man had arrived...and all was well in my world.

Sandy came over to my office and waved her hand in front of my face. She laughed. "Earth to Laci! Sister, you might as well call it a day and go home because I *know* you aren't here anymore!"

I laughed too, realizing she was right. "No, I can do this! At least two more hours anyway. I'll just take a short lunch and leave early. I don't think I could eat right now even if I tried." It was a beautiful, warm, sunny day and my insides matched. Nothing could spoil my good mood. Every call, email, and push of the computer keys ended with a smile as I thought about the night ahead. But first things first—I had to make arrangements for my kids, otherwise our first date would be a little overcrowded. I dialed Teri's extension.

"Loans, this is Teri," she answered.

"Hey, girl. I need a *huge* favor," I pleaded in my most pitiful voice.

"Let me guess. Does it have something to do with you and Airplane Man?" She laughed.

"Well, yes, duh. Obviously he's a day early and wants our first date to be tonight!" I yelped in desperation, and she took pity on me, "Fine, fine. I'll watch the kids tonight. How can I refuse?"

"You are the best friend *ever!*" I said, squealing with joy! "Yep, and you'd better not forget it when true love comes knocking on my door!" She laughed and we said goodbye. I was relieved to know that she would be with the kids tonight.

At two o'clock, my stomach was churning, my nerves were shot, and I was a full-fledged, walking, hot mess, so I decided to call it a day. I popped in and told Sandy goodbye.

"I'm taking off, Sandy. I can't function anymore," I said with a laugh.

Sandy got up and came around to give me a hug. "Well, good luck, sweetie! Don't be nervous; just have fun tonight and enjoy every minute of it. He seems like a really great guy, and he's definitely nice on the eyes!" she said in her fun-loving way. "And why don't you plan on coming in around ten tomorrow morning, okay?"

"I will! Thank you, Sandy. I appreciate you so much. See you tomorrow!"

and the courting begins

At home, I poured myself a glass of wine to calm my nerves, then I walked upstairs to contemplate my wardrobe. As I tore through the endless options of nothing, my phone rang. It was the school.

"Hello?" I answered nervously.

"Hi, Ms. Kramer. This is Brenda at Olympic Elementary. I've got Emma here in the nurse's office. She's complaining of an earache but she doesn't have a fever. Did you want her to go back to class or would you rather pick her up?" Immediately, my heart grew heavy, and I knew in an instant that my evening with Mitch would no longer become a reality.

"Of course, I'll be right there." I replied. I hopped into the car and drove to the school. I signed Emma out of the nurse's office and decided to pick up Travis too since I was there, then we headed home. Back at the house, I followed Emma upstairs and tucked her into bed.

"Lie down and rest okay, sweetie? I'll get you a heating pad for your ear and some pain reliever. Do you need anything else?"

"No, thanks," she said in a sad little voice.

"What's wrong, Em?" I thought maybe her symptoms had grown worse.

"You look sad, Mom. Did I do something wrong?"

I tried so hard to not let my feelings show, but apparently, I wasn't doing a very good job. I took a deep breath to keep myself from having a meltdown, and said,

"You've done nothing wrong whatsoever. But I guess I am a little sad, for two reasons. One, because you're not feeling well; and two, because I won't be able to see my friend tonight. He came into town to visit me. But don't worry, you are much more important, my love. I just want you to get well. I'll be right back with your medicine okay?"

She grabbed my arm. "Mom, if I feel better, can you still see your friend?"

"I don't think so, but I'll see him another time. You shouldn't worry about that now okay?"

I left to get her the heating pad and medicine. While I was downstairs, I sat on the couch for a minute to collect my thoughts and the tears started pouring. The disappointment of not being able to go consumed me and I let it all out. After a few minutes, I wiped my face and stopped feeling sorry for myself. I looked out the window and watched as it began to rain. Strangely enough, it made me feel better, just like it did when I was little. I pulled myself together then decided to call Mitch and tell him our date was off. As I dialed his number, I hoped his voicemail would answer so I could avoid talking to him. Naturally, he picked up on the first ring.

"Hello, Ms. Laci! Are you ready for tonight?" he asked with the excitement of a kid. I hesitated to answer, overwhelmed with sadness.

"Actually, that's why I'm calling. I'm afraid tonight isn't going to work out, Mitch. The school called earlier and I had to go pick up my daughter Emma. She was in the nurse's office with an earache. I'm so sorry." There was no answer from him at first. I imagined he was reconsidering this whole "dating a mom of three kids" scenario. "You're not about to get out of this date that easy, darlin'," he said with a chuckle. "If we can't go out, then we'll stay in! I'm a parent too, remember? I remember what it was like when they were little. Life happens, so we'll work around it. Our date is *still* on, and I'll be at your house around six thirty as planned. Don't eat and don't worry about fixing anything for the kids. I'll take care of everything."

We said goodbye and hung up. I was in a complete state of shock. How was that going to work? Our first date…at my house. That wasn't exactly what I had in mind of course, but I wasn't about to nit-pick. From his reaction, he didn't want to miss out on our evening any more than I had. Once again, my innermost parts were singing and my heart was light. Even the butterflies were back!

I went back upstairs to give Emma her heating pad, feeling better after having talked to Mitch, and smiling from ear to ear. She looked up at me and said, "Mom, if you go see your friend tonight, maybe Teri could come and watch us?"

"Well, that was the plan originally, yes. Why, are you feeling better?" I wondered if the illness was just a ruse to keep me home. "My ear still hurts, but not as much. I think I'll be okay if Teri comes over to watch me. I want you to go see your friend. It's a date isn't it?" She gave me a sweet smile. Knowing her, she was

just saying that because she heard me crying downstairs earlier. "Yes, it's a date. But don't worry, it's all taken care of now. I just called Mitch, and I think we're going to have our date here tonight so I can stay with you."

Emma's eyes lit up and she grinned, reaching up to give me a hug. "I can't wait to meet him! I promise I'll be good," she said, giggling.

"I know; you're always good. Now get some rest." She lay back down and closed her eyes as I stepped out of the room. I went to my room and sat on the edge of my bed, now rethinking my wardrobe options for a "stay-in" date. The red dress was definitely out of the question, which was quite disappointing. I had sincerely hoped to turn his head a *little* bit with that one. Sadly, I would have to save it for *another* rainy day. All of a sudden, it hit me. Mitch was coming here—to my house! To my messy, cluttered house! In a hot second, I was flying around from room to room, picking up toys and clothes, throwing dishes in the dishwasher, dusting furniture, and sweeping floors, and all the while, the clock was ticking faster and faster. Travis and Todd came down to see what the fuss was all about. I shared the plan with them, and they both pitched in to help where they could. By the time we were done, I only had thirty minutes left to get ready. My phone rang. It was Teri.

I quickly answered the call. "Hi! I forgot to call you—change of plans."

Worry in her voice now, she asked, "What? What's going on?" "Emma came home sick from school so I called Mitch to cancel our date, but now he is coming here. He wants to have it here—at my house!" I shouted, my voice obviously showing severe signs of stress.

"Oh no! That won't do at all! I am coming over and you two are going out!" She demanded.

"It's too late. I've already talked to Mitch and he's got some- thing up his sleeve, I can tell. Emma is ecstatic that we are staying home, even in her weak state, which I'm almost sure is ninety percent in her head. She doesn't even have a fever, but her ear does hurt. I can tell."

Teri laughed. "He's crazy about you, you know that, right? You two spend one day together, a hundred phone calls and emails over the last two weeks, and now he is moving heaven and earth to make sure you can be together tonight. You are the *luckiest* woman I know and I hate you right now. I do!" she said, still laughing. Teri cracked me up and I laughed right along with her. Then I checked the time and screamed.

"I've got to go get ready, girl! I'll see you tomorrow okay? I'll be in late."

"You'd better be there! Have fun tonight!" She said and wished me good luck.

Back in my closet, I was once again staring into the abyss of crappy outfit choices, struggling to decide on what to wear...at home...on our first date. I settled for black capri pants, a cute black-and-white sleeveless blouse, and little black patent leather sandals. Luckily, the hours on a tanning bed had paid off; my arms and legs were a nice golden brown for a change. I fluffed my hair and touched up my makeup. My hands were shaking, so I avoided my eyes altogether, afraid I would look like Cruella de Ville if I tried.

Travis ran into my room, looked up at me, and said, "You look pretty, mom!" I smiled, then bent down and hugged him.

"Thank you, sweetie. Are you going to be good and watch a movie upstairs with Todd while Mitch is here?"

He gave me his little pouty look. "Yes. I won't bother your dating." I laughed and hugged him again, realizing I needed it more than he did. I was so nervous I could barely breathe. The clock now read 6:30 and I made my way downstairs, turned on some music, and checked everything one last time, praying that he wouldn't be too disappointed in my humble surroundings. But if he was even *half* the man I thought he was...he wouldn't care. The doorbell rang and I froze. I took a deep breath and tried to steady my knees, and then I opened the door. Mitch stood on the porch with an umbrella in one hand and a bouquet of wild flowers in the other. He took my breath away. He was so handsome in his black pants and simple pale blue dress shirt, his tan chest peeking out from a small opening at the top. I feared my heart had stopped completely at the sight of him, so I checked my pulse for good measure. Luckily, all was good.

"Come in, come in! Get out of the rain," I said, escorting him inside.

"Hey, darlin'. Happy first date." He gave me a sweet smile and looked at me like he was seeing me for the first time. "You look beautiful," he whispered as he handed me the flowers. These are for you." He leaned in and kissed me softly on the cheek. The smell of his cologne drifted by me and a quiet whimper accidentally escaped as I exhaled. My eyes flew open and I prayed he hadn't heard me.

"Are you okay?" he asked, obvious that he had heard.

My cheeks flushed, and I cleared my throat, "Oh, yes. I'm fine.

Just a...frog in my throat. No worries."

He just smiled. "Okay, well I've got a few more things to bring in. I'll be right back." He walked out to his car to retrieve a basket and a small cooler. I opened the door for him and laughed, wondering what they contained.

"You don't travel light do you? Can I help you carry something?" "Nope, I've got it covered. Just point me to the kitchen and I'll

show you what comes next!"

I led him into my little bistro styled kitchen, then I sat down at the snack bar and watched as he unpacked. First he pulled out some type of cheese, then a bunch of grapes, two wine glasses, and prosciutto, and from the cooler he pulled out two beautiful salmon filets, fresh asparagus, and a bowl of prepared rice. My mouth fell open as I looked at all the beautiful food, realizing the thought and preparation he'd put into making the night special. Words could not begin to express the amount of joy I felt. I was simply amazed. Tears filled my eyes as I looked at him from across the bar.

"Mitch, this is too much. I never expected you to cook for us! I feel bad. And I'm sure this isn't what you imagined for our first date, cooking in my house with three kids upstairs." I tried to hold the tears back, but a few escaped and rolled down my cheek. I turned my head and wiped them away so he wouldn't see, but it was too late. He walked around the bar and stood directly in front of me, cupping my face in his hands.

"Being here right now, cooking for you, and spending time with you is exactly where I want to be, where I'm supposed to be." His thumbs glided across my cheek, wiping away the remnants of a few tears, and then he brushed a strand of hair away from my eye. It suddenly became hard to breathe. He gently tilted my face up and leaned down. It was about to happen…our first kiss! And I closed my eyes…

Suddenly, a tiny voice from behind me asked, "Hey, mom. Can I have some juice?" Travis had made a stealthy and sneaky entrance into the kitchen.

Mitch smiled and winked at me. He raised himself up and walked back around to the other side of the counter, his cheeks now a tad pink. "Of course you can, sweetie. By the way Travis, this is my friend, Mitch. Can you say 'hi'?" Mitch offered him his hand, and surprisingly, Travis knew to shake it. I had no idea he had ever done that before. Travis was a little shy, so Mitch started off the introductions.

"Hi, Travis. It's nice to meet you. I was wondering if you could you help me with something?" Mitch asked.

"Sure, I guess." Travis said, shrugging his shoulders. His curiosity was up now.

"Great! Are you hungry?"

Travis's eyes grew to the size of half dollars. "Yeah!"

"Well, it just so happens that I have something in this basket for both you and your brother, but you have to promise me one thing first." Mitch smiled, knelt down, and whispered something in Travis's ear. Travis looked at me and grinned, then ran over and threw his hands up, asking for a hug. I laughed and reached down to give him his hug. He ran back to Mitch for a high five.

"Way to go, little man!" Mitch said enthusiastically, and he pulled two frozen dinners from the basket, one kid-sized cuisine and one for a "hungry man." He put them in the microwave. I couldn't help but crack a laugh as I watched this manly display unfold. The timer went off and he took them out.

"Okay, Travis. How about you show me up to your man cave? You carry your dinner and I'll carry Todd's, if that's all right with Mom." Mitch looked at me for approval.

"It's fine. Just be careful okay, buddy?"

"I will, Mom!" Travis took off upstairs, showing Mitch the way. My head was spinning! He had not only thought about our dinner, but my kids' too. Never having met them before that night, he had managed to score big points with the small one— that wasn't easy.

Mitch walked back downstairs and into the kitchen. "Well, when I brought Todd's food in the room, he said 'you rock, dude.' I'm hoping that's good?" he asked with a chuckle in his voice.

"Oh, that's very good!" I said, shaking my head in amazement. "Thank you, for bringing them dinner. That was so thoughtful." "It was my pleasure. I couldn't very well show up without something for everyone. Which reminds me, I brought chicken noodle soup for Emma. I wasn't sure what she would want to eat, not feeling well and all."

"She'll be thrilled. That's her favorite. And speaking of Emma, I should go up and check on her. Are you okay down here by yourself?"

"Of course, go! I do know my way around a kitchen, Ms. Kramer. I'm sure the boogeyman and I will be fine down here, all alone." And he gave me his Dr. Evil laugh just for spite. I laughed and walked upstairs. I remembered back to our flight, how he had talked about his love for cooking. I never thought it possible that he would actually be downstairs cooking in *my* kitchen!

When I got to Emma's door, she was in bed but still awake. "Hey sweetie, how are you feeling?"

"About the same, I guess. Is your date here?"

"Yes, he's downstairs cooking dinner for him and me, and he brought something for you too: chicken noodle soup."

Her tired little eyes lit up. "My favorite! How did he know?" "Hmmm...I'm not sure, but I'm guessing Mitch's son used to love chicken noodle soup when he was little and he'd get sick. Maybe he thought it would make you feel better too. Do you want some?"

She nodded. "Yes! I'm super hungry!"

"Okay, lie back down and I'll go warm it up. Be right back." And I stood up to leave.

"Mom," Emma said, stopping me before I left her room. "Can he come up with you when you bring my soup? I want to tell him thanks."

I smiled at her. Emma had such a caring soul, a priceless trait she got from her dad. "Sure, I'll bring Mitch up. That's very thoughtful of you, sweetie."

I went back downstairs. Mitch had put our dinner in the oven and had already warmed up Emma's soup, so we took it up to her room and I introduced them. She smiled sweetly and said, "It's nice to meet you. Thanks for my soup. It's my favorite!"

He walked over next to her bed and knelt on the floor. "You are most welcome, Emma. It's very nice to finally meet you too. Your mom has told me how creative you are. I hope you feel better soon so I can see some of your arts and crafts."

"Thanks! I will. And…umm…Mitch? Thanks for bringing your date to our house," she said and slurped her soup.

Mitch laughed. "It was my pleasure, Emma."

He stood up, took my hand, and we walked back down to the kitchen. I wasn't sure, but if I had to guess, I would say my daughter had just developed a crush on my…boyfriend? Friend? What was he? Was he anything? Would he even want to be? *Ugh!* I decided it best to wait until *after* the date was over before I made too many assumptions.

"It looks like you have charmed your way right to the top around here. I'm impressed. Do you have any other surprises in your bag of tricks, Mr. Young?" I laughed and started to peek into his basket.

Swiftly, he closed the lid on my hand. "Just one more if you must know, but you'll have to wait until after dinner. Now, if you'll kindly hand me that bottle of wine I sent you earlier today, we'll begin your first wine tasting lesson." He smiled.

I passed him the Pinot. He took me by the hand and led me to the snack bar. He pointed to the barstool, and I sat down on his cue. He slid the other stool over next to me and sat down. He handed me a glass and as he opened the bottle, I noticed the wine label for the first time. It read, "Rainstorm 2009 Oregon Pinot Noir." Quite appropriate for our evening since the rain continued to pour down. And it was also then that I realized the wine bore the same year we had both lost our spouses. A shiver ran through me as I thought how truly fitting it was; how the rainstorm had washed away our past and made things new. That night was a new beginning indeed.

Mitch poured a small amount of wine in my glass, then in his. "Wine needs to breathe," he said as he swirled it around in the glass. No wait, that was *me* who needed to breathe...I didn't care about the wine! Being so close to him like that, my senses were on high alert and I could feel my heart pounding.

"A good wine is about the color, the smell, and the taste. Pinot Noir pairs best with a meal, like our salmon. But first, you need to taste the wine by itself." His voice was soft and low, slowly explaining each step one at a time. I quickly became very attentive to him.

"Close your eyes. Smell the aroma and take a small sip. Let the wine sit on your tongue for a moment, then swallow."

Listening to him made every nerve in my body tingle and cry out for more. I was definitely under his spell—in a trance-like state even. If he had asked me to cluck like a chicken right then, I probably would have done it! My eyes were closed and I did exactly as he said, rolling the wine around slowly in my mouth, then letting it slide down my throat.

"Now, tell me what you taste." he whispered.

I opened my eyes and he was staring at me, smiling and waiting for my reply. I could barely think straight, let alone tell him how it had tasted. Finally my words found their way out, though my voice was shaky. "It was bitter, at first. I could swear I tasted cherries for a minute. Then a light, sweet taste came through and it was kind of smooth as it went down my throat," I said, my cheeks blushing again. "I liked it." And I looked down, smiling.

His eyes never left me. He even looked a bit stunned. "I'm… impressed! A *very* nice description indeed." He smiled, proud as a peacock.

"Well, I had a good instructor," I said. I was so shaky that I dropped my glass and spilled my wine! I was utterly embarrassed and immediately became upset. I apologized, scolding myself under my breath, then got up and started cleaning my mess. My face was forty different shades of red by then. I couldn't even look at him.

He laid his hands on mine. "Laci, stop. It's fine, really," he said, laughing softly. "Mercy, you're cute when you get mad." We laughed and finished wiping up the counter then sat back down. "Now, let's have a toast shall we?"

He lifted his glass toward me and spoke in his soft, sweet voice. "Here's to divine intervention, chance encounters on a plane, to layovers, to the Crawdads, to late-night phone calls, good books, surprise text messages, great wine, the rain, and to this first of hopefully many more dates to come. And last but not least, to you, Ms. Laci Kramer. You've turned my world right side up since the minute I laid eyes on you and I think it's only fair to tell you that…well, I've fallen for you."

His words made me swoon and I could barely remember what came next. I was fairly sure our glasses clinked and I took a sip of wine, but it was somewhat of a blur. And I knew it wasn't the wine. I shook it off and was again fully engaged in what was going on around me. Mitch set his glass down and slowly leaned his gorgeous face towards me. My hands shook so I set my glass down, watching it wobble all the way. He moved in and his lips gently brushed over mine. They were so warm and soft. He lifted his hand to caress the back of my neck and pulled me deeper into the kiss. The sweet cherry taste from the wine still lingered on his lips. I wrapped my arms around him and let my fingers dance slowly through his soft, thick hair. His strong arms moved behind my back, but his hands never wandered. He was the perfect gentleman and my heart overflowed. He pulled away slightly and broke our kiss. He opened his eyes to look at me. "I hope your heartbeat is an indication that you enjoy kissing me, if not, I'd better call 911," he said with a soft laugh. My face turned bright red again.

"Yeah, you could say that. It has a habit of doing that when you're close by. Actually it does that even if you're within a fifty- mile radius."

He reached up and ran his fingertip across the edge of my bottom lip. "You're lips are even sweeter than I imagined. I've wanted to kiss them since the day we met, but figured that was a bit too soon," he said.

Okay, maybe that 911 thing wasn't such a bad idea after all – crash cart, paddles, *anything!*

"I'm glad we waited until now too, this was much better. Although I normally don't kiss on the first date, so you should consider yourself very fortunate," I said and smiled at him. I could still feel my heart racing.

"I consider myself very blessed, darlin'," he said, then he reached down and lifted my hand, kissing the top softly like he did the day we met. The oven buzzer went off and I jumped ten feet. He burst out with a belly laugh, and I found the nearest hand towel to throw at him for spite. Dinner was ready so I got up to set the table while he plated everything. Then he walked over to his basket and pulled out two candles, put them on the table, and lit them. He had thought of everything...

We sat down at the table across from one another, and he reached over and took my hands in his.

"Would you mind if we say grace?"

My jaw dropped to the floor, and I stuttered a reply. "Of course…yes, please."

We bowed our heads and closed our eyes, though I peeked once at his handsome face. His prayer was short, simply thanking God for our food, our many blessings, for me and my family, and for the rain falling outside as he prayed. He had given me another reason to want him in my life even more. Not to mention that the dinner he made was out of this world! The salmon was mouthwatering with a cherry chipotle glaze on top, perfect with the Pinot Noir. I looked over at him and smiled, gloriously happy with our first date.

After dinner, he cleared the dishes then said, "I have one more surprise." Going back to his basket of surprises, he pulled out a DVD: *The Count of Monte Cristo*. A happy squeal escaped my mouth, and I jumped up and down like a little girl.

"Ah! Sweet! I can't believe you brought this. Is there *anything* you haven't thought of, Mr. Young?"

"Well, actually there is *one* thing I forgot." He hesitated and a pouty look appeared on his face.

"What's that?"

"Dessert. I forgot our dessert. I'm so sorry."

I had to laugh a little because as it turned out, I had made a treat for the kids the previous night and they had hardly touched it. I walked over to the fridge, somewhat cocky in knowing I had saved the day. I took it out and put it in the oven to warm.

A quirky grin covered his face. "What is that you have there, Ms. Laci?"

"Why, it's dessert of course. I made some homemade hot fudge cake last night and there's quite a bit leftover. It's better warm though."

"You bake?" he asked, a surprise tone in his voice. He began walking towards me with a slow, yet determined stride.

"Why does that surprise you? I'm not totally inept in a kitchen, you know. I have kids to feed. And I like to make desserts, so sue me," I said with a giggle.

"Not surprised, but most certainly pleased. I'm a big fan of dessert, you know. However, I don't think I've ever had hot fudge cake," he said in his deep southern voice, still inching his way toward me.

Where was that oven mitt when you needed it?! Between the heat from the oven and the heat coming from him, I had to fan myself for some relief. He was still moving toward me, so I toyed with him a little and started walking backwards away from him. "I also have vanilla ice cream. It pairs nicely with the cake," I said in a playful tone. I laughed, knowing I had cracked a small joke on his wine etiquette.

He laughed too, then walked towards me, grabbed me by the waist, and pulled me into a warm embrace. "I think you're the one full of surprises now," he whispered softly in my ear. I would definitely have to crank up that AC soon!

"Maybe one or two. Now go put our movie in," I said, smiling and pushing him away.

He walked over to the TV and got the movie ready while I prepared a bowl of cake and ice cream. I watched him and wondered how all of this could be happening after just one day on a plane together. I could easily get used to him being around on a more regular basis, but it's a little soon for that...or was it?

Before he pressed play on the remote, I decided to go up and check on the kids. Travis and Todd were perfectly content watching their movie, and Emma was sound asleep; her empty bowl of soup was on the floor. Back downstairs,

Mitch was already on the couch holding the remote. I smiled and sat next to him.

"How is everything upstairs? Is Emma feeling any better?" "The boys are zoned out with their movie and Emma is

already asleep. She even ate all her soup, so that's a good sign." "Of course she ate her soup. I made it!" He laughed, all proud of himself.

The movie started to play while we enjoyed our dessert. He finished first and set his bowl on the table in front of us. "That

was delicious, Ms. Laci. You have some serious baking skills," he said with a sweet smile.

"Why thank you. I guess I'm still full from dinner." I set my half-full bowl on the table. There was no way I could eat one more bite – the butterflies had already taken up too much space in my stomach.

Immediately, I started to worry about our proximity to each other on the couch. There was an ocean between us! We looked like teenagers at our first movie, when the guy was about to fake a yawn and put his arm around the girl. But if *I* scooted closer to him, he might think I'm expecting something…which of course I was! Luckily, I didn't have to stress about it too long. Mitch started to slouch a little and leaned over my direction, the edge of our shoulders barely touching. Then, slow as southern molasses, his arm slid across the couch toward my leg. He was either trying to sneak a cookie from the cookie jar or trying to hold my hand – it was still up for debate. My hands were on my lap, but that didn't stop him. Finally, he reached over and took my hand, pulling it over onto his leg and covering it with his other hand.

My heart was pounding and it was hard to concentrate being so close to him, but after a few minutes, I calmed down and was able to enjoy the movie. At one point, he looked over at me and I was utterly engrossed in mouthing the characters' lines during a scene.

He laughed. "Wow, you *really* like this movie!"

"Are you laughing at me, Mr. Young?" I asked with a snarky voice. "Because if you are, that's not very nice and I think you deserve some payback." And without another thought, I reached over with my free hand and started poking his side quarters, hoping to find a weak spot I could pursue. But to no avail, because he wasn't ticklish! He laughed at my feeble attempt and never flinched once.

"Oh, darlin', you should never start something you can't finish." He smiled.

Then at that moment, the tables turned. Recognizing right away that I was extremely ticklish at the slightest touch, he took full advantage of the opportunity to pinpoint my weakest spot, sending me into a fit of laughter to the point of tears. Small tears spilled from the corners of my eyes from laughing so hard, and I begged him to stop. He looked at me and paused, then pulled me close. My eyes were fixed on his face and I melted into his warmth. The laughter that escaped my lungs just seconds ago had now been replaced with shallow, unsteady breathing, rendering me paralyzed by his touch. I laid my head against his chest and lingered inside his arms.

The last line of the movie played and my heart sank knowing our date was about to end. In response to that thought, I sighed and pulled away.

"I don't want this night to end," I said sadly. "I know. Me neither."

As he echoed my sentiment, I realized that I didn't know when we'd be together next, which made it even worse. We stood up and took our dishes to the kitchen. Then, to make matters worse, I yawned. I was totally embarrassed and I worried that he might think I was growing bored of his company.

"I'm so sorry. It's not you I promise. I've been pretty tired lately, too much going on at work, I guess." I laughed at myself to cover up the fact that I was more than a little tired; I was achy too, but I just wrote it off to recent stress.

"It's okay. It's late, and I should probably head out anyway." Mitch packed up his bag of surprises then helped me clean up a little. "Did you have fun tonight?" he asked while washing our dessert bowls. I was completely taken with him.

"I can't even begin to describe what an amazing night this was. It was unbelievable." Feeling a little bold, I walked around the counter and wiggled my way in between him and the sink, then curled my hands around his neck. His wet, soapy hands folded around me. "Thank you," I whispered. A tear rolled down my cheek.

"It was my pleasure. And I can't wait until we do it again," he said softly. He brought his lips down to meet mine once again, pressing me firmly against the edge of the sink and sending me to another place entirely.

Reluctantly, I helped him take everything out to his car, and then we came back inside for one last goodbye. Emma had woken up and she and Travis were now standing at the top of the stairs, watching and giggling at the two of us.

"Bye, Mitch, thank you!" they yelled down. Todd even peeked around the corner to say "See ya, dude," which was quite impressive.

"Bye guys. It was nice to meet you. Get well Emma," Mitch replied.

That was one huge stress off my shoulders at least – the kids liked him! Well, three out of the four anyway. I walked him out to the front porch. The rain had stopped and I could see a few stars peeking out from behind the clouds.

Looking up at him, I asked, "So, where do we go from here, Mr. Young?" Without hesitation, he wrapped his arms around my waist and pulled me close, brushing the hair from my eyes.

In his charming, warm southern voice, he simply said, "Anywhere you wish, darlin'. But I'm hoping you'll at least accompany me to a winery on Saturday, after you recover from your event Friday night, of course. It's not far from here. Would you be interested?"

"I'd love to! Just to be clear though, is this date number two or a casual invitation? It could make a difference you know." I laughed.

"Well, we wouldn't want any confusion in that area, now would we? So, I'm inclined to go with date number two, if that's all right with you." He played with my hair and the scent of his cologne swirled around me in the gentle breeze. I drew in a deep breath and created a memory of the moment. Stored away now with the others; like the scent of that cheap hairspray that always made me remember my high school flag corps team primping in the bathroom after our half-time show. "That's more than all right with me. So I guess this means you kind of like me, huh?" I asked in a mischievous tone. Thankfully, my blushing cheeks were hidden by the black night.

"Hmm…I might," he said as he kissed me softly on the top of my head. "But it could be a long courtship." He kissed me on my forehead. "And we'll have to keep practicing." He kissed me on the cheek. "To be certain." Then he kissed my other cheek. "This part especially." Then he kissed my chin. "To make sure I have enough information." He kissed my bottom lip. "To base my final decision." And in one swift, strong motion, his lips were pressing hard against mine, full and deep, no longer holding back. Everything we had felt that night and had saved for each other was poured into that loving, passionate kiss that lingered on. I was lost in him and didn't want to be found. Every muscle in my body was shaking and I could feel my knees about to give out. He must have felt it too because his embrace tightened and he lifted me up off the ground, never removing his lips from mine. Gently, he pulled away and leaned his forehead against mine as we quietly caught our breath. He held me until I was steady, and then sat me down.

"I don't want to say goodnight, but I need to. I'm heading down to Oregon in the morning to visit a couple of wineries. I'll be back in town late Friday night, but I'll call you in between, okay?"

"You'd better. And please be careful driving. I'm kind of sensitive in that area." I smiled, looking down. "Thank you for everything. This first date was amazing, even if it was with a creepy stalker guy." We both laughed. He took my hand in his, kissed it softly, and said goodnight.

He drove away and I smiled, finding it hard to move. That entire day and my night with him had me wound tighter than an eight-day clock. If he only knew what he did to me! I went back inside and finished cleaning up what was left of our evening together. I picked up a wine glass and remembered the taste on his lips and how they felt against mine. I smiled as I felt the heat rise in my cheeks. After I finished, I turned out the lights and went upstairs to check on the kids. Emma had fallen back to sleep and the boys were groggy, nearing the end of their movie.

I walked over to tuck in Travis. "Goodnight sweetie. I love you. Thank you for being such a good boy tonight," I whispered. "Love you too mom. Did you have a nice dating night?" he asked, yawning.

"I certainly did. Now get some sleep, okay?"

"Okay. I think I kind of like Mr. Mitch," he said sweetly. I smiled and kissed him goodnight. Todd whispered down from the top bunk, "Night, Mom."

"Goodnight, hon. Thanks for keeping Travis entertained for me."

"You're welcome. He was pretty cool. You really like him, huh?"

"I really do. He understands what it's like to lose someone; he lost his wife several years ago. And he makes me feel special," I whispered. Travis was already snoring below, and it made me giggle.

"I'm glad. But you won't forget dad, will you?" Todd's question knocked the wind from my lungs; it was the last question I had expected. I hadn't even considered their feelings about me dating again. The entire time I had been consumed with my own feelings for Mitch, caught up in the whirlwind of it all, thinking only about myself.

"Todd, your dad was my whole world and the love of my life. I will never forget him as long as I live. Every day when I look in your eyes, when I hear Travis's laugh, I know he's with us. He's part of you. I think he would want me to be happy and find love again, find someone I can grow old and share my life with after all of you are grown and gone. Don't you?"

"Yeah, he would. I want you to be happy too. It's just weird seeing you with someone else I guess," he admitted.

"That's perfectly normal. All you've ever known is me and dad. It will take time to adjust, I know. Just promise me that you'll keep talking to me okay? You and your brothers and sister will always come first for me—always! Don't ever forget that," I said, and I reached up to give him a half hug as he leaned down over the bunk.

Lying in bed, I hugged the pillow next to me then gave in to the wave of emotion I held captive inside. The tears fell like a hard rain and I cried to the point of being breathless. I missed Andrew all the time and I felt guilty for liking Mitch. Was I doing right by my kids? How could I be deliriously happy one minute, and feel the world crashing around me the next? Was I meant to be happy? I took a deep breath and let it all out until my eyes could cry no more. I sat up, turned on a lamp, and pulled out my little Bible. It fell open to the book of Jeremiah and my eyes were drawn to a highlighted verse I knew all too well: "For I know the plans I have for you, declares the Lord. Plans to prosper you and not to harm you, plans to give you hope and a future" (Jeremiah 29:11, niv).

After I read the words, a weight lifted from my chest and I literally felt God set me free of the guilt I had harbored for so long. A sense of peace came over me, and immediately, my urge to cry was taken away. God's plans for me were so much better than my own! I closed my eyes and asked God to guide me, show me his plan, and keep me on track. Then, Mitch's face appeared in my mind. Oh good grief! I couldn't even pray without thinking about him! Yet I wondered (and hoped) if Mitch was part of his plan. I decided it best to trust God with everything and turned off the light.

cinderella and the "beach" ball

I woke up that next morning and felt different, like I had come alive in ways I never thought possible. My enthusiasm to begin the day overflowed a bit and I was pretty sure my kids were wondering what planet their mom was on. I didn't care. I was too happy to let anything or anyone ruin that day. I dropped the kids off at school and headed straight to the coffee shop. My eyes were still a little puffy from my midnight cry, but despite that, today held nothing but joy and new possibilities. My phone rang and recognizing Mitch's number, I let out a little squeal of joy.

"Good morning, handsome!" I answered cheerfully.

"Mercy, someone is in a good mood this morning," he said with a soft laugh.

"Yeah, must have been that wine I had last night. It was so good."

"I see. Well remind me to get you more of that wine." His deep voice gave me happy chills. Selfishly, I didn't want him to leave town at all, but I knew he had places to go and grapes to see. "Yes, that would be very nice, but only if you promise to deliver it in person."

"Now that is one promise I can easily make, darlin'."

"So, are you on the road yet?" I asked, now sad at the thought of him getting farther and farther away.

"Yep. I just stopped to fill up my gas tank then I'll be on my way. I should be in Oregon by eleven o'clock or so, but I'll call you when I get there, don't worry. You miss me, huh?" he asked, gloating.

"Hmm...maybe a little bit," I answered in a silly tone. "Okay, maybe a lot."

"Good, glad I'm not the only one. I can't seem to get you off my mind, Ms. Laci. Last night was rather wonderful. I hope it was just the beginning..." The beginning? That word made my entire day! I was so happy I could have jumped through the phone and...well, hugged him or something!

"I hope so too. I like new beginnings."

"Are you still planning to join me for the winery tour on Saturday?"

"I wouldn't miss it, Mr. Young. But right now I need to go. I'm at the coffee shop and my order is up. Be careful driving okay?" I asked, trying not to be that nagging girlfriend.

It was different now, right? Did I mean something more to him now that our first date has come and gone? I supposed it was too presumptuous of me to say 'girlfriend'. Maybe I was sim- ply a bright, caring lady that sat next to him on the plane. Or maybe I had become the annoying girl that likes the rain. Either way, I would happily wait and see what this 'new beginning' had in store.

"I will. Have a good day, Laci."

We hung up and his sweet voice lingered in the air for a minute. It was surprising how much my insides already ached with- out him there. With coffee in hand, I drove to work.

The first part of my morning was spent chatting with the girls, and I gave them the scoop about how my date went. Their laughter and occasional squeals were heard all the way down the hall, especially when I shared the part about me spilling the wine.

I found work to do for a while, but my mind was elsewhere. After lunch, Lena stopped by my office to get a file and shared a few sentiments with me.

"It's written all of your face, you know," she said, smiling. "What is?" I asked, playing dumb. Of course I knew exactly
what she meant, but I pretended otherwise.

"You've already given him your heart, girlfriend!" She winked at me then walked out, leaving me to ponder her observation. Was I that transparent to everyone? If she noticed, had Mitch too? My heart had belonged to Andrew for so long, I worried that I might never give it away again. But Lena was right. I had given him my heart...and he held it in the palm of his hand.

The rest of the day went by pretty fast, thankfully. I left work early to prep some décor at the event site, and then went home for the night.

Mitch left the gas station feeling good after his morning call with Laci. She was on his mind 24/7. So much so that getting the winery up and running had fallen behind schedule. Making the best use of his drive to Oregon, he decided to call his brother Brad and work over the phone.

"Brad, hey. What's going on at home?"

"Oh, it's my little brother and business partner, or is that ex- partner? How nice of you to call. I wasn't sure you even remembered who I was with your Airplane Girl there and all," Brad said, obviously frustrated with Mitch's new distraction.

"I deserve that I suppose, but you'll be happy to know that I'm on my way to the Willamette Valley for my first of not one, but two tours." Mitch's confidence and current efforts hoped to change the tune of the call. "And her name is Laci, not Airplane Girl."

"Laci, whatever. And that is good news, unless of course she's with you. If she is, you won't get anything done—"

"No, Brad, she's not with me. She has a big event for work tomorrow."

"Wow, and you're still breathing? I'm shocked." Brad's voice was sharp with sarcasm.

"Look, I was hoping we could go over some business while I drive, but if you're going to be a jerk the entire time, then I'll hang up."

"Fine, fine. I'm just messing with you, little brother. Okay, we need to talk about a name for the winery and pick a name for our first label, and you need to decide on an ad agency when you have time to look over the proposals I sent to your email."

"You couldn't give me something easier to start with?" Mitch laughed.

"All right. I suppose you could tell me how your first date with Airpl——, I mean Laci, went. I know you're itchin' to anyway."

"Why thank you, that's much easier!" Mitch paused, smiling at the memory of their night together; he missed her already. "And since you asked, it was an amazing night. She's unbelievable, Brad. Her kids are too. And she's got a gift when it comes to wine, but she doesn't even know it. She picked the cherry notes out of the Pinot after one taste last night."

"Impressive. Let's get her on the payroll. Oh wait, there is no payroll because we're not open yet, silly me." Brad's smart aleck comments and dry wit continued to drag the conversation down. "Do you want to know how our date went or not? Jeez, Brad.

You're acting like a jealous teenager! I thought you wanted me to date again, find love, be happy," Mitch said, growing tired of his brother's attitude.

"I did. I do. I guess I didn't think it would happen this fast. You just met her dude, and you're already acting like she's 'the one.'"

"Brad, you know me. You know I don't rush into things, and I'm pretty picky when it comes to finding someone after what I've been through. You should also know that Laci is special. There's something strong between us that I can't explain, nor ignore.

When I'm with her, I feel whole again. And I know it's only been a few weeks, but I'm falling in love with her—there, I said it. So yes, to use your words, I do think she could be 'the one.'" Saying it out loud for the first time felt good. He had known it ever since he first sat down beside her on the plane.

"Whoa, little brother, let's slow this love boat down a little!

Have you declared your revelation of love to her yet?"

"No, of course not, I don't want to scare her off. I'll know the right time when it comes. But you need to get off my back and deal with it. She's in my life and I want her to stay there. Got it?" Mitch's tone was strong enough for Brad to know he was serious.

"Okay, okay, I got it. Airplane Girl in."

If Mitch had to guess, Brad probably just rolled his eyes as he said that last comment.

"Thank you. Now, I've got an idea for our winery name. How about 'Three Young Vines'? I figured Caleb will probably be running it one day, and he's already working there, so it's only right to include him.

"I like it. It's good."

"And I have an idea for our first label, but before you get all 'judgey,' please hear me out. I was thinking either 'Laci's Rain' or 'Hope's Rain.' And yes, it's for Laci. She believes that good things come with the rain or right after it rains. And if I remember correctly, it rained the day I stumbled onto our winery. So who knows, maybe there's something to her theory." Mitch's memory of that day brought a smile to his face, how he'd felt that God had guided him to that very spot, showing him a glimpse of his new future—a future filled with hope and promise.

Brad laughed out loud. "Well, since I'm the 'judgey' type, I'd have to say that they both stink! Who is going to buy a bottle of wine named 'Laci's Rain'? It sounds like she cried in the bottle and made wine from her tears or something. You can't be serious?" Brad's comments bruised Mitch's ego a tad, but he knew
 once they met each other that things would be different; they had to.

"All right, just keep them on the list for now and give them some thought, okay?"

"Yeah, yeah. They're on the list. I had a label idea too, you know. Want to hear it?" Brad asked.

"Sure, shoot."

"I was thinking 'Rowdy Boys.' How do you like it? It's on the list right?" Brad's hearty laugh followed.

"Wow, Brad. I'm sure that holds tremendous emotion and meaning for you. It must have taken you all of, what, five seconds to come up with that?" Mitch laughed and at this point realized the "working" phone call had come to a screeching halt.

"Listen, I've got some heavy traffic up ahead. I'll call you after I get to the winery okay?"

"Sounds good. Talk to you later, little brother."

Mitch pulled into Carlton, Oregon, around eleven thirty, sent Laci a text to let her know he had arrived, then spent the rest of the day at the first winery on his list. The tour went great, but he was anxious to leave and move on to the next vineyard in Gaston before evening set. That one held the most promise. For the last several months, he'd been reading about their success online and it was the one he really wanted as a grape supplier for their Pinot Noir. It wasn't until recently however, after meeting Laci, that he'd realized the vineyard shared her last name. It was called Kramer Vineyards. That was no accident; it was just God being God, full of surprises and affirming once again that his future was about so much more than just wine. It was about a new beginning, a life with Laci.

He checked into his hotel and tried to sleep, but his mind was racing with thoughts of Laci and their possible future together. He hoped she wanted one with him as much as he did. In an effort to find rest, he decided to call her and say good night.

Evening arrived and I still hadn't heard anything from Mitch except for his one text that morning to let me know he had arrived. I lay in bed and felt sorry for myself, wishing I could be there with him. I'm sure he's deep in wine country with no cell phone signal. Saturday wouldn't arrive soon enough! I was too exhausted to sleep; my mind spilled over with thoughts of Mitch, my wine tasting, his arms around me, and then my phone buzzed and I saw Creepy Stalker Guy flash across the screen. My heart leapt inside my chest. That man sure could flip on my electrical system!

I answered the call. "Well hello, Mr. Young. I was hoping to hear your voice tonight." I was certain he could hear my smile right through the phone.

"Hey darlin'. Hope I didn't wake you. I wanted to say good- night. I've missed you today." Once again, his sweet, southern voice raised every goose bump on my body. The mere fact that he had the ability to do that shouldn't even be legal, but I decided to let it slide that once…maybe twice. Okay fine – let's just say I was willing to suffer any and all future offenses as a community service!

"I miss you too. I couldn't sleep. I just kept tossing and turning, thinking about you. I would have called, but I figured you'd had a pretty long day and I didn't want to wake you. I wish I was there with you though."

"Well, in a matter of speaking, you are. You're never going to guess the name of the vineyard I'm touring tomorrow."

With a gentle laugh, I replied, "You would be right. I'll never guess because I'm horrible at games, so please just tell me!"

"Oh all right. I can't wait for you to guess anyway. It's Kramer Vineyards. Pretty cool, huh?"

"You're kidding me! It really has my last name?"

"It really does. I'll send you a picture of their sign tomorrow. So see, you really are here with me, in more ways than one." Mitch yawned, exhausted from his long drive that day.

"Well, you're definitely there for a reason then. It must be a good sign since they used my name. I hope things go well tomorrow. You'd better get some sleep now though. I can hear how tired you are. Sweet dreams, Mitch," I said.

"Goodnight, darlin'." Mitch replied. *My dreams are always sweet when you're in them*, he thought, and within minutes his head fell silent on the pillow.

———⎯⎯⎯⎯⎯⎯⎯⎯———

The day of the beach party event had finally arrived and I woke up feeling both anxious and excited. The weather was perfect; it was hot and sunny, which was rare for late in August. I arrived at the museum and found a place to park, then walked around to find Sandy when I heard a familiar chime from my phone. I closed my eyes and inwardly wished it was Mitch. It was!

<Good luck tonight, darlin'! Have fun, but not too much fun since I'm not there. Ha Ha. Miss you!>

I was bouncing off the walls, hyper-happy since I'd already heard from Mitch. I was pretty sure I was driving Sandy a little nuts, but it was fun nonetheless. For the better part of the morning, we decorated tables, set up vendor areas and fluffed the auction items to make them look good. By midafternoon, I hadn't heard anything more from Mitch and my "hyper-happy" feeling had turned into more of a "ho-hum." I wrote it off thinking he probably didn't want to bother me while I was working or maybe his cell phone was dead. I took a short break to rest and grab a snack, but even the smallest lull in activity caused me to lose focus. Instead of recharging my batteries, I decided to throw a mini pity-party and beat myself up for not inviting him there that night. Then I took it a step further and tried to make sense of my intense feelings for him and how they could develop in such a short time. That break just kept getting better by the minute! What's next? Oh yeah…the 'mini-melt-down'…those were always fun. Okay, break over…it was time to get busy and stay focused on my job.

A few short hours later, we added the last-minute touches and lit the tiki torches. As the guests arrived, I couldn't help but notice the sunset; it was breathtaking. Tables were adorned with crisp, white linens wrapped with colorful ocean-blue sashes and miniature sandcastle candles were glowing in the center of each one. The band announced their presence with a jamming beach tune that officially kicked off the event, so Sandy and I left to freshen up and change into our party clothes. I was all dressed up with no Airplane Man in sight…that figured. But there was no time to pout, I had work to do. I walked around to check on the stations and found the dessert station understaffed, so I prepped their table then made my way back to the auction site to work the "wine wall" when my phone buzzed with a message from Mitch.

<Great tours. Finally on the road back to you. Miss you! See you tomorrow.>

My heart jumped from the absolute happiness I felt just reading his words. I couldn't wait to get the night over with so I could finally be with him the next day. A smile spread across my face and I typed my reply.

<Tomorrow won't get here soon enough. Miss you too!>

The evening was more than half over and a complete success. Everyone was having a great time. Sandy, her husband John, and I decided to enjoy a signature cocktail with some friends. Suddenly, Sandy asked, "Where is your Airplane Man tonight? I thought he was coming?"

My face reflected the answer clearly. "He drove down to Portland yesterday morning to visit a couple wineries. He's on his way back now but won't be in until really late tonight, unfortunately. Besides, I'm sure he would have been a distraction any- way—I am working after all."

Sandy nodded, then looked past me and smiled, recognizing one of her many friends or colleagues no doubt. Then suddenly a deep voice erupted from directly behind me and said, "So I'm a distraction now, huh? And here I thought we were moving on to the next level in our relationship."

I jumped at first, startled by his sweet, deep southern voice, but then I froze and my eyes grew to the size of half dollars. I would recognize that voice anywhere. Sandy looked at me and smiled, and then I slowly turned around to see Mitch standing right behind me. He looked utterly irresistible in his khaki pants and short-sleeved tropical shirt that was unbuttoned to reveal a black T-shirt underneath. But it wasn't just any black T-shirt. It was a tight black T-shirt! I nearly shouted Amen right there. His eyes sparkled like the stars that hung in the sky above.

"You're here! I can't believe it! How are you here? I don't care. I'm just so happy you made it!" I rambled, now quite nervous with his arrival. I didn't waste any time though. I walked over and threw my arms around him, hugging his neck so tight he could hardly breathe.

"I left early so I could surprise you and be here for moral sup- port," he said softly in my ear. "You look wonderful, by the way." His compliment didn't even register at first. I was still a bit woozy from the sight of him in that T-shirt.

Sandy and John clapped for our little reunion. Sandy said, "Hi, Mitch! Glad you were able to figure out my directions and find your way here."

My mouth dropped open. Wow...even my *boss* had been in on the surprise arrival.

Mitch laughed and peeked around me. "Hi, Sandy. Thank you; they were very helpful," he replied. He looked back at me. "You look surprised that I consorted with your boss to crash your party. I hope that's a good thing. I know you didn't really want me to come but I couldn't resist."

"Are you kidding me? Of course it's a good thing. I've been driving her crazy all day. All I've done is wander around and think about you, wishing I had just invited you. It's been more than a little difficult trying to stay focused on my job, let me tell you." I shook my head, looking down to hide my flushed cheeks. "Well, I'm here now. Truth be told, I had always planned on coming even after you said not to. Sandy gave me directions while I was in your office on Wednesday. I wouldn't have missed being here with you for anything, Laci. Not even for a winery tour. I knew how important this night was to you, which means it's important to me too. And, you did an amazing job; every- thing looks great," he said proudly, then leaned down and kissed me softly on my cheek. His lips were as warm as the summer sun. "Go dance, you two! The night will be over before you know it," Sandy yelled over the noise.

"Shall we dance, Ms. Laci?" Mitch asked in his most charming way, offering his hand to me.

"I would love to, Mr. Young."

I took his hand and he led me over to the dance floor. It was one huge sand box full of overgrown kids dancing and having a great time. Mitch slipped off his deck shoes and tucked them under a table nearby. I followed his lead. My pumpkin had become a magnificent coach and my prince was right in front of me. Everything was picture-perfect, including the night sky above, clear and covered with a quilt of stars as far as I could see. As we danced, the warm sand squished between my toes and I couldn't help but stare at him, utterly amazed that he was there with me.

The 50s beach songs that were playing were fun and we acted silly, doing the jitterbug and the mashed potato. He twirled me around, making goofy faces at me while attempting to keep his rhythm, a very difficult task in sand indeed. I was happy to learn that he could dance, and dance well. I wondered if there was anything he *couldn't* do. With my luck…he could probably sing too. And if he could, I was in much bigger trouble than I imagined. At one point, I was laughing so hard my sides hurt. Then, the slow song began. I felt like I was back in high school and was just asked to dance by the guy I had crushed on all year. I was scared to death that I would step on his feet and I never knew exactly where to put my hands. Well, that wasn't entirely true… My palms were moist with sweat and my nerves were amped up, firing on all cylinders. Maybe this is how it happened for the Incredible Hulk. Instead of turning green however, I favored more of a blush red.

Mitch pulled me close and gently wove my right hand into his, then tucked them in between us. His other arm wrapped around me and his hand rested on the small of my back. I lifted my arm up onto his shoulder, caressing the back of his neck with my hand, and slowly, I ran my fingers through his hair as we danced. Then he moved his striking face in close and pressed his cheek against mine. It was his sweet, old-fashioned charm that kept pulling me in even farther. We swayed slowly with the music, barely moving our feet. The night air was cool and I shivered as I felt his breath blow softly against the nape of my neck. I closed my eyes and let the music and noise of the crowd simply fade away. All that remained was his heart beating against my chest. I wanted to stay in that moment forever. He was my fairytale prince come to life, and he had brought me out of the deep sleep I'd been in since I lost Andrew.

The music played on, but he stopped and raised his head to look in my eyes, the glow of moonlight on his face. Both of his arms were now wrapped around me, and without a word, his soft lips met mine. He kissed me gently, an intense fire coming from within him. I was powerless to resist him. I knew, without a doubt, that I had fallen for him.

Sadly, the music came to an end, and the emcee wished every- one a good night as the band played their final song. We couldn't seem to leave the sand pit. Mitch pulled his head up and looked at me with a smile. "You're not going to take off running and leave behind a shoe are you?" he asked, laughing.

That's where Cinderella and I would have parted ways...she was crazy to leave her prince behind! "Very funny, Mr. Young. I'm not going anywhere, trust me. Besides, I'm still barefoot, remember? Our shoes are over there under the table," I said with a smile, and we walked over to retrieve our footwear. The party had ended and the guests were leaving, so Mitch stayed to help me clean then he walked me to my car.

"So, is tomorrow date number two or three? I mean, you *did* crash my party tonight. Technically that could be considered date number two," I asked, teasing him.

Then Mitch's phone rang and he looked to see who was calling. "It's my brother; he's probably worried about me. Do you mind if I answer this?" he asked politely. I shook my head no.

"Hey Brad, what's up? Sorry I didn't call you when I got back," "Let me guess. You're with Airplane Girl, aren't you?" Brad asked sarcastically.

Apparently, Brad didn't realize how loud his voice was coming out of Mitch's phone and that I had just heard every word he'd said. Who did he think he was calling me 'airplane girl'!? It sounded like some superhero sidekick name. Ugh! Obviously he wasn't too thrilled that Mitch was here with me. That's great, Laci – you are already causing a rift in his family, way to go!

"I am with Laci, yes. So I'll call you in the morning before we head out to the winery okay? Okay, good night." Mitch hung up. "Sorry about that. My brother's annoying, but as my business partner he's downright obnoxious at times. All business and no play. He means well though."

"I understand. All part of running a winery I suppose. I hope he's not upset that you're here with me. I don't want to get in the way of your work," I said. I looked away feeling a bit defeated. Mitch lifted my chin with his finger and forced me to look him in the eye. I melted into his touch; if made of snow, I would have been a pool of water at his feet.

He smiled and said, "You don't get it do you? I *want* you in the way, in *every* way possible. And to answer your question before we were interrupted, tomorrow is still date number two. Crashing a party never constitutes a proper date. I'll see you in the morning around nine. We have a full day ahead of us so go home and get some sleep." He smiled and then leaned down, leaving a sweet kiss on my lips. "Sweet dreams, darlin'," he whispered.

detour ahead

Saturday morning arrived. We found ourselves on our way to a little place in Woodinville called Chateau Ste. Michelle, Washington's oldest and most acclaimed winery, and the maker of my favorite Riesling. Our drive was filled with both fun and serious conversation. Many questions were asked and answered, and there was lots of laughter. Part of me wanted to keep driving, just skip the winery and spend the day doing nothing together. But we stopped, and that was okay too.

During the tasting, Mitch got a kick out of watching me make various faces after I tried each wine. My eyebrows rose slightly after I tasted a good one, my eyes popped open wide after sipping a really good one, and a sort of "sour lemon" look appeared after a few others. I wanted to learn as much as possible so I could share in that part of his life.

Our time together was flying by faster than I would have liked. I tried to stay in the moment, but it was getting hard to avoid the thought of him leaving the next day. Mitch packed a picnic dinner for the two of us, so we found an empty gazebo on the grounds and took advantage of the incredible scenery around us. Evening had arrived and we got up to watch the sunset behind us. The view was breathtaking, but it was hard to enjoy.

My heart started to ache; I didn't know when we'd be

together again. I had four kids; I couldn't just jump on a plane whenever

I wanted. He had a winery to run; I couldn't expect that of him either. Maybe I was crazy to ever think this could work. How could it? The shift in my mood became a little more obvious.

"What is it Laci? You're so quiet all of a sudden."

This wasn't the time to hold back. I had to tell him the truth or I would always regret it. "It's just that, well, spending these last few days with you has meant more to me than I ever imagined possible, and now it's about to end. You leave tomorrow and I miss you already. I don't want you to go."

Like a slow burning fire, Mitch began to smile like the Cheshire cat. That *wasn't* exactly the reaction I had expected after having just bore my soul to him, but at least he didn't run. I thought that was a good sign. His arms lay atop the half wall of the gazebo; his hands were folded together and he looked out at the sunset. I was growing quite nervous about what he would say. "You just said the magic words, darlin'," he said, and then he turned and walked back to our table. My eyes followed.

"What do you mean? I'm not seeing the magic in your impending departure," I replied, now a little ticked off by his lack of concern for my feelings. He laughed softly and pulled out an envelope from the picnic basket, then walked back over to me.

"The part you said about 'missing me,' those were the magic words. And, I have a little surprise for you. Open it." He handed me the envelope and I looked at him curiously. I opened it and out slid what looked like plane tickets to North Carolina, leaving the next day! I looked up at him wide-eyed and with my mouth wide open, but not a word came out. I was utterly speechless.

He continued. "Okay, before you say anything, hear me out. I know this seems a little forward and crazy and foolish, and a hundred other things, but I want you to come back home with me tomorrow. Just for a few days." He moved closer and took my hands; the goose bumps on my arms stood at attention. "You were the most beautiful and unexpected surprise I could've received that day on the plane. I remember walking to my seat and you looked at me, like you were saying hello with your eyes. I couldn't wait to get to my seat and thought how lucky I was to be sitting next to you. Then after you returned home and we made contact again, I couldn't wait until I got your next email or phone call or text. And once I arrived here, all I could think about was spending time with you and holding you." He took me in his arms. "So you see, I can't leave without you; it's too soon. I want more time with you, Laci. I want my family to meet you and get to know you."

He gave me a look, as if he was shielding himself from an oncoming blast, and waited for my reply. However, my reply came in the form of tears, overwhelmed from the shock of his offer.

It was time for an emergency session of the 'itty-bitty-committee'. First, he didn't want to leave me…that alone spoke volumes to my innermost parts and I was totally jumping for joy! But meeting his mom for the first time so soon? Probably not the smartest idea, but I would love to meet her. I think Caleb liked me, but I wasn't so sure about his pretentious brother. What about my kids, and work? Teri would probably stay with the kids if I asked her, and I knew Sandy would give me the time off–a much needed break now that my event was over… And with that, it was settled. My 'itty-bitty-committee' had made a unanimous decision…I was going!

He must have thought his offer had upset me because he apologized immediately. "I'm so sorry, Laci. If it's too soon, I understand, but please keep the ticket. When you decide it's the right time, you tell me and—"

I quickly interrupted his apology.

"Mitch, I'm not saying no. I'm crying because I'm happy, because I'm saying yes! I would love more than anything to visit your home and your family." And he scooped me up in his arms, hugged me tight, and twirled me around the gazebo, belting out a "Woohoo" so loud that the neighboring picnic parties started laughing at us.

Then he stopped and whispered softly in my ear, "Thank you, thank you, thank you."

"I should be thanking you. You're the one taking all the risk by bringing your girlfr—— umm, I mean, bringing me home." My face flinched, completely embarrassed by my mishap with the *g* word. "Sorry. I didn't mean to assume that I was your girlfriend." I looked away, my rosy cheeks filled with heat. Where was that sock when I needed it?

"Laci, look at me," he said softly. I did as he instructed. He continued. "Let's just settle this now, shall we? Will you be my girlfriend, Laci Kramer? And I mean exclusive girlfriend. I don't want to see or date anyone else but you."

"I thought you'd never ask, Mr. Young. Yes!" I shouted. "I would love to be your one and only girlfriend!" I jumped into his arms and kissed his wine-soaked lips to make it official.

"Well okay then, darlin'. Let's get you home; looks like you have some packing to do." He smiled.

"And some calls to make. I have to find a sitter for my kids and clear this with my boss, remember? I may not be going if those two don't work out."

Mitch took my hands and smiled. "Yeah, about that, I have a small confession. Your boss already knows. I told her at the event last night. She said to tell you to 'have fun and be good.'"

"You can't be serious? Again? You two are a real piece of work you know, conniving behind my back twice now. I'm impressed!" I laughed.

"Yeah, she kind of likes me. And she is totally okay with you going, I promise." He smiled, all proud of himself for having my boss on his side.

"Oh I don't doubt it. You're quite the charmer I must say— lured me in from day one."

And it was finally official! That step was huge for me, as I'm sure it must have been for him. I hoped this was part of the Lord's big plan for me…because I certainly wanted it to be part of mine!

Mitch dropped me off at home and headed back to his hotel. The little ones were already asleep, and Todd was on the computer talking to his friends, so I poked my head in the den to say hello.

"Hi sweetie, were the kids good today?"

He yawned. "Yeah, they just played all day with the neighbor's kids. After dinner, they put in a movie and fell asleep."

"Thanks for hanging out with them. I'm glad you're still awake actually. There's something I want to ask you. Mitch has asked me to come back to North Carolina with him tomorrow. He wants me to meet his family. It's just for a few days, and I'd be back Thursday night. Would it bother you if I went? I want you to be okay with this, or I won't go."

"Mom, you're crazy about him. You should go. I don't mind, but will you at least ask Lena or Teri to come over and cook for us?" Always thinking about the important things in life that one– heck with mom…just feed him and he's good!

"That's the plan. I'll call Lena in the morning. I would imagine she'll just stay here while I'm gone to make sure you don't go hungry. You're sure about this?"

"Yep, I'm sure. Go, have fun. It will be good for you. You're always stressed out and tired from taking care of us by yourself. You deserve a break, Mom." He's grown into such a wonderful young man…I always assumed I had hidden my stress from them, but apparently that wasn't working out so well.

"Okay, sweetie. Well, I'm going to go up and pack. I'll fix us all a big breakfast in the morning and tell the other two then. Good night and thank you. I love you."

"Love you too, mom" he said, yawning again.

The next morning, I woke up, showered, threw on some sweats, and a T-shirt, finished packing, and then headed down- stairs to start breakfast. I called Lena first thing to fill her in on my pending travel opportunity.

"Okay, girl. I want all the details. Don't leave anything out!" She was full of questions about the recent events with Mitch, so I quickly brought her up to speed. There was no time to waste chatting.

"So can you be my nanny for a few days? I'll pay you, buy you lunch for a week, whatever it takes. I'm not above bribery to make this happen."

"Will you stop already? You know I'll watch the kids! I'll be there in a couple of hours, okay?" Lena said.

"You are truly the sweetest person on earth. I don't know how to thank you. Saying it doesn't seem like enough, but thank you anyway."

"You're welcome! Anything for you, 'darlin'." Lena said, laughing as she poked fun at the name Mitch called me at times.

———ᘐᓂᓂᘇᘂᘇᘂᘇᓂᓂᘐ———

Lena arrived and ate breakfast with us, and then I told the kids about my trip. Travis wasn't too happy about it, but the fact that Lena would be there helped to appease him. We went over a few more details together, and then I went upstairs to get ready and do a final check of my bags. Just then, my phone rang.

"Good morning," Mitch said. My heart leapt a mile at the sound of his sweet voice. "Were you able to get everything worked out for the kids?"

"I did. Lena is already here and she'll be staying with them while I'm gone. I'm free and clear to go!"

"That's what I was hoping to hear. And you're absolutely sure about this, right? No second thoughts?"

"None whatsoever. I can't wait to meet your family! Well, most of them anyway," I laughed. On the inside, I was already a basket case, nervous and unsure about what they would think of me—a woman he barely knew who lived clear across the country and had started a relationship with after meeting me on a plane. "Don't worry okay? I'm crazy about you, and I know they will be too. I'll see you in an hour."

I ran upstairs, fixed my hair, threw on my comfortable yet fashionable black leggings, a cute pink T-shirt and matching jacket, and put on my pink-and-white sneakers. No fuss—I kept it simple. It's just another flight sitting next to the man that has completely captivated my heart. What was there to fuss about? Nothing...everything!

An hour later, on the dot, my doorbell rang.

"Hey there." I smiled and greeted him cheerfully. He had dressed down too in faded jeans and a pale yellow polo shirt. That whole 'eye candy' thing had taken on new meaning entirely!

"Hey darlin', all set?"

"Yep. I just need to go up and get my bag." "Lead the way. I'll get it for you," he said politely.

I took him upstairs and stepped inside the door of my bed- room. He followed me in, quickly closed the door behind me, grabbed my hand, and pulled me over to say hello with a sweet kiss. He held me in his arms, reluctant to let me go.

"So you're about to purposely sit next to a creepy stalker guy slash Crawdad fan on this flight. Think you can stand it? It's not a short flight, you know," he said with a smile.

"I can stand it if you can. Just one small difference though." "Oh yeah, what's that?"

"This time, I'll be able to hold your hand, lean over and give you a kiss, snuggle inside your arm, or even fall asleep on your shoulder. Think you can handle that?" I asked. I poked his mid- section, trying once again to find a ticklish spot.

"Darlin', I wouldn't have it any other way. You look so cute and sassy today in your little pink and black outfit, I'm liable to let you have your way with me." And he kissed me again softly. I stopped in my tracks, sure that my flushing cheeks had given me away. We loaded the car, said goodbye to the kids and Lena, and then we were on our way.

his home sweet home

From my window seat in the plane, I looked down at the Raleigh airport. It was lit up with soft, white lights. It was actually quite beautiful and had stunning architecture for an airport; it was a work of art by itself. As we got closer, my stomach started to knot up and I wondered if I had made the right decision coming here. It was a little late to turn back now though.

It was a lovely warm evening when we landed, and since our connecting flight was a small commuter plane, we disembarked outside on the tarmac. The sky was barely light. Shades of blue stretched across the horizon and a thin strip of orange glowed from the recent sunset that had passed. It was ten o'clock at night and still eighty degrees. We were no sooner off the plane when Mitch said, "Welcome to North Carolina, darlin', or should I say, welcome to Crawdad territory." He smiled and winked at me.

We walked inside the terminal, collected our luggage, and found our way to his car in the extended parking area. He loaded everything in the car and we were ready to go— to his home where he grew up, to where his mom lived, and where his wife once lived. Had I really thought this through? If his family doesn't like me, that could mean the end of our new beginning. The look on my face must have screamed out "nervous wreck here" like a neon sign. I think "scared to death" would have been an accurate description at that point. Mitch closed the lid of the trunk and pulled me close.

"I know you're nervous, but I'm right here and won't leave your side, okay?" His sweet words spilled over me, starting at the top of my head and working their way down to the tip of my toes, calming every part of me. I stood inside his arms and realized that, outside of being with my kids, it was the only other place I'd rather be.

"I know," I said, smiling and giving in to his words. "Besides, how could you leave? My side is the winning side."

"True, and I am growing rather fond of your side—all your sides actually. They're quite impressive." He laughed, then leaned down and brushed my lips softly with his, a kiss for the road. He walked me around and opened the car door to let me in. I had to admit, that part of his whole *courting* thing had really started to grow on me. And we were on our way.

It was now pitch-black outside so enjoying the scenery while we drove was impossible. Mitch put our windows down a little, and the warm summer air wafted inside, gently blowing on my face. I could smell summer; it reminded me of home. The smell of a recent rain still hung in the air, along with the scent of fresh flowers and a little scent-of-cow here and there. I was tempted to lay my head back and close my eyes, but I knew if I did I would surely fall asleep, and probably drool. That would *not* be good!

"How far away is your town?"

"Crystal Creek? Oh, it's about an hour and a half from the airport, not long. Get some sleep if you want to, I don't mind. I'm sure you're tired."

"Thanks, but I'm fine, really. I've got you all to myself right now. I'm not going to miss out on that."

"Is that what you're worried about? That I'm going to throw you to the wolves when we arrive and say 'have a nice time'? I haven't planned every minute of our time with family, trust me.

We'll have plenty of one-on-one time while we're here. Actually, I have a surprise for you!"

"Oh really? Do I have to wait to find out or can you tell me now?"

"You're definitely waiting. It's bound to be the highlight of your visit here, so I wouldn't want to spoil anything." He laughed.

"Not even a hint?"

"Let's just say that you've been asking for this since the day we met."

"That's not much of a hint in my book. I'm even worse at riddles."

"Well, it is a surprise for a reason. I'm not giving it away with the first clue."

Over the next hour, we talked a little, laughed a lot, and even during the few moments of silence, it felt as right as rain to be there with him. Then out of nowhere, a fleeting thought ran through my mind and I began to panic. Where was I staying? I hadn't booked a hotel for myself! Was I staying with him and Caleb...in their house? I couldn't believe I hadn't thought about this earlier! I started twisting my hands around together, stressed about how I would approach the subject.

"All right, what's up? You're clenching your fists. That can't be good." He reached over and took my hand.

"It's nothing really. I...I was just thinking that I didn't have a chance to book a hotel or anything, and it's so late now that it may be hard to—"

He laughed, then he brought my hand over to his lips, kissing it softly.

"You can't stand this whole 'courtship' thing can you? First of all, you're crazy if you think I'm going to make my guest, my *girlfriend* at that, stay in a hotel! Second of all, Caleb and I both want you to stay at the house with us. If you want to, that is."

After a long pause and a deep sigh of relief, I started to breathe normally again. "Well, I guess because you don't stay at my house when you visit, I just assumed that you wouldn't want—"

"No, no, no. You've got it all wrong, darlin'. I want to stay with you when I'm there, trust me. It takes everything in me to walk out your door at night. But it's different. I'm a stranger to your kids, and the last thing I want is for them to think I'm trying to move in and take their dad's place. It's hard to explain. Your kids are smaller and it's just different somehow. But Caleb is older and it's only the two of us, plus we have plenty of spare bedrooms. It's kind of like being in a hotel, except I'll be down the hall," he said with a little smirk on his face.

"I guess that makes sense. I would like to stay with you, as long as it's not an inconvenience to you or Caleb." Again he laughed at my comment.

"Trust me, Caleb had a guest room set up and ready the same day I told him you were coming. He can't wait to meet you, Laci. He is always saying how you made his life better when you came into my life. It's true you know." He squeezed my hand and smiled.

"Mine too."

After he mentioned Caleb, we talked about our kids and the struggles they shared since losing a parent. It made me even more thankful to have Mitch in my life. Before I knew it, we had crossed the border into the little town of Crystal

Creek, North Carolina. "Well, we're here. It's only a few more minutes to the house."

My hand tightened again, but this time from excitement and anticipation about what the week would hold for us.

At first, the houses looked fairly similar to those in my own neighborhood. As we kept driving, they grew farther apart. They also got bigger, at least from what I could make out in the dark. Then the car slowed down, and he turned into a driveway, but I couldn't see the house for the trees that lined the front. The driveway was rather long, but finally I could see the house up ahead. Landscaping lights lined both sides of the driveway, and a few flood lights pointed directly up at the house. I looked at it and sucked in my breath. I felt like I had traveled back in time. The driveway made a circle in front of the house, but he went past the house, turned, and drove through a carport up to the detached garage. He pushed the button on the garage door opener and slowly pulled inside. It was dark, but even in the night I could see that it was a much older, Victorian-style house. The full wrap-around porch on the bottom level was breathtaking. There was even a turret ceiling over what I figured was some fancy room inside or maybe the kitchen. I'd never seen anything like it outside of magazines and the film *Gone with the Wind*. It wasn't a huge house, but it was big enough. The yard was probably professionally manicured and kept in pristine condition to match the rest of it.

I felt like a duck out of water already. All I had to worry about now was trying to keep myself from knocking over some valuable, antique heirloom that had been in their family for a hundred years or more. No pressure. Seeing his home only increased the amount of butterflies in my stomach, but I kept telling myself that it was just a house. It was Mitch and Caleb's house; it was Karin's house. Then I felt sad for them, living here all alone with- out her. It was a little different for me because Andrew never lived in the house I was in now. I was glad that we didn't have those images to contend with during our first date.

Had Mitch thought this through? Were they really prepared to see another woman walking around their kitchen where his wife had cooked their breakfast? To have me in their home where they laughed and cried together? I hoped so. If not, the next few days were going to be more difficult than I had anticipated. We got out and went around to the trunk to unload our bags. Caleb was already jogging out to greet us. I was sure he'd missed his dad a great deal.

"Hey, dad!" He hugged his dad right away. It was no surprise to see how close they were with everything they'd been through together. I couldn't help but smile at them.

"Hey Caleb, how are you bud?" Mitch patted him on the back. "Good, good. Can I help you carry your bags inside?" He had his dad's sweet, southern charm without a doubt. Before he picked up a bag though, he looked right at me and smiled.

"Hi, Ms. Laci. I'm really glad you're here." Without hesitation, he hugged me right there in the garage! His sweet gesture made me feel right at home and nearly brought me to tears.

"Hello, Caleb. It's nice to be here and finally meet you in per- son. You look like your dad, so tall and handsome."

"Well, thank you ma'am. Let me help you carry those," he said, taking my bags from my hand.

Mitch and Caleb carried the bags inside through the side entrance of the house into a mudroom. That's what I called it, but I wasn't sure if that's what they called it in the south. I followed them through the mudroom, through the kitchen, past a formal dining room, then on around to a large open foyer at the front of the house. Every light in the house was turned on—it was like Christmas! I did a full 360-degree spin to look around and came back to the gorgeous front door; it had to be at least ten feet high, but I was pretty short so anything over six feet seemed tall to me. It was made from an antique white wood of some kind. Everywhere I looked were beautiful, antique pieces of furniture, lamps, and decorations. But the most amazing part was the stair- case. It was in the center of the foyer and it curved slightly as it went up. The spindles were made from the same white wood as the front doors. The hand rail was a stark contrast, made from a dark cherry red wood that had been weathered from age. I had never seen anything like it, and couldn't wait until morning to see the whole house with sunlight pouring in through the windows. Before we started upstairs, Mitch looked at me and smiled.

"I'm so glad you're here, darlin'," he said softly.

"Me too," I replied.

Caleb cleared his throat. "Your room is upstairs, Ms. Laci. Turn left at the top, and it's the last room at the end of the hall. I'll be right behind you with your bags."

"Thank you, Caleb." Mitch and I both laughed and we started up.

Caleb sat my bag in the door, said good night, and then went to his room. Mitch gave me a tour of my room, then he showed me the bathroom down the hall that apparently no one used now, so it was all mine while I was there. We walked back to my room and he stood just inside the door.

"It's been a long day and you look exhausted, so I'll let you settle in and get some sleep." He took me in his arms, and in similar fashion to how he said hello that morning, he said good night.

I didn't want to let him go; his arms felt so strong and safe. His kiss stayed with me long after he had left my room. I put on my pajama top and shorts and walked down the hall to wash my face, then headed back to my room and slid into bed. I lay there thinking about the day and pondered how the events of the next day would play out until sleep found me and I gave in.

The next morning, I woke up to the smell of bacon and coffee – my favorite combination. I got ready and went downstairs expecting to find Caleb and Mitch cooking up a storm, but instead, I was greeted by a much different scene. Mitch's mother was in the kitchen cooking, and Mitch was setting the table, at which sat his brother, Brad. Really? I had to face his mother *and* brother first thing out of bed? I stopped dead in my tracks and immediately gave Mitch the look, hoping he would get the hint and save me from whatever was about to take place. But unfortunately, he wasn't fast enough. His mother was already making a beeline for me.

"Good morning, Laci. I'm Marjorie, Mitch's mother, but please call me Maggie. It's so nice to finally meet you, sweet- heart! How did you sleep?" she said in a sweet, southern drawl as she walked over to greet me. She had spunk and I liked that. She was Mitch's mother, so of *course* I wanted to like her more than anything. I wanted her to like *me*. But I sensed that this southern Mama was a force to be reckoned with in some way.

She put her arm around my shoulder and led me into the kitchen, waiting for my reply. She had all the charm of a true, southern belle, but she wasn't your average sweet, old-fashioned grandma. She was saucy. Her hair was all fixed up; although she could have possibly been a brunette at one time, her hair was mostly silver with a few darker strands showing through here and there. It was quite beautiful though and it shaped her face well. Her makeup was just right, and she wore a sassy little summer pantsuit, which probably came right off Nordstrom's racks, and matching orange dress sandals.

"I slept well, Maggie. Thank you." My eyes searched around for the nearest coffee cup.

Mitch walked up behind me and put his arms around my waist. I wasn't sure that was the smartest thing to do right in front of his family, but he was quite sure of himself as he pulled me toward his chest and peaked around to kiss me on the side of my cheek. I was never more embarrassed than I was at that moment.

"Good morning, darlin'," he whispered. "Sorry for the ambush. Can I get you some coffee, milk, tea, me?" He laughed, and some- how that made everything all right

"I thought you'd never ask. Coffee, please."

We walked over to the coffee pot. Everything was all set out—cups, a variety of creamers, several types of sugar and sugar substitutes, stir sticks, and even a small dish for my coffee trash. At my house it's a spoon, a sugar bowl, and a carton of half and half...and you'd be lucky to get a cup that wasn't made of paper. I guess I had missed the coffee etiquette class. I fixed my fancy coffee, took a few sips, and let the caffeine do its thing. I knew it would take me several cups to get through the morning.

"Mrs. Young, I mean Maggie, may I give you a hand with something? I don't mind helping." I thought it best to offer my assistance in the kitchen rather than taking advantage of their hospitality. I was never good at setting back while others cooked in front of me.

"Absolutely not, dear. You just sit right down with Mitch and Brad and enjoy your coffee. Those two need a good referee when they're together and I have a feeling you're perfect for the job," she said with a smile as she shooed me away from the kitchen.

In the morning light, his beautiful house took on a whole new air and its character became more evident. I took my coffee to the informal kitchen table that sat inside a large nook area with large picture windows all around and crown molding framing. I sat next to Brad. By the look on his face, I could tell he wasn't thrilled to be there. Mitch thumped the newspaper to get his attention. Brad lowered the paper a bit and gave Mitch a big, cheesy smile. Good looks definitely ran in the family, but Brad was the polar opposite of Mitch in every other way. His tousled, dark black hair was streaked with a few gray hairs here and there, and it probably hadn't been combed once that morning, maybe not even since the previous day. His scruffy, unshaven face was tan, weathered by age and the sun. But his most appealing features by far were his eyes. They were the lightest shade of blue I had ever seen, and they sparkled like little blue diamonds. Although quite happy with my choice, I had to admit he was quite good looking if you liked that manly, rough-around-the-edges kind of guy. I mean, I wasn't dead – I enjoyed taking in a little southern scenery like any respectable woman!

Now that he had Brad's attention, Mitch made the introductions. "Brad, this is Laci. Laci, this is my sometimes insolent, yet mostly loveable brother, Brad."

Brad looked over at me with the same smile, and I instantly got the feeling that he wasn't too hip on me. "Well, well, if it isn't Airplane Girl. It's so nice to finally meet the woman who stole my brother's heart and my business partner's brain. Thanks for that." Brad said.

My jaw dropped a little at his cold and callous greeting. It had caught me completely off-guard. I wasn't even sure how to respond, or if I should just get up and walk back to my room. But I was a tad riled up. He was being a pompous and arrogant... ugh! I wasn't about to give up that easily. Airplane Girl, indeed! I would show him–he doesn't even know me!

Mitch became defensive and started to say something, but I didn't let him have the chance. I smiled and looked at Brad, then replied in a calm, collected manner.

"No, Mitch. It's okay. Brad was just making small talk, weren't you Brad? Airplane Girl, very funny. I remember you calling me that once before when you were talking to your brother on the phone. Sounds a little like a superhero sidekick name, which I'm not, last I checked." I offered my hand to him as a greeting and hoped we could start over. "My name is Laci, I'm dating your brother and I care about him more than you know, so let's start there, shall we? It's very nice to meet you."

Brad smiled and shook my hand firmly. Mitch laughed out loud, and then reached over and squeezed my hand. "That's my girl!" he said proudly.

Behind me, I heard Mitch's mom clear her throat. I was suddenly embarrassed at my lack of self-control and I'm sure she was none too pleased at the display she had just witnessed. Not a great first impression. She walked up behind Brad and laid her hand on his shoulder, ever so gently.

"Bradley, you will apologize to Laci right now for your rude comments and greet her properly, or you can eat your breakfast outside from the horse trough," she said in her soft, sweet south- ern voice. I couldn't help but chuckle softly. And it was good he couldn't see my little victory party going on inside...I'm sure that would have really ticked him off.

"It's nice to meet you, Laci. I apologize for my rudeness. I'm glad you were able to join us for a visit.

Maybe you could persuade Mitch here to bring you out to the winery later, give you a tour." Then he leaned in toward me. "And by the way, he is a bit of a superhero to me so that kind of makes you his sidekick in my book." A little smile appeared on his face like he had just won the battle. He must be the black sheep of the family. He definitely seemed protective of Mitch, and for that I had to admire the guy, but I didn't have to like him!

"Don't worry Brad, that's our first stop after breakfast. Does that sound okay, Laci? I thought I'd show you around and we could have a picnic lunch out there." Mitch said.

"Sounds great! When do we leave?" I asked, a bit anxious and ready to get out of the house.

"Mitch, let the poor girl eat before you rush her out," his mom commented as she sat down at the table. I smiled. We ate our delicious breakfast and talked about the weather and the winery. I answered his mom's many questions about my job and the kids. Brad, a mere spectator at the table, finally gave up and left. After Mitch and I finished, we cleared the table and washed the dishes. Shortly after we finished, Caleb stumbled downstairs looking for food, still half-asleep. Typical teenager.

"Mornin' sunshine!" Mitch said to his son, messing up his hair. "Laci and I are headed out to the winery. Will you be out later?" "Uh, yeah. I'll see you in an hour or so." He yawned, fumbling in the cupboard for a coffee cup.

the wedding barn

We hopped in the car and headed to the winery. The sun was shining; it was already eighty degrees outside, and forecasted to turn hotter as the day went on. I took in the scenery as we drove. Outside the city limits, Mitch took an exit onto a rural highway and the roads became hilly and winding. Everywhere I looked, I saw green, rolling countryside dotted with cows and horses. Small and large farm houses were spread all around. Other homes were mansion-like and had beautiful fences lining the perimeter of their land. A few minutes later, we entered a more wooded area; the trees were tall and majestic. I couldn't imagine how old some of them were.

Mitch slowed the car down a bit and that was when I saw the most beautiful wooden bridge out my window. It was set back in the woods a little. The color of the wood was light and natural, showing every knothole. It was long and arched in the middle, and the rippling creek move swiftly below it over the rocks. I couldn't stop staring, and I turned my head to keep it in view until we drove on past.

"That's an old truss bridge. Beautiful, isn't it?" Mitch said, knowing exactly what had caught my eye. "We'll see it again. That bridge sets on the backside of the winery, which means we're almost there."

My eyes grew in size at the excitement of being able to see it up close. "Can we walk to it?"

"Of course we can, I own it."

"It's beautiful out here, Mitch. I would never want to leave if this was what I had to look at every day."

"I can leave it, but only for something ten times more beautiful than this place."

"What's that?" I asked, thinking it was some other place. "You." He smiled and took my hand in his. I dropped my head to hide my blushing cheeks then shook my head in disagreement, unable to respond.

He slowed the car and turned into a long drive. Hanging above our head over the entrance was a large wooden sign connected by two tall wooden poles. An old name plate dangled down, broken but still readable. It read "Seven Oaks Winery," the original winery name. We drove on up and parked between two buildings. One, I guessed, was the main winery area, and another barn-type building sat across it. Both were rustic, weathered, and aged, but I could see where they had already made some repairs. They had added a new porch and steps, outdoor lamps, benches, and new landscaping. It was slowly being transformed from something old to something new.

"Well, Ms. Laci, welcome to the Young Family Winery. We don't have a formal name yet, so that's just what I'm calling it for now."

"I'm honored to be your first visitor. It's wonderful."

We got out of the car and he took me on the grand tour. I saw Brad wandering around from time to time, throwing out a comment now and then like, 'Hope you're having fun,' or 'Don't mind me, I'm just working here'. He seemed so bitter and jealous of the time Mitch spent with me and I couldn't understand why. After everything Mitch had been through, you would think he would want Mitch to be happy. Did he think I was going to take him away from here forever?

The winery was a huge structure with rafter ceilings inside. They had just added three huge chandeliers that hung down from the center beam. Bistro tables sat around and were already covered with dark red linens. The inside was almost finished; it featured new windows, a handcrafted wine tasting bar, and wooden floors that had just been resurfaced and stained. Strands of white lights lined the rafters and decorative grapes and vine leaves were wrapped around the poles throughout the building. I walked over to a barstool sitting beside the wine tasting area and admired the *Y* that had been hand carved into the back, with grape leaves etched around the edge.

"My uncle made those. He's a carpenter by trade, but he doesn't do much these days because of his health. He wanted to do these for me as his final project and gave them to me and Brad as a gift. He's talented, isn't he?"

"I've never seen anything like them. So intricate. I can see the love he put into each one." Tears welled up in my eyes when I thought about what that gift would mean to them in years to come.

"Well, let's go look at the wedding barn next door and then we'll walk out to the bridge and have lunch. Sound okay?"

"Wedding barn?" I asked, puzzled as to what that meant. We walked outside and headed over to the other building.

"Yes, wedding barn. Years ago this barn was the most popular place in town to get married. They would run white Christmas lights around every pole and rafter, hang candelabras from the ceiling, and line the inside with flowers of every color. I've only seen pictures, but it looked like the event of the summer was being held in here. I want to start that tradition again. My mom is pretty good at decorating, so she is going to take care of that part for me. What do you think?"

I looked around and imagined a wedding being held there, what I would want if it were my own. My head was filled with so many ideas. I could see it decorated with colorful flowers every-where, with family and friends sitting all around. It could be an experience like no other.

"It's going to be amazing, Mitch. I can't imagine a more romantic, serene location to get married in." I walked around, stared up at the ceiling, and visualized how it could look. I then proceeded to share my vision. "If you show it off and promote it at your opening, be sure to entwine the strands of white lights inside some white tool first, then drape it across these rafters; it will create a beautiful, soft glow. And bring in bales of hay to create dimension with the flowers."

Mitch just stood there and shook his head, smiling at me. "Sorry," I said, suddenly embarrassed. What was I doing? I had no business telling him how to promote this place.

"Don't be sorry. You have a knack for this. I forget that it's part of your day job."

"It's the best part of my job. I can see the images in my head and it's hard to shut them off sometimes. I didn't mean to tell you how to decorate. I know your mom will do an amazing job." "Well, two heads are better than one right? I'll be sure and share your ideas with her. I loved them." He took my hand and we walked to the car to get our picnic lunch and blanket.

The bridge didn't seem that far away, but even if it was I hadn't noticed. We talked nonstop while we walked through the woods. Mitch shared more about his plans for the winery and how they planned to open up in the spring.

The bridge was just up ahead and even lovelier up close. I walked onto the bridge, stopped in the center, then leaned my head down over the rail and closed my eyes. The restless sound of summer was all around me. I heard the birds chirping high above and the rippling water below, mixed with the soft rustle of the trees. It was a place right out of a child's storybook. While I admired the surroundings, Mitch spread a blanket behind me and set out our food.

"Come on, let's eat, girl. I don't know about you, but I'm starving."' He sat down and patted the spot next to him, inviting me to sit beside him.

"How can you be hungry after that gigantic breakfast you ate this morning?" I laughed and sat down.

"I'm a growing man, what can I say."

We filled our plates and he poured us a glass of wine, then we toasted to a beautiful day together. I knew it was crazy, but I hoped this would be the first of many lunches we would share together on this bridge.

"We have a few projects left to finish, but the grand opening is tentatively scheduled for March 21, the first day of spring. It seemed like the perfect day to open, a good day for new beginnings."

"That is a perfect day, and it's also Todd's birthday, so he would definitely agree with you on that. I'm so happy for you Mitch, and for Brad too. I know you've both worked so hard to get things ready." I leaned over and kissed him, overwhelmed with such pride for him and what he had accomplished.

"Laci, I want you to help with the wedding barn, the decorations, and getting everything ready. Would you be interested?"

I hesitated at first, somewhat confused by what he was asking. "Umm, that's very generous, but I'm not sure how that would be possible. Don't get me wrong, I would love to help, but how can I? I can do some things from my house, but it's not the same. I'm a very visual person so I would have to be here in order to figure out what's going to work. Besides, I don't want to interfere; it's not my place. Your mom has ideas of her own already, I'm sure. Plus I don't think Brad would be all too thrilled if I was helping out either."

"This isn't about my mom or Brad. It's about us—me and you, creating something special together, something new and wonderful. I want you to make that wedding barn come to life and I know you can. But it's more than just the barn, Laci. It's..." He fumbled around for words and suddenly seemed anxious, nervous even. And he was so darn *good looking* when he became nervous. He was good looking all the time actually, what was I thinking? I could hardly look at him without my heart forgetting to beat.

"Laci, you should know something." His face became serious and I began to worry. Was it something I had said? Oh for flip- sakes...I've made him mad. Great.

"Mitch, what is it? What's wrong?" I asked, and he scooted closer to me, took my hands, and squeezed them tight.

"Nothing is wrong. For the first time, everything is right, because of you. I know it's only been a little over a month since we met, and it's crazy how I can feel so close to you already, but I do! I remember that it poured down rain the day we boarded that plane, and I wasn't even supposed to be on that flight. Did I ever tell you that?"

"No...I...you never told me that." I thought to myself that only God could be that creative and sneaky, bringing us together that day. My heart wouldn't slow down as I thought of what was yet to come.

"I don't know if it was the rain, or God, or some other cos- mic force—"

Unable to control my mouth, I decided to butt in and add my thoughts.

"Well, God is the only cosmic force and he made the rain, so really it was all those things!" I smiled, all proud of my definition, and Mitch just laughed. "What? It's true!"

"You're right, it is true!" he said in an excited voice.

He stood up, helped me up off the blanket, and we walked over to the side of the bridge. He looked around for a second then he put his arms around me. As we held each other close, I could hear the water swishing below. The wind picked up a little and he brushed the hair out of my face. Rays of sunlight were scattered around us, coming through the trees in different places. One shone down behind him, and for a second, it looked like his head was glowing. I laughed softly. He looked at me, eyes intense and warm all at the same time, and a smile plastered all over his face.

"What's so funny?"

"It's nothing. The sun was shining behind you and it gave you a halo-like glow. It's gone now though. Too bad; it looked good on you."

"Well, if you liked that, just wait until you see my wings," he said, laughing.

But in a matter of seconds, the sun hid behind the clouds, the sky darkened, and the wind gained even more strength. The temperature also dropped about ten degrees or more. Mitch had no sooner looked up when I felt a drop of rain on my arm.

"Ah for crying out loud, not now!" he yelled out.

"It's just a sprinkle. I'm sure it'll pass. What's the big deal?" "It's just that…I wanted to tell you—"

Thunder rumbled in the distance, but it wasn't just any thunder; it was rolling thunder and it announced itself with a loud crack, then weakened as it grew more distant until it finally stopped. Then it cracked again, even louder this time. Mitch took a step back and looked up to assess the situation. Dark, black clouds in the distance were racing toward us and I could already smell the rain in the air.

"This storm is coming up fast, Laci! We'd better pack up and get back to the winery." We jumped over to our picnic area, shoved everything into the basket, and took off running.

Before we had made it to the barn though, the sky unloaded. I saw a flash of lightning from the corner of my eyes and the hair on my arms rose from the current in the air. It was about to be my first Carolina gulley washer! The warm rain came down hard and fast and we were drenched in seconds. I could see the barn up ahead and we ran inside for cover, laughing hysterically as we gasped for air from our marathon run. Not only was I out of breath, I was also quite chilled by the cool winds blowing about, made evident by my chattering teeth. Mitch found an old blanket and wrapped it around both of us so we could warm up as the rain hammered down on the roof above.

"This is awesome!" I exclaimed over the noise. I wanted to go back outside and run around in it, but now wasn't the time.

"You're something else, Laci Kramer. You and your rainstorms. If I didn't know any better, I'd think you arranged this," Mitch said, smiling. Droplets of water fell from his hair.

"It's good luck, you know. There are good things in store for you and this winery!"

"It's more than that, Laci," he said, raising his voice over the rain.

"What do you mean?"

"I wanted to tell you this before…on the bridge, but this storm interrupted everything, and I need you to know." A serious look came over his face. My heart began to pound even harder than before our little 5k run from the bridge. I couldn't catch a break! "It's just that, I've not felt this way about another woman in a long, long time." He stammered, searching for the words, then continued. "I'm almost forty-six, Laci, and I'm not a man to take things lightly or make foolish decisions on a whim. I'm the consummate business professional, always the last one to approve something because I take so long to do my research first. It took me over a year to finish the deal on this winery." His hands slid behind my neck. He looked outside at the rain for a brief second, then back at me. Tears sat on the edge of his eyes and my knees were about to buckle under me. He stepped out of the blanket and wrapped it around me, tucking it in so it wouldn't fall, then he cupped his hands around my face and looked at me with determination. I kept telling myself not to freak out, even though I had a feeling of what was about to come. "Laci, what I'm trying to say is, I love you, darlin'! I love you with all my heart! I realize we still have so much to learn about each other, and I want to know everything there is to know about you and your kids. You have completely stolen my heart and I can't hold it in anymore." For a second, I couldn't breathe! It wasn't exactly the best time for a long pause, especially since I knew I felt the same way. My mouth dropped open and all I could do was cry. I was caught completely off-guard by his unexpected words. He didn't even wait for my response; he just pulled me close and kissed me with a fierce passion I hadn't felt until then.

My skin was on fire; I melted in his arms. Tears rolled down my cheeks and I could taste the saltiness seep in between our lips. He pulled his head back and wiped my tears, then smiled.

"I love you too, Mitch. I have since the day we met. I love you so much!" I said, my teeth still chattering.

"You do, you really do? You're not just saying it because I said it first?"

I gave him the look and said, "For crying out loud, do I look eighteen to you? I think I know what it means to be in love, and I'm pretty sure I loved you first even though you did say it first. Now stop talking and kiss me!" I smiled.

"You got it, darlin'."

I savored his warm, sweet lips. I didn't want that moment to end, but I lifted my head for a brief second and said, "See, I told you good things come with the rain." I smiled then returned to his kiss.

family drama

A few intimate minutes later, the rain was still coming down in sheets. Mitch and I had moved to a small bench to sit and wait it out when we saw Brad standing on the front porch of the winery looking at us. He didn't look happy.

"He really doesn't like me, does he?" I said, as we watched him walk back inside.

"He's worried I'm moving too fast. He's just looking out for me, that's all. His bark is much worse than his bite. It will take some time, but he'll warm up to you, I promise." Mitch's eyes looked sad, and I wasn't sure if he believed his own words.

"I'm not worried." I smiled at him. The heat inside our blanket felt good, although my legs were still shaking. I looked around the barn and thought about all the things I could do in there. "I want to help with the barn, Mitch. I don't know how I'll do it from Washington, but I'll figure something out."

"I know, and it will be amazing when you're done. I have faith in you." He smiled and then kissed me on the nose. "Your nose is so cold. Let's make a run for the car and head back to the house. We need some dry clothes." We got into the car and Mitch cranked up the heat for me.

"I'm going to go tell Brad goodbye. I'll be right back." He got out and ran inside the winery.

"Brad, we're taking off man. We're soaked and Laci is shivering out there," Mitch said.

"Skipping out on work again, huh bro? Are you ever going to stick around and help me out around here?" Brad said in a snide tone, his voice cold and tight.

"Brad, what is your deal? You're acting like a big baby. I bring my girlfriend home to meet my family and you can't even be civil to her? What's going on?"

"You need to slow down, Mitch. You don't know nearly enough about this woman! It's been, what, three weeks, four, tops? How can you be in love with her? Have you even thought that maybe she's just after your money? She obviously knows you're rich."

"I've told you before; she's not like that. You're unbelievable you know it?" Mitch laughed in exasperation. "You have been begging me for months to find someone, move on with my life. Now that I'm finally doing that, you're looking for every excuse you can find to keep us apart. Why? What's really going on and don't tell me it's about the winery. I know better than that."

"I don't know, I can't explain it. I just get a vibe that's all, like she's going to hurt you. I won't stand by and see you get hurt again Mitch. I won't. You'll end up falling in love and moving to Washington to live with her and her kids and then I'll lose you and be stuck running this place by myself. I can't lose you, man. I want this winery to work and I want us to run it together until we're old and can't see or walk anymore." Brad's face was ashen; his fear of losing Mitch was evident.

"That's crazy. She is not going to hurt me. And for the record, I do love her! I told her so today and she loves me too. Look, I know you're my big brother and it's been your job to watch out for me for a lot of years now, but I'm all grown up if you hadn't noticed. I can take care of myself. I will never be able to thank you enough or repay you for standing by me when I was going through all that pain and heartache from losing Karin. I know I wouldn't even be standing here today if it weren't for you. But I need you to trust me on this, big brother. She's the one. She's the reason I got on that plane and the reason I'm so incredibly happy and ready to start over again, to love again. She's that special. And if you're going to make me choose between you and Laci, then you should know that she wins. She'll always win. I'm not about to let her become the one that got away, I can promise you that. I won't leave you or this winery; I'm not leaving North Carolina. For now, she understands that and we'll figure the rest out as we go. I don't know what the future holds for us, but I know I want her in my life, forever. I haven't shared the 'forever' part with her yet. I almost proposed today, but it didn't feel right—it's too soon, and I'm sure it would have freaked her out. Besides, I want your blessing before I make it official. I love you, brother, and I need you to support me on this...so what's it gonna be?"

There was a long pause and Mitch stood there, staring at his brother and waiting for his reply.

"I'll do my best, but I can't promise that I won't stop looking out for what's best for you. It will always be my job. I can't help it; Dad's orders, you know?" Brad smiled, then he pulled Mitch over and hugged him. "Now go, get out of here. I'll stop by later tonight. There are some things I need to go over with you but it shouldn't take long."

"Thanks, Brad. I'll call you after we get back from dinner."

Mitch came running outside and quickly got inside the car. "Hey, sorry about that. Brad was just going over a few invoices with me. Are you getting warm?"

"Toasty! Now let's go. I think my bones are even soggy."

After we got back, I took a nice hot shower, fixed my hair and makeup for the second time today, and then threw on my good jeans, a sleeveless, yellow blouse, and my taupe heels. The rain had ended and the temperature was back up to a balmy eighty- five degrees again.

Mitch and Caleb gave me a tour of the town, and we made a visit to Caleb's high school. I had to shop a little too, of course. The little shops were amazing, and I bought way too much. The afternoon went by fast, and before long, we were exhausted and hungry, so we headed over to Pizza Vino, Mitch and Caleb's favorite place in town, and stuffed ourselves like ticks. The food was delicious and the atmosphere was warm and cozy. Almost everyone that walked in the door knew someone else inside. I felt like I was part of a revolving-door family reunion. I loved it. I really enjoyed spending time with Caleb and Mitch. They had such an open relationship, and it was nice to watch them together. We talked about Caleb's girlfriend of three months who was starting to annoy him, his lifeguard job at the local recreation club, and many other things before dinner had ended. Learning about his life made me feel like part of their family in some way.

Before we knew it, it was eight o'clock, so we went back to the house and Mitch called Brad to meet us there.

"I hope you don't mind, but I asked Brad to stop by tonight so we could work on a few things for the winery. I need to make some decisions so he can move forward tomorrow on a couple of items. Is that okay?"

"Of course! You have a business to run, Mitch. I understand that. Please do whatever you need to do. If you need to work tomorrow, I can keep myself entertained. The last thing I want to do is interfere with your business or come between you and your brother. I'm a big girl. I can handle being alone."

"I'm not about to work while you're here, he'll survive. But thank you. I'll just be an hour or so. Besides, tomorrow I have a little surprise for you," he said with a smile.

"A surprise again? And still no hints?"

"Nope. No hints, sorry. You'll find out soon enough."

After we got back to the house, Caleb jumped out of the car and announced he was heading over to his friend's house for the night. Brad was waiting on the front porch for Mitch, so I went straight to my room and changed into my fuzzy, coffee-cup pajama pants and a T-shirt and turned on the TV. I couldn't find anything to satisfy me, so I decided to call Teri and the kids to check in since it was only a little after dinner time there. After a brief chat with everyone and an update on work and home from Teri, I tried to relax, but I couldn't help wonder about my surprise tomorrow. He had mentioned it on the drive here, how I had had it coming since the day we'd met. What did that mean?

After about an hour of random thoughts and boring TV, I went downstairs to fix myself a cup of coffee and sit on the front porch, and maybe read for a bit. As I rounded the corner going into the kitchen, I saw Brad standing in front of the refrigerator and holding the door open, staring at its contents as if it would change in the next few seconds. I thought he had already left. Let me rephrase that, I was hoping he had left! I walked in and had no plans to engage him in conversation, figuring he would rather have it that way too. I wasn't sure where Mitch had gone, but I went about my own business and found myself a cup, creamer, and a coffee pod.

"Didn't your mother ever tell you that drinking coffee before bed would stunt your growth?" Brad said in a sarcastic tone. I debated whether or not to be contrary in my reply, but in the end I decided to keep things civil.

"Nah, she was too busy telling me how to save energy by not standing in front of the refrigerator with the door open and let- ting out all the cold air," I replied flippantly. I turned and flashed him a big grin just for kicks.

"Ha-ha. Very funny, Airplane Girl." His voice was cold, some- where between trying to be funny and actually being a bully. It didn't take long to determine which one he was. "Are you dating my brother for his money?" he asked bluntly, once again completely throwing me off-guard. He had also interrupted my evening coffee time – not smart! *This* time, I immediately went on the defensive.

"Where on earth did you get that notion? You don't know the first thing about me, and yet you assume I'm only interested in your brother for his money? You've got some nerve! And to answer your lame question, no. I'm not after his money. I am in love with your brother for more reasons than I can even state, but mostly for just who he is, how he makes me feel, and for who I am when we're together. I know it sounds crazy having only known him a few short weeks, but I do. Whether you choose to believe it is your problem. Any other stupid questions you'd like to ask me?"

My face was probably beet red at that point. I felt the veins in my neck bulging out as I spewed my answer at him.

"Only one. What will it take for you to walk away? Just back off and let him find someone else, someone closer to home." Shocked by his words, my mouth dropped open. Surely I had misunderstood!

"Seriously? You didn't just ask me to dump your brother, did you? Get it through your thick skull, *Brad*, I'm not about to give him up. I love him! He's made my life worth living again. We lost our spouses in different ways, but the fact remains that we still lost them. The three-year span of gut-wrenching agony that followed that loss is finally coming to an end, don't you get that? He taught me that life can go on and it's okay to love again. I want to spend the rest of my life with him, although he doesn't know that exactly and it's a bit too soon to tell him." I lowered my voice, embarrassed by my statement. "Please don't tell him I said that." I cracked a little smile, realizing what I had voiced out loud. Oddly enough, Brad started laughing too for whatever reason. A few seconds passed in silence and then Mitch walked through the kitchen door and stood behind Brad staring at both of us. It felt like I had just been caught with my hand in the for- bidden cookie jar.

"Hi, guys. Am I interrupting?" Mitch asked, walking into the kitchen quietly. Oh for flip sakes! How much of that did he hear? That day just kept getting worse. I've not only insulted his brother and confessed my love for Mitch all in the same breath, but most likely had become the source of a small Young family feud. Yep, great visit so far. I was sure to get a gold star for that one!

"Brad and I were just getting acquainted, weren't we, *Brad*?" "Yep, getting acquainted. And I think it's about time I head out. Thanks for the chat, *Laci*," he said with a snarky voice. "I'll walk you out." Mitch said and followed him outside.

I worried about what Mitch might have heard me say, but I figured there was no sense in making a big deal about it until I knew for sure. I finally made my coffee, picked up my book, and walked out onto the porch just in time to hear the squeal of Brad's tires against the pavement as he pulled away. Mitch was leaning over the porch. His arms were crossed in front of him resting on the ledge, and he looked deep in thought. I walked up next to him, sipping my coffee and being quiet. But I wasn't very good at *staying* quiet.

"I can't remember the last time I've seen this many stars. My view is always covered by clouds. I rarely get to see the moon, let alone the entire Milky Way. It's breathtaking." But no answer came, just silence. "Mitch, I—"

"It's nothing you've done. I don't know why he's behaving this way toward you." His gaze never left the night sky.

"He's protective, I get it. Our *relationship* is only a few weeks old. I'm guessing you told him you loved me, am I right?"

"Yeah, I told him at the winery earlier. He wasn't very receptive and told me I was moving too fast. He'll come around though, I know it. He's got some crazy idea that I'm going to leave all my responsibilities here and move to Washington with you." He laughed softly.

"But you wouldn't, even I know that."

"No. I wouldn't. I…" The gravity of his own words came crashing down and he looked at me with regret in his eyes. "I'm sorry, Laci. I didn't mean that the way it sounded."

"Yes, you did, and you have nothing to apologize for, silly. We are still dating, remember? Long-distance relationships are always complicated, but they're not impossible." I stepped over to a small table behind me, set my coffee and book down, then walked back over to him and hooked my arm through his, resting my head against his shoulder.

"I love you, Mitch Young. Let's start there and take it one day at a time. Deal?"

He turned and lifted my head up with his hand. His eyes drank in the moonlight above; a silver glow surrounded them.

"You've got a deal, darlin'." He sealed his promise with a sweet, little kiss. Little being the operative word there...I could have used a big one myself. "It's late; we should head back inside and get some sleep. Big day tomorrow!" he said, with an 'I-know- something-you-don't-know' smile.

"Oh yeah, my surprise! I had nearly forgotten about it. When are you going to tell me what it is?"

He turned and started to walk back inside, so I grabbed my coffee and book then followed behind.

"Tomorrow morning, after breakfast." I stopped across from the living room and he looked at me.

"In that case, I'm going to stay up and read for a little while, take my mind off the suspense of my surprise. I'm not sure I could sleep right now anyway, after everything."

"All right, don't be up too late. I'm sorry about Brad. Don't let him get to you, okay? I'll see you in the morning. I love you, Laci," he said softly, and he pulled me into his arms.

"I love you too. I love saying 'I love you,' is that silly?"

"No, I feel the same way," he said, smiling. I cupped his face in my hands and gave him a nice, long, proper kiss.

"Goodnight, handsome."

He walked up to his room and I retreated to the living room with my book. It was my favorite room in the house so far, with its doily-covered Queen Anne chairs, Tiffany lamps sitting on small antique tables, and a beautiful old rug in the center of the room. I imagine that room had a few stories to tell. It was peaceful there. I felt Karin in that room, and in some strange way, I think she had welcomed me into her home and even approved of me and Mitch being together. Maybe she was happy to have someone love him again and take care of him. I chose a chair next to the ornate mantle and fireplace. It was too warm for a fire, of course, but I pictured one in my mind—wood cracking and pop- ping as it burned, flames dancing about as they threw an orange glow all over the dimly lit room, the smell permeating the air. I wondered if I would ever see it burn, or if what Mitch and I had was real enough to last. At some point, we would have to make some big decisions about the future. But it was much too soon to think about all that.

I opened my book, *One Day* by David Nicholls, to the part I had left off on the plane, chapter ten. Naturally I was reading about star-crossed lovers! What a poetic ending to the day.

in crawdad territory

Tuesday. I woke up with a heavy feeling in my stomach, already bummed about leaving the next day in spite of the surprise that awaited me. I crawled out of bed, feet heavy and still half-asleep, then headed to the shower. I decided to go with my scrunch-and- go look that day. I have naturally curly hair, so every once in a while, I would give the flat iron a rest and keep it sassy and fun. I wrapped a robe around myself, walked back to the bedroom, and shut the door. Before I could pick out my clothes, I was startled at someone knocking at my door and I squealed like a mouse. I could hear Mitch's hearty laugh at my response.

"I'm not dressed yet, what's up?" I asked through the door. "Hmmm, I am happy to provide any assistance if you need it," he joked.

"Very funny. What do you want?"

"I just wanted to tell you to dress cool and very casual. It's supposed to be a real scorcher today and we'll be out in the sun for most of the day."

"That's it? Just 'we'll be out in the sun most of the day'? Nothing else? No hints?"

"Nope. But hurry up, breakfast is ready."

I heard him laugh as he walked away. If he only knew what my wardrobe challenges would be now after having made that comment! Men! I decided to take note of the 'very casual' part and went with short denim shorts, a pink T-shirt, ankle socks, and my white tennis shoes.

I walked downstairs and followed the smell of freshly brewed coffee. Mitch was already pouring himself a cup, so I just stood there and watched, enjoying the view from behind. He looked rather yummy in casual khaki shorts, a red-and-white t-shirt, and a black baseball cap. He turned around to greet me, and I noticed his hat displayed the letter *H* with a little red crawdad wrapped around it. That was when I knew. He was taking me to a Crawdad game! Sweet! I couldn't let on that I knew though, it would totally spoil the fun.

He walked toward me with coffee in hand and smiled. He was totally checking me out as if he had never seen me before.

"Wow, very nice! I like the hair, too. If you don't mind me saying so, it's quite sexy. You pull off the cool, casual look really well." He leaned down to give me a good morning kiss on the cheek, and then whispered in my ear, "And pink suits you; it matches your cheeks." It would be nice if I could get through just *one* day without neon cheeks!

I made my way to the cabinet and pulled down a coffee cup. "Thank you, and no, I don't mind you saying that at all. Flattery will get you to 'first base' at least." I laughed at my sly attempt to be humorous, and then poured my coffee. I sat down at the table next to him. That morning's breakfast was a stark contrast to the one Mitch's mom had made us the previous day. The menu was yogurt, fresh fruit, cereal, and milk. It was all very healthy and colorful. After about twenty minutes of eating and small talk, he looked at his watch.

"Well, I have one stop to make and then we have a forty-five- minute drive to your surprise. But before we go, I have a little present for you." He reached under the table, pulled out a gift bag, and handed it to me.

"Ooh, a present for me? Yeah! I love presents!" I squealed and ripped into the bag like it was Christmas morning. I pulled out a pink baseball hat with a letter *H* on the front to match his, the same crawdad wrapped around the leg of the *H*. I looked up at him and smiled, knowing what it meant of course.

"Ah, I love hats! Especially pink. It matches my outfit; nice touch! Thank you." I leaned over to give him a kiss and wrapped my arm around him in a half hug. "Is this a clue to my *surprise*?" "Yes, as if you didn't know. I'm taking you to your first official Hickory Crawdads game today. I hope you're up for a little minor league baseball action; Single-A at its finest!" He boasted.

"I *knew it*! I can't wait to see your Crawdads play! And yes, you kind of gave it away with your hat. Not too hard to figure that one out. What time does it start?"

"It starts at one, so we have plenty of time. I wanted you to have the hat because most of the seats are right in the sun. I didn't know at the time, however, that it would match your outfit. I think I scored a 'homerun' on that one!" He laughed. "Nice 'first base' comment earlier by the way. I figured you had caught on when you said that."

"I try." I smiled at him then got up and took our dishes to the sink. I ran some soapy water to wash them and he looked over and just stared at me. "What's up? You look lost."

"Nothing. You just remind me of someone, standing there doing dishes."

"Oh yeah? And who would that be?"

"My mom." I looked a little stunned, not sure if I should be flattered or grossed out by his comment.

"O-kay. Is that a good thing or a bad thing?"

"It's a good thing, of course. The way you always ask to help or get up and wash the dishes without batting an eye.

You like taking care of people, like she does." He smiled and came over to help dry.

"It's a mom thing, I guess. When you're so used to doing this for your kids and there is no one else around to do it, it becomes second nature. I don't even think about it. I love to help others. Makes me feel useful."

We finished the dishes and Mitch went upstairs to get some- thing. I walked out onto the porch and felt a gentle breeze blowing, the sun already heating things up nicely. The trees rustled and swayed back and forth gently. I closed my eyes to listen, letting the wind swirl around me like a warm blanket. I didn't get many days like this back home. Summers in Washington are beautiful and we do have some hot days, but they are few and far between. That day, I planned to enjoy the heat, the sun, the sweat, and whatever else I could think of to help me remember my time with him. I opened my eyes and the world was spinning around me. I stumbled back a bit and landed in a rocking chair. I sat there for a little bit and heard Mitch come outside.

"Are you ready?" he said.

"Let me run up and get my purse and sunglasses. I think I'm going to need them today."

I got up slowly, but he didn't seem to notice. I collected my things and threw a migraine pill in my purse for good measure. I hadn't suffered one in several months, but with the uneasy start to that morning, I thought it was best to be prepared.

We ran some errands and then headed off to Hickory, North Carolina, home of the Crawdads. It was a short drive for the most part, which I didn't mind on such a gorgeous, sunny day in August. Labor Day was the next weekend and I thought about what the kids and I might do when I got back. Probably the usual: a small BBQ with Lena and Teri and their husbands. A few of the kids in the neighborhood would wander in, and if it was warm enough, we would have a water-balloon toss and end the day with s'mores on the outdoor fire pit. It was bittersweet to think about it. I looked forward to spending good, quality time with my kids, but I knew that Mitch wouldn't be with us. After that weekend, I would miss him more than ever before, especially in light of our new status and having just declared our true feelings for each other. The next phase of our relationship would take on a different feel entirely. We were closer, more in-tune with one another, and more in love. I didn't want to think about leaving yet.

Mitch parked the car and we made our way into the grand Hickory Crawdads baseball field. I had somewhat expected a dirt field and metal bleachers, but that wasn't the case at all. The stadium was beautiful! They played in the L.P. Frans stadium. It had a nice brick front entrance and a gorgeous green field inside. I think my Rainiers would even be jealous! We found our seats just to the right of the home plate and down close to the field. He was right about being directly in the sun. I was already thankful for my pink Crawdads hat and sunglasses.

"I'm going to go up to the Crawdad Café and get us some popcorn and drinks. Do you want a coke?"

"Yes, a coke would be great, and a hot dog? Please?" I smiled at him.

"A woman after my own heart. Be right back, darlin'."

I mouthed "thank you" as he walked off. While he was gone, I threw my hair up in a ponytail and put on my new hat, poking the tail out through the back of the hat. The team mascot, Conrad the Crawdad, was the center of attention and entertained the crowd until game time. Finally, with my colossal dog and drink in hand, the game began, and boy was it a nail-biter. We were playing against the Legends and they were good. We scored, they scored, we scored, and then they scored again. The crowd was loud and fired-up, cheering for their Crawdads. There were some major fans in the stadium! That was one thing I loved about minor league baseball; it was about the love of the game, not the love of money. Mitch and I went back and forth holding hands, clapping, and jumping up to cheer when the Crawdads scored. I was having the time of my life. I felt like one of their own. The last two innings were the best. Hickory player Gallo came out onto the field and the crowd went wild. On the second pitch, he belted one out of the park for a towering home run to tie things up! He was obviously a fan favorite, along with Brinson, but you could tell the entire team was loved by all. In the top of the 9th, the Legends scored another run and took the lead, but we were up at last. Bases were loaded and Edwards was up to bat. One good swing to right field and the game was over! The Crawdads won, 10 to 9. It was a great game and one I would never forget, as I was there with the man I loved.

"Now that's what I call good baseball! What did you think?

Are you an official Crawdad fan now?"

"I hate to admit it, but I am! Just not a creepy *stalker* Crawdad fan; that title is reserved strictly for you."

We laughed, thinking about our conversation at the airport the day we met. So much had happened since then. I was so thankful to God for bringing him into my life. I never dreamed I would be that happy again. I took his hand and we walked to the car to leave. The drive back home was quiet. The sun had taken its toll on me and I could feel my skin burning. I realized how useful sunblock would have been.

"I hope you're okay with dinner at my mom's tonight. I know it's your last night here, but she really wanted us to come so she could see you again. Our weekly family dinner, you know."

"I remember. I like your mom and dinner at her house sounds great. What's she making?"

"I think she's fixing fajitas. She lays on a spread to feed an army, as you know from her breakfast yesterday." I laughed, recalling fondly the massive pile of bacon she'd served.

"Sounds great! What time? I may need to freshen up a bit." "Not until seven or so. If you want, we could go by the winery

one last time before we go over? I can have Caleb meet us there." He reached over across the car, took my hand, and squeezed it. I could tell he was starting to dwell on the inevitable goodbye.

"I would love that. Maybe a quick walk to the bridge if it's not raining?" I smiled, thinking about our mad dash into the barn.

Back at the house, we quickly changed clothes. Mitch came out wearing his Dockers and a light blue polo. I went with a loose-fitting, spaghetti-strapped tank and my long beach skirt to stay cool. The less material sitting on my beet-red arms the better. We arrived at the winery and Brad was nowhere in sight. I was grateful. The walk to the bridge was quiet but nice. We stood on the bridge, looking out over the water.

"I don't want you to go, Laci," he said. He turned to face me, pulling me to him.

"That makes two of us, but you know I have to. My kids need me and I have a job to do. This is the worst part." Although I tried to hold my emotions back, tears escaped and rolled down my cheek.

"Don't cry. I'll be up soon. I'll try to visit at least once every few weeks if I can, maybe more. I have a lot of frequent flyer miles to use; they'll just be shorter visits from now on. Brad is getting aggravated with me because I'm not around to help with the business. I was thinking about spending Halloween up there and trick-or-treat with Emma and Travis. What do you think?"

"That would be great, Mitch! They will love that! Emma has a Halloween party you know; she'll rope you into helping her with it so be prepared." I looked down, holding back the tears.

"Hey, look at me," he said. I looked into his eyes and that was all it took for the water works to begin. "You're beautiful even when you're crying, you know that?" He held me tight against his chest and I could smell the cologne on his shirt. I breathed him in, making a memory of the scent so I could take it with me. "We have tonight together, so let's enjoy every minute of it. I'm sorry we have to spend it with my family," he added.

"It's fine, really. I like your family, they are wonderful. Except Brad maybe, that one I'll have to work on." I smiled.

It was just a little before seven when we pulled into his mom's driveway. The house smelled like a Mexican cantina; the aroma of bell peppers and onions filled the air. Before dinner, I was standing in his mother's living room looking at all the pictures of Mitch and Brad when they were little, laughing at some of the photos.

"That was Mitch at age ten, stealing home plate with his little league team. He was a baseball all-star by the age of fifteen," Mitch's mom said, as she walked up behind me. Pride was evident in her voice.

"They were so cute. You must be very proud of them."

"Oh yes, they are my pride and joy as a mother. I owe them both so much. They spoil me, though. I can be a bit needy at times." She paused for a minute. "You love him don't you?" she asked me bluntly.

I looked directly in her eyes and replied, "Yes, ma'am. I love him dearly. He changed my life when he got on the plane that day."

"He says the same about you, sweetheart. But please be careful." Not her too! What was it with his family?

"What do you mean, Maggie, if I may ask?"

"I can see how much you love each other, but long-distance relationships are hard. A few days after his trip, he came over for dinner and had a different look about him. I knew then that something had changed. Turns out it was you. It's been nice to see him smile and I credit you for that. But it won't be easy, darlin'. He has a life here and you have a life there. If this continues to get serious, one of you will have to give up your life. Are you prepared for that?" She seemed so cold and I didn't know how to respond for a minute.

"I'm not worried. If that day comes, I will do whatever it takes to make him happy, even if that means moving to the moon. He means that much to me, Mrs. Young. Please believe me. I would never hurt your son."

"I do, sweetheart. I do. Now let's go have dinner, shall we? I've got key lime pie for dessert!" she said in her sweet, southern voice and a smile appeared on her face as big as Texas.

I entered the dining room and saw Caleb sitting at the table with his dad and Uncle Brad. Oh *joy*. My appetite suddenly left, but seeing as how Mexican was my favorite, I forced down my food and a small piece of pie to be polite. Everything was delicious, but his mother's sweet, southern hospitality had made my stomach a little sour. I was ready to go and I think Mitch finally picked up on my subtle hints of no eye contact, no smiles, and a complete lack of conversation on my part.

"I think we're going to head out, mamma. We have an early morning tomorrow. Laci has to be at the airport by ten. But thank you for a delicious dinner, again. You're the best," he said, and he gave her a hug and kiss goodbye.

"Yes, thank you Maggie. It was such a pleasure meeting you this week and so nice of you to invite me into your home. Everything was delicious. I hope to see you again."

"I have a feeling you will, sweetie. And Laci, thank you for giving my Mitch his smile back. Let's keep it there, shall we?" She walked right up to me and gave me a big hug and a little peck on the cheek. I should've been happy about that, but Jesus was kissed on the cheek too and as I recall, that didn't turn out so well for him. Forgive me if I didn't consider this little visit a success just yet…

Back at the house, I slid into my pajamas and went downstairs. It was early yet and I heard Mitch rustling around in the kitchen. He had on his lounge pants and a tight T-shirt, showing off his nice six-pack. I swooned over him for a second, but I soon realized that I was actually dizzy. I slowly stumbled over to the table and sat down. Mitch saw me and came rushing over naturally.

"Laci, are you all right?" he asked, helping me sit down.

"Yes, I'm fine. Just tired I guess. That sun really kicked my butt today. Could you get me some water?" The last thing I wanted was for him to worry or make a fuss over me. He poured me a glass of water and came right back.

"Here you go. You do look a little pale, despite the sunburn. Maybe you should call it a night, as much as I don't want you to." He sat down and took my hand while I drank my water.

Sadness washed over me at his comment. "Thank you for asking me to come home with you and meet your family. I had such a good time and I…" The tears came again, but I quickly wiped them away. "I should get some sleep. Walk me up?"

He escorted me to my room and we said goodnight. Sleep didn't come for a few hours; my stomach was in knots. I was thinking about having to leave and say goodbye to him, how it would be much harder than the other times since I was on his turf. I was leaving *him*….

The morning was rushed because I had overslept a little, but it was also quiet. Too quiet. I said goodbye to Caleb after break- fast and then we left. The long drive to the airport seemed much shorter that time around. We parked and made our way inside; the airport was already dense with travelers. Mitch walked me in, toting my bag behind him, but there would be no waiting around with me. I had security lines ahead to wade through, so we walked over and stood by a wall to say our goodbyes. He put my bag down on the floor and wrapped his arms around my waist, pulling me close.

"I'll see you in a few weeks tops, okay?" he said.

"Promise?" He looked in my eyes and I put my hands around his neck, not waiting any longer for my goodbye kiss. My lips drank him in like sweet tea and I didn't let him up for even a breath of air. I couldn't let him go. I ran my hands through his hair as we kissed, tears streaming down my cheeks. Finally I let him loose, wrapping him up in my arms in a tight hug.

"I love you, Mitch Young," I whispered in his ear.

"I love you too, darlin'," he laughed and shook his head. "God, I love you more than I ever thought possible after only four weeks." We stood there and simply held each other.

"I'd better go."

"I know. Have a good flight. Call me the minute you land and when you get home," he said, as he let go of me. I looked into his tear-stained face, laid one hand on the side of his cheek, and said goodbye.

I picked up my bags and walked away, making my way towards security. As I stood in line, I turned back to look at him one more time. He was still there, watching me, and he blew me a kiss.

I returned home from our weekend together filled with an over- whelming joy that penetrated my bones. With that came the sense of security of now being exclusive to one another. That weekend spurred a courtship like no other I had ever experienced, not even with Andrew. It was long-distance courting in its rarest form—phone calls, texts, emails, and even the occasional hand- written letter. Those were my favorite! It was like living inside a Hallmark movie. Each visit held something new and wonderful, as we learned more and more about each other. I had a bad case of the Cinderella syndrome! I didn't care though. Mitch had become the center of my universe in such a short time. The hardest thing for me to admit was that I didn't think I had ever been that happy in my life, not even when Andrew was alive. There was such a deep connection with Mitch; it was unlike anything I had ever known. I was head over heels in love with him! When he was with me, everything was right in my world; and when he left, it became hard to breathe. I was at the point that I could barely fall asleep without hearing his voice first. We even had a virtual coffee date every Saturday morning when we would go to our favorite respective coffee shops and talk on the phone while we sipped a cup of joe together. The time difference made it a little challenging, but it was the thought that counted. It was my favorite day of the week.

Every couple of weeks, Mitch would fly up to visit me and the kids, and never once did he ask to spend the night. He would say, 'I'm not about to mess up a good thing; we're doing this the old fashioned way, darlin'."

So he would always stay in a hotel and left each night around midnight or so depending on what we were doing. We had our exclusive movie nights and dinners together. But each time he visited, I noticed him wanting to spend more and more time at the house and being part of our family. Before I realized it, Mitch had become the new normal in our life. The kids grew more excited to see him before he arrived and sadder each time he left. One of the highlights of each visit was Mitch's rather unique and hearty laugh that made the kids giggle incessantly when they heard it. Making him laugh became their mission in life.

As we created new memories together, each moment became as precious as gold to us. For the first time in years, I was living life without guilt or thoughts of being unfaithful to Andrew. There were times I could even feel him looking down and smiling, knowing that his family was happy again.

an autumn to remember

Halloween had finally arrived, and next to Christmas, it was my favorite holiday! I could still remember when my mom and my aunt had dressed up for my elementary school costume con- test years ago. My aunt's costume had been an outhouse, complete with a moon carved out of the front of her refrigerator box painted with gray and black stripes to look like old wooden boards. My mom's outfit was a bit more complex; she had large pillows to create a large belly as well as a crazy old woman mask, her hair was up in curlers, and she carried a rolling pin. I was never so proud! She had made my costume too, Raggedy Ann, and the boy I had a crush on was Raggedy Andy. We were in third grade and I was in love! It was all so sweet an innocent back then. I couldn't wait until it was time to hold his hand and walk in to parade around the gym. He, on the other hand, was totally grossed out. We won first place that year, unlike the year she made my skunk costume. That had a very different outcome all together! Things were much different back then.

Now the Halloween parties were called 'fall festivals' and homemade treats were no longer allowed in the candy sacks. Some days, it would be nice to rewind life and go back to a time when things were simpler. Of course, I wouldn't last a single day without my smart phone, so I would have to settle for present day.

Most of the colorful fall leaves had fallen to the ground or blown away. Mornings started off with a visit from Jack

Frost, leaving sparkling white crystals clinging to each blade of grass and hanging on bare tree limbs. Pumpkins and bales of hay were strewn across lawns throughout the neighborhood announcing that autumn was in full swing. I was excited to spend Halloween with my kids, minus Evan of course, Mitch, and Caleb– the complete package. It's still hard to believe that three months have already passed since we met – seemed like only yesterday that he walked onto that plane and into my heart.

Travis and Emma were beyond excited to see Mitch. He would arrive later that afternoon, but the kids had no idea he was bringing Caleb – he wanted to surprise them. That would be the first time they'll have met his son since we started dating. Plans had already been made to ask Mitch to go trick-or-treat with us and help throw our annual 'monster bash' for the neighborhood. There was a lot of work to be done, so I took a vacation day so I could get everything ready for tonight and the weekend, plus go to my doctor's appointment later that day. I'd been working in our garage since seven o'clock that morning – magically transforming it into a splendiferous conglomeration of black curtains to hide the 'stuff ', fake cobwebs, spiders, homemade tissue ghosts hanging from the ceiling, orange and white lights strung all around, and a black-light to give everything a nice eerie glow when the lights went off. I could hardly wait to see Mitch's reaction! Emma was using every minute she had before the bus arrived to help me setup.

"Bring me the hot glue gun, Emma! I've got to glue this bat's wing back on."

"Here you go. When will Mitch be here? I want him to help us carve our pumpkin tonight!" she said, so excited and impatient. I couldn't help but laugh at her enthusiasm; it made me happy that she liked him so much.

"He should arrive before you get home from school, if his flight is on time. If you'd get busy and help me decorate, the time would go by faster, you know."

"Time doesn't go faster, mother. It just feels like it sometimes." That girl was becoming such a smarty pants!

"Yes, I know that Emma, but let's pretend like it will go faster just for kicks, shall we?"

"You're in love with Mitch, aren't you, mom?" Emma's question threw me for a loop and I choked myself right into a coughing fit.

Her question was so matter-of-fact; it sounded as if she already knew the answer to it. I had been dreading it somewhat, but knew that eventually one of them would ask. I took a deep breath and answered.

"Yes, Em. I'm definitely in love with him. How do you feel about that?"

"I think he's great! And you are so happy now. When he's here, it feels kind of good, like before. You know, before Dad died. So if you marry him I'd be okay with that."

She was just going to throw out *all* the big questions today wasn't she? I've thought about marriage, but I've only known him a short time. It would be crazy to get married that soon! Would I say yes if he asked? Then again, I wouldn't be in my right mind if I said no! Oh good grief...what was I thinking? We were moons away before that question would be asked, if it was ever asked at all. I wasn't about to get my hopes up.

"What? No, no, no. We're nowhere close to talking about marriage yet, sweetie. We haven't even known each other that long!" "Well, you might. Just sayin'," she replied. I laughed at her cute tween slang response.

"I'm glad you like him and it's good to know that we have your approval. If there's any talk of marriage, you'll be the first to know. But please don't ask him about this okay? That might be a little awkward and I don't want you to put him on the spot."

"I won't, don't worry." She rolled her eyes at me.

"You need to go get your backpack, grab your brother, and then head to the bus. I'll keep decorating for a little while and then you can help me finish up after school."

"Ugh, fine! Why can't I stay home today and help?" she whined. "Because you can't that's why. I have a ton of things to get done today and a doctor's appointment this afternoon to boot.

Now go or you'll be late!" She stomped out of the garage with a huffy attitude and went back inside to get her things.

⸻ ∿∘⊙⟲⊙⟲⊙⟲∘∿ ⸻

The ob-gyn's office wasn't too crowded—just a few pregnant mothers and a few of us on the other end of that life stage. Although, there seemed to be more and more women my age that had waited until later in life to have children. I guessed they were career-minded early on or maybe hadn't met the right per- son yet. Many reasons for that I suppose.

They seemed to be running on time thankfully. While I waited, I sent Mitch a short text to let him know where I was in case he landed while I was with the doctor.

<At the doctor. Can't answer phone for a while. Text me when you land. Back before you arrive hopefully. Love you!>

It was my least favorite appointment of the year, as it was for most women. A necessary evil, I suppose. For the most part, my appointment was like that of any other year.

My doctor was really nice, so it was tolerable. She scolded me though for waiting two years to come in for my exam. Since Andrew died, I'd had a few other priorities. I always had normal results, so I didn't see the harm. We talked about "the change" and all the fun symptoms ahead of me, boring stuff. After my exam, she sent me over to the other side of the clinic to have a mammogram. I wondered how men would feel to have their most sensitive part squished to a pulp between two pieces of cold, hard plastic. At that thought, I cackled so loud that the sonographer had to come over and reposition me. I shared my internal thought with her and we laughed about it together.

I've often questioned God on this thought; how women ended up with PMS, periods, childbearing (as joyous as it was in the end), mammograms, Pap smears, and the ever popular hot flashes, night sweats, and mood swings. Maybe whoever named it "the change" thought that would make it sound less horrible, but he was quite wrong. What did men have to deal with? I'm sure there was something, but I couldn't think of one thing. I believe God said he would never give us more than we could handle, so I suppose it's a compliment to women that we must endure those things, as awful as some were. And if that's the case, I was okay with it.

Luckily, I was in and out of the doctor's office within an hour. I headed home and my cell phone beeped. It was a text from Mitch telling me he'd landed. The image of his handsome face appeared in my mind and the anticipation of seeing him caused my heart rate to shoot up. Then my lead foot pressed down even harder on the gas pedal...a little too hard. The siren blared and the blue-and-white lights flashed behind me. Ten minutes and a 115-dollar ticket later, I decided to send Mitch a text before I pulled out on the road. He was certain to beat me to the house thanks to that little setback. The kids were already home from school by then, and Emma would no doubt be thrilled that she got to see him before me.

I typed him a message and hit send.

<Running late.
Be there in twenty minutes.>

He replied a few minutes later.

<Everything okay?
You sick?>

<Oh no, just a checkup. All is good. You at the house yet?>
<We're about ten minutes away. Will be waiting with open arms!>
<See you soon!>

I pulled into the driveway to find Emma escorting Mitch and Caleb around the garage, giving them the full tour of the Halloween events to come. I felt so bad that I wasn't home when they arrived, especially with Caleb there to surprise the kids. But from the looks of it, the introductions went fine without me. Then my eyes found Mitch and I let out a little "woohoo" in the car before getting out, taking in the view. So happy in fact, that I quietly sang the first few words of the Hallelujah chorus just for grins! He stood tall, wearing his snug blue jeans and a creamy white sweater that showed off his handsome, tan face and sandy- blonde hair. He took my breath away. As I opened the car door to get out, he walked my way, and a bright, beautiful smile spread across his face. He didn't hesitate as he scooped me into his arms to say hello. I nearly melted right there on the driveway like a snowman in July!

"You are a sight for sore eyes, darlin'. I've missed you," he whispered softly. His hands moved up and cupped my face and his soft, warm lips covered mine in a strong, passionate kiss. I could feel how much he had missed me. His arms slid behind my back and he pulled me tighter into him, but when I heard tiny giggles drift out of the garage, I backed away a little, realizing we had an audience watching. I was somewhat embarrassed, but it was worth it.

"I missed you too, but right now we are on display so let's say hello again later when we're alone." I smiled and kissed him again quickly. "Sorry I wasn't home to greet you when you arrived. In my excitement to get home and see you, I, umm, overdid it a bit and grabbed the attention of a local police officer on the side of the road." I pulled out my ticket to show him, ever-so-proud of my efforts to get home. He looked at it and let out a big laugh, then hugged me again.

"I like that in a woman, not afraid to take a risk and go after what she wants."

"Why, Mr. Young, are you encouraging me to break the law to see you?" I laughed.

"Whatever it takes, darlin'." He took me by the hand and we walked inside. Emma was bending Caleb's ear with all her plans for the weekend. We went inside and had a snack then spent the rest of the afternoon getting costumes ready and adding more decorations. Mitch and Caleb were both good sports, doing pretty much whatever Emma wanted them to do; she knew good help when she saw it. The trick-or-treat hour was upon us, and after a quick trip around the neighborhood, we headed back home to get the last-minute items set out for the party.

Guests were due to arrive around eight after the porch lights went out. Caleb and Todd were bonding over the Xbox, playing the latest games and yelling at the other online players to take a shot, whatever that meant. I finished icing the ghost- and bat-shaped sugar cookies. Mitch was standing right next to me, slicing green olives to use as eyes on the deviled "bug" eggs. He looked over at me and smiled.

"What?" I asked.

"I could get used to this, you know—you, me, cooking in the kitchen together. After I spend time here, my desire to go back home grows less and less because you're not there. Nothing is as good when you're not around." He put his knife down and slid over beside me. I looked up at him and my thoughts drifted for a second as I thought about how good that icing would taste if I were kissing it off of his lips. It was a most distracting thought, indeed, but I quickly regained my composure and focused. "I want you to spend Thanksgiving with us, Laci. The whole family. I want to fly all of you down. My mother wants to cook a huge dinner to celebrate us finding each other and the progress we're making on the winery. What do you say?"

My eyes grew to the size of half dollars and I jumped into his arms to show my excitement.

"Yes, yes, yes! I would love to spend Thanksgiving with you and your family, more than anything! I'm sure the kids will feel the same!"

"Really? Because I want you to be sure. Visiting over a major holiday gathering can be a little overwhelming. Make sure you talk to the kids before you make your decision okay? But selfishly, I want you there." He squeezed me tight and every part of me quivered. I was completely in love with that man – no question about it!

"I will talk to the kids, don't worry. But I can't imagine spending another holiday without you, Mr. Young." I smiled. I had one hand around his neck and the other held my icing tool, so I leaned back and swiped a little icing on his lips, then proceeded to kiss it off. That's what I would call a 'sweet' victory!

"You are full of surprises, Ms. Laci! The things I could do with you, mmm!"

"Well, as a matter of fact, you'll get to do something with me tonight. Didn't I tell you? We're both dressing up for this little party tonight and I have a costume with your name on it waiting upstairs." I snickered and watched his face give way to a new look altogether.

"A costume? You're not serious, are you?"

"Do I look like I'm kidding? I take Halloween very seriously so if you want me for Thanksgiving, then dressing up tonight is part of the deal. It's a dignified costume though, nothing too crazy."

"Blackmail is very unbecoming on you, darlin', but for you I'll pay the price. Just remember I may decide to charge interest on any repayment." He smiled, then his hand came up to my face swiftly and he rubbed a huge dollop of icing all over my cheek. The icing war was on and it got messy fast, but man, it was fun!

A few minutes later, Mitch went upstairs to clean up and change into his costume. I heard the doorbell ring and I figured it was a late trick-or-treater, but when I opened the door, Evan was standing there with a huge grin on his face, bag in hand and wearing a silly monster head hat.

"Trick-or-treat, mom," he said loudly, and I screamed out with joy! I couldn't open the door fast enough. He stepped inside, tossed his bag to the floor, and I threw my arms around him. I gave him the longest, tightest hug I could muster. Of course the waterworks began shortly thereafter, and I was sobbing happy tears on his shoulder. My firstborn was home and life was good. "What are you doing here? You're supposed to be at school!" I let go of him so he could talk.

"A buddy of mine lives up here in Puyallup, and he was coming up this weekend for his mom's birthday. He was supposed to bring his girlfriend, but she got sick so he asked me if I wanted to use her ticket knowing I lived up here too."

"Well that was so nice of him! Please tell him thank you for me when you see him okay? I'm so happy to see you sweetie, you have no idea how much I've missed you. How long are you staying?"

"We fly back on Monday. Will you be able to take me the airport?"

"Of course, but let's worry about that later. Umm, there is something you should probably know though. I have guests here. Well, you know, my friend Mitch that I told you about. He and his son are up here visiting. They won't be sleeping here though, so you can still have your room. I hope that's okay."

"It's fine, mom. Are you two getting serious?"

"I like to think so. I hope so anyway. Yes, I believe we are. He's a wonderful man, Evan. I care a great deal for him."

"Okay, that's good. You don't have to give me all the gory details, mom. I get it." He laughed.

"Well, why don't you relax for a while? Emma and Travis' party is tonight in the garage, so I'll be a bit preoccupied with that for the next hour or two. As soon as Mitch comes back down, I'll introduce you. He's getting into his costume, which I need to do myself, but first let me introduce you to Caleb."

We walked down the hall into the living room. Caleb and Todd were still fighting the aliens on their video game, oblivious to us standing there.

"Hey boys, Evan is home," I said in a loud voice. They didn't even flinch! I walked over to Todd and pulled his headphones away from his head and let them snap back.

"Mom, what the!" Todd yelled as he turned around to look at me. Then he saw Evan and jumped up.

"Evan! Hey man! What are you doing here?" Todd asked with a big smile on his face. Evan walked up and hugged Todd with his manly, "not too close, not too long" brotherly hug.

"Just passing through; got a free plane ticket, so I'm here for a couple of days. Is James playing online with you guys?"

"Yeah, he and Lamar both. We're totally kicking their butts." Todd laughed. I listened to them and just smiled. It was so nice to have him home, being big brother for a while. Todd needed it more than me, I think.

"Caleb, this is my oldest son Evan. He just flew in from college for the weekend as a surprise. Evan, this is Mitch's son, Caleb." Caleb had already stood up and reached out to shake Evan's hand.

"Hey man, nice to meet you. Your mom's told me a lot about you. So you're up at NYU huh? What's it like in New York?" Thus their "guy chat" began.

Emma and Travis came running inside from the garage and saw Evan standing there, and the chitchat was over. They attacked him with hugs and kisses. Emma went on and on, telling him how much she missed him. Travis was just trying to wrestle him to the ground like he always did. I was the happiest mom in the world at that moment, watching my kids play and laugh together. I interrupted for one last comment. "I'll let you all get to know each other. I have a costume to put on, so I'll be back down in a few minutes. Boys, help yourself to food in the kitchen!" I yelled as I walked upstairs. It was nice that Caleb and Evan were so close in age. I hoped they could become friends, maybe even become as close as brothers. Upstairs, I knocked on the door where Mitch was changing and he let me in. He was dressed in the old-fashioned, pinstriped baseball shirt I had found online. It was made to look like an old White Sox uniform, complete with an embroidered baseball on the left front shoulder and matching ball cap. I had left him a note to just wear his jeans with it so he wouldn't feel completely awkward. He was completely adorable and quite hard to resist.

"My, my, Mr. Young, you do look very nice as a White Sox player, or is that 'Black Sox'?" I winked at him. "Thanks for being such a good sport, and I'm sorry you don't have matching pants, but I wasn't really sure what size to buy." I snickered.

"Funny. You keep laughing, darlin'. Where on earth did you find this get-up? It's not bad, don't get me wrong. But I don't think I've dressed up for Halloween in fifteen years or more." He fiddled with the ball cap in the mirror. "Did you have more trick or treaters at the door? I heard your doorbell." He turned and pulled me to him, wrapping his arms around my waist.

"Not exactly, it was actually Evan, my oldest. He wanted to surprise me. I guess he got a free ticket from a friend that lives up here. Can you believe it? He and the boys are getting acquainted downstairs. Now you'll finally get to meet him!" I said, a huge smile spread across my face. Finally, we were all together for the first time. But suddenly, my stomach felt a little queasy. I desperately wanted Evan to like Mitch, but I got the sense that it wasn't going to be that easy. "That's wonderful, Laci! No wonder you looked so happy when you walked through the door. I am looking forward to meeting him, but I'm a bit nervous about this one for some reason. He's been the man of the house for some time now, how do you think he'll take me being here?"

"Evan is a mature, young man. I think he knows how I feel about you and recognizes that you are in my life now. It will be good for him to see that this is real and not just a short-term fling. But will you stay up here while I change? I want to be the one to introduce you."

"What are you dressing up as anyway?"

"The sooner you let me go, the sooner you'll find out! Now sit, read a magazine. I'll be out in ten minutes." I stood up on my tippy toes and kissed him quickly, then hurried into my bath- room to change.

A few minutes later, I came barreling out of the bathroom wearing a somewhat form-fitting, white, long-sleeved fuzzy sweater; a full, knee-length red skirt; white bobby socks; my white sneakers; and a red pompom in each hand. My hair was pulled back into a ponytail tied up with a wide, red ribbon hanging down. It was my attempt at a vintage cheerleader outfit.

"Rah, Rah, Rah! Let's go have some fun, baseball boy!" Mitch stood there and I watched his mouth fall open and then smiled.

"What?" I asked.

"Ummm…it's just…well, that's not exactly what I expected as your Halloween costume I guess…but you look incredible! I'm not sure I want to share you with everyone though." He smiled.

"Well, I'm afraid you'll have to. Emma is probably freaking out because we're not down there helping her, so get your mind from out behind the high school bleachers and focus. We have a party to throw, mister."

"Okay, okay, just one thing though before we go down." And he curled his warm hands around the back of my neck and pulled me in close. His kiss was so soft and tender, radiating through me like an electrical pulse. I longed to stay there and bask in it forever but the party was waiting, so we headed downstairs.

As we entered the living room, all three boys had controls and were now engrossed in the online world of Halo. It was Travis's favorite game and he was right where I expected him, sitting on Evan's lap telling him how to shoot the aliens. My heart over- flowed with joy as I stood there, amazed at how happy I was today compared to this time last year when I was drowning in sorrow.

"Evan, this is Mitch. Mitch, this is Evan." Evan stood up and shook his hand, like a gentleman.

"Hello, sir," Evan said politely. He was such a wonderful young man, and it showed through.

The two of them began to exchange simple conversation, and I decided to head out to the garage and greet the guests. A few minutes later, Mitch came out to join me, Travis following close behind. Emma was already laughing and visiting with all her girl- friends. Michael Jackson's "Thriller" song came on and I cranked up the volume. The entire group started doing the Thriller dance. Evan, Caleb, and Todd came out a few minutes later, all wearing their monster masks and trying to scare the kids. A few of them screamed, but most of them laughed or ignored them altogether. As the music played, the kids ate, danced, and had fun bobbing for apples. Mitch and I moved to the corner and snuck in a dance or two, rocking back and forth to whatever monster song was playing. I couldn't remember the last time I felt that happy with my life. Emma and Travis were having a blast at their party. It was a magical night, filled with innocence and fun, a complete success. Everyone finally left around ten, hyped up on the biggest sugar rush of the year. I wished those parents luck getting them to bed!

Mitch and I cleaned up the biggest part of the mess, and then headed inside. The boys had switched from playing the Xbox to talking about music and girls. At one point, Evan was cackling so loud I thought he would pass out right on the floor.

"Hey Caleb, we should head back to the hotel, bud," Mitch said to his son.

"Aww, Dad! Right now?" Caleb asked in protest. He was obviously having a good time visiting with Evan and Todd. It gave me a good feeling inside to know they had hit it off so well.

"Yes, now. Laci's had a long day and would probably like to visit with Evan for a while. Head on out to the car." Caleb said goodbye to everyone and even gave me a hug, "Bye, Laci. Thanks for letting us hang out," he said in his charming, teenage way, then he headed outside.

Mitch gave the kids a hug goodbye and shook Evan's hand. I walked him to the door.

"You look pale, darlin'. Are you feeling all right?" Mitch asked. "Oh yeah, just a long day. I probably overdid it, packed too many things into one day as usual."

"Well, get some rest. What time do you want us back tomorrow morning?"

"Be here by nine, if that's not too early. You can help me with breakfast for this crew." I smiled and lifted my head up to give him a goodnight kiss.

"I'll be here at eight," he laughed, then he kissed me again, lingering a little longer and wrapping his arms around me to give me a hug. "Goodnight, Laci. I love you," he whispered.

"I love you too, Mitch."

I watched through the front door as they drove away. I thought my heart was going to burst from the joy that I felt at that moment. I walked back into the living room and visited with Evan for the next two hours. We caught up on his school, job, girlfriends, and more. Travis and Emma had fallen asleep on the couch next to us so Evan carried them up to bed, a perfect ending to the day.

Mitch and Caleb showed up around eight-thirty, and I gave them a hard time about being late. I had already started the meat and had the coffee ready when they arrived. Caleb found the couch and was back asleep in less than ten minutes. My kids were still sleeping too, so Mitch and I cooked a big country breakfast together. It was a breakfast that would have made his Mama proud. Not only because of my stellar cooking ability, but also because I had managed to keep that smile on 'her Mitch's face', just as she had instructed. We laid the spread of scrambled eggs, biscuits, gravy, hash browns, bacon, sausage, coffee, juice, and milk out onto the table. It looked like an IHOP breakfast on steroids!

After breakfast, we went to the park and played football all afternoon. A few of Evan's friends even drove up to join us. It was a perfect fall day—the first day of November already—sunny, mid-fifties, and amber leaves all over the grass, with some still falling from the bigger trees. Later that afternoon, we had a BBQ dinner, then everyone came back to the house and stayed up late watching movies. The weekend was going by much too fast. As Saturday came to an end, I said goodbye to Mitch and felt my heart sink knowing that tomorrow would be our last day together for several weeks.

Sunday arrived with a bang and I woke up with a king-sized migraine. Lately, they had been happening more often for some reason. Mitch had never been up here when I had one before, but today it couldn't be avoided. I took my medicine and hoped it would subside before he and Caleb arrived.

Evan knocked on my door then poked his head in my room. "Hey mom, you feeling all right?" he asked, watching me take my pill.

"I'm fine sweetie, just a headache. Some things never change. Mitch and Caleb are on their way over. I think we're just going to relax around the house today. I may not be up for much if this headache doesn't go away soon."

"Sounds good. Sorry about your headache. Do you need me to do anything around the house before they get here?"

"No, not at all. Will you be around most of the day? It would be nice if you and Caleb could hang out. I'm sure he's bored out of his mind up here and misses his friends."

"Yeah, sure. Maybe we can meet Lamar and James at the mall and hang out," he said, stalling at the door. I could tell he wanted to talk to me about something, but he was nervous to say it.

"What is it, Evan?"

"It's Mitch. I know you're in love with him, and he seems nice and all, but I don't...I just don't like it, mom. I miss Dad. It doesn't seem right, him being here, hugging and kissing you all the time."

"That's what people in love do, hon – they hug and kiss. I shouldn't have to tell you that. Is it something Mitch said or did to make you feel this way, or is it the idea that I'm moving for- ward with my life?"

"That's it, I guess. I do like him, and Caleb too. I can tell he loves you a lot. I think the dude would walk on hot coals if it made you happy. I know it's silly to feel this way. I can tell you're happy too and I'm glad, it's just weird, that's all."

"Evan, it's okay to feel what you're feeling. Todd went through this too, at first. But he's around him more and it didn't take him long to get used to the idea of us being together. It's part of life, sweetie. People come in and out of our lives for all different reasons. I like to believe that God had a plan for us from the beginning." Evan walked over and gave me a big hug, voluntarily. I normally only get them on Mother's Day and Christmas, so it was a treat!

"It's all good, mom. I'll get there. See you downstairs. I love you."

"I love you, Evan."

He walked out of the room. Between the headache and worrying about Evan liking Mitch, I had a mini-meltdown, but it was short-lived. Mitch would be there soon so I pulled myself together.

Mitch and Caleb arrived, my headache still in full swing. Evan grabbed Caleb and Todd and they were off to the mall. Mitch could tell I was hurting from the minute he said hello, so he ordered us to spend the entire day lounging on the couch, watching movies, and eating junk food. We didn't talk much, just enjoyed each other's company. The kids ran around the house and popped in once in a while. We would flip over to a kid movie now and then to make them happy. At one point, my head was lying in his lap and he was playing with my hair, stroking it softly with his hand. It gave me goose bumps. The throbbing finally subsided, but I stayed still and enjoyed being in his care. Before long, the day had ended and it was time to say goodbye again.

They were becoming more difficult to say each time and I wondered if we would ever truly be together.

"I'd better go, darlin'. I wish I could stay until you felt better, but I have to get back. Will you send me your outline on the wed- ding barn décor next week? I need to get started on that pretty soon. And for the record, my mom really liked your ideas."

"Whew! That's good. I was sweating that one a little, I have to be honest. I'm not sure she really likes me either. Such family drama, huh?"

"She likes you, don't worry. Oh, and tell Evan to drop Caleb off at the hotel if he doesn't mind. He's a great kid, Laci. Very grown-up and responsible. He's very protective of you. I think he was glad he didn't have to hang out with me again today though." "He is a good kid, isn't he? And he'll come around, Mitch, don't worry. He and I had a talk this morning. He's just having a harder time seeing us together than he thought he would. I guess we're both waiting for our families to get used to this." I laughed. "I know. I still have to remind myself that it's only been three months. It seems like only yesterday. Time flies when you're having fun," he said, and he scooped me up into his arms like a little girl, twirling me around.

"You love this, don't you? Holding me up in the air, in your arms, completely helpless and at your mercy." I laughed.

"You haven't seen anything yet, darlin'." He bent his face down, pressing his lips gently to mine. He kissed me tenderly, like it was our last, not letting me move an inch.

It was over too soon and he left. Another weekend had gone by and I would have to wait until the next time. Caleb and Evan came in about an hour later and I asked Evan to take him to the hotel. I was able to say goodbye to Caleb and give him a hug at least. After Evan got back, he sat and talked to me for a few minutes on the couch, but I was fighting sleep.

"Go to bed, mom. We'll talk tomorrow. I got a call from my friend; he wants to stay up here one more day."

"What about school? Won't you miss your classes?"

"I'll only miss two days counting the travel day, and I can catch up pretty easy. I'd rather be here with you anyway. I'll take care of the kids in the morning so you can sleep in. You're not going to work, are you?"

"No, I don't think I'll make it in tomorrow. Thank you for helping, sweetie. Good night." I kissed the top of his head and went to bed.

when it rains, it pours

The next morning I got a text from Mitch that he and Caleb were getting ready to board the plane. I'm fairly sure a Mack truck had run over my head at some point during the night because I could barely lift it up off the pillow. I sent Sandy a text to let her know I was taking a sick day and sent Mitch a last minute text to say goodbye, then went back to sleep. Evan took care of the kids for me, got them up, packed their lunches, and sent them off to school. Around eleven, I finally dragged myself out of bed, my neck still stiff from the lingering migraine, but overall, I felt much better. I went downstairs and ate some yogurt and had a cup of coffee. Evan was sitting in the den working on his laptop, so I poked my head in to say hello.

"Hey sweetie, I'm going to grab some coffee and hit the shower. Thanks for taking the kids to school for me."

"No problem, Mom. You feeling any better?"

"Yeah, the worst part is over. Now it's just an annoying ache in my neck which isn't too bad. You're headed back tomorrow, right?"

"Yep, Charles is actually picking me up so you don't have to worry about taking me to the airport. He'll be here in the morning around seven. Are we going out for dinner somewhere tonight?" he asked, looking at me with those puppy dog eyes. I knew he wanted to go to the Fuji Japanese steakhouse. His favorite place.

"Yes, yes. Fuji-rama here we come!" I replied and he jumped up to give me a hug.

"Sweet!" he said softly.

"Oh, and you get to unload and load the dishwasher for me since we're going to your favorite place. Deal?"

"Deal."

I refilled my coffee cup with some more caffeinated good- ness and headed upstairs to shower. Before I was completely undressed, however, my cell phone rang. I hurried to answer it thinking it was Mitch, but instead it was the nurse at the ob-gyn office asking me to hold while she put my doctor on the line. I thought that was odd, but I immediately got a sick feeling in the pit of my stomach. The doctor came on the line and said she had some results from my mammogram and wanted to review them with me in person. She asked me to come in to the office, adamant that I come as soon as possible. Hearing those words, my expectations were not good but didn't want to worry needlessly. I showered and got dressed, then I told Evan I was going to the doctor for my headache and would be back soon.

I pulled into the parking lot and looked at my phone, wishing I could hear Mitch's voice to calm my nerves. I was certain he was in the air by then. I sent him another quick text to let him know I was home sick and would call him later tonight after he got home. I walked inside, checked in at the front desk, sat down and waited for them to call my name, all the while trying to assure myself that it *wasn't* what I thought it might be. While I waited, I thought about my best friend Laura, and how she was forever impacted by the breast cancer that took her mom at the age of forty-seven. That was in the early 70s, back when breast cancer wasn't talked about like it is today, when there was no special meaning behind a pink ribbon. She still misses her every day. Then, as fate would have it, Laura herself was diagnosed at the age of forty-six, expecting the same fate as her mother at first, but she beat it. And I'm so thankful, because her life has now forever

impacted mine. She's been my best friend for nearly seventeen years now and I am so grateful to have her in my life. I wish she was here…

I sat there thinking about my kids, my parents, my friends, Mitch, Caleb, my work, everything! A few minutes later they called me back and escorted me to an exam a room with an X-ray machine hanging on the wall. Dr. Walker came in, put my ultra- sound films in the viewer, then came over and stood next to me. The look on her face was all I needed to confirm my suspicions and I immediately felt sick to my stomach.

"Hi Laci, it's good to see you again. I wish it were on better terms, however the results of your mammogram were a bit concerning to me. If you look up at your results on the light board, you'll see several pin-sized dots on your left breast here. They're very small, however my fear is that they will migrate together and become one lump or spread out farther. It's too early to say until I run more tests, but we should consider the possibility that it could be cancer. If it is, I think we've caught it early enough to manage it with minimal treatment and hopefully beat it all together. I would like to do an MRI and biopsy today if you have time. This can't wait, I'm afraid. It doesn't take long, and only requires a local anesthetic; you'll be back home in a couple of hours."

I was stunned, and speechless. My hands started to shake and I opened my mouth to talk, but nothing came out. I wanted to scream out in anger, but I could barely move. Finally, I answered her.

"Yes, I understand. I can stay for the tests. I need to call my son first, let him know I'll be late." She left the room to give me some privacy.

My hand shook as I dialed his number, and after a few rings, I was grateful it went to his voicemail. I left him a message and hoped my shaky voice wouldn't tip him off to something more, and then hung up. I stared at the floor, void of any reaction to the

news I had just heard. My world would be forever changed from that moment forward.

A few minutes later, a nurse came in and she escorted me around the corner to another hall and into Procedure Room A. She left while I changed into a gown filled with holes. With all of that open space, I wondered the point of wearing a gown at all. I climbed onto a table covered with white, sterile paper, already freezing. Did they purposely set the temperature at twenty below zero in those rooms just for kicks, knowing I would be half naked? The room was dark and smelled of alcohol and an annoying beep was echoing from a machine down the hall. The shiny silver tools on the tray next to me made me nervous. My stomach responded and threw out a nice, loud rumble as it churned. The nurse came back in and prepped me for a biopsy of my left breast. All in all, the test was relatively painless, and it was over in a few short minutes. My mind was still numb; it spun out of control as I worried about the results and how they would affect the road ahead.

After the procedure, I was escorted back to the doctor's office and waited. Dr. Walker came in, stood in front of me, and placed her hand on mine, giving it a gentle squeeze.

"Thanks for waiting, Laci. Are you feeling any pain from the procedure?"

"No, just a little tender but no pain."

"Good. I won't know the results for a few days, so for now, go home and try not to worry. Easier said than done, I know, but until we find out more, we shouldn't assume anything. Call a close friend or tell someone you trust to get it out of your system and I'll call you the minute I get the results. Expect to wait a few days, okay?"

"Yes, thank you, Dr. Walker." She said goodbye then walked out. I sat there for a minute, took a deep breath, then got up and left.

I didn't remember the drive home, but somehow I got there. Evan wasn't around and there were still a few minutes before the

kids were out of school, so I went up to my room and locked the door. Laura would want to know – she was the only one who would understand. I took my cell and walked into my closet to call her. It rang.

"Hey, what's up girlie-girl?" she asked in her chipper, sweet voice.

"Hi sweetie. Oh, not much." I struggled to find the words. "Ummm, so do you remember how I always seem to follow your lead when it comes to hair color, new haircuts, buying a new out- fit, stuff like that?" I said with a soft laugh, trying to play it cool at first. My hands were sweaty and my voice shook.

"Yeah, I do the same thing to you, why? What's up, you sound funny? Are you going to follow my lead and get a new car now because I just got a new Mustang convertible?" She asked, laughing a little. I paused, and then broke down. My voice gave way to sobs and my lips quivered uncontrollably.

"Not exactly, although a convertible sounds much better." I mumbled and began to cry.

"Laci, for heaven's sake! What is it? Tell me! What's wrong?" "I had a biopsy today, Laura. My doctor suspects it may be breast cancer. What do I do?" And I continued to cry quietly.

Silence followed at first, then her strong, beautiful voice came through loud and clear. "Well, why don't you tell me about it? Did they find something on your mammogram?"

"Yes, several little dots. She said they were small, but they could grow together if we don't treat it. But there is a chance it might not be cancer, I guess. Right?"

"There's always a chance. How do you feel? Have you been sick or tired?"

"Not sick really. Tired yes. I've had some dizzy spells the last couple of months, off and on. I figured it was stress. I had a bad migraine yesterday and it was the worst one I've had in months. Besides that, I feel fine. How did you get through it?"

"I had a lot of people that loved me and supported me. Like you. Without that, it would have been much harder to keep going. But mostly, it was God and my faith, and my sweet husband, of course."

"So, if you were to give me one piece of advice going from here, what would it be?" I asked.

"You pray through it! You get up every day and smile that you were blessed with another day. You get dressed, hug your kids, kiss your sweet man, have a Starbucks coffee, do what you can do at your job until it becomes impossible, and you pray. Every day. You hold your head high and believe that God will see you through this to the very end, whatever that may look like, do you hear me?" Her matter-of-fact tone carried through to every fiber inside of me. I knew then that she would become my source of encouragement and strength as I was for her years ago.

As we talked, she even reminded me about my offer to shave my head if she had ended up losing her hair, which thankfully for both of us she never did. I did have an awesome wig picked out though, just in case. My how the tables have turned. Laura and I talked for over an hour. When we hung up, I felt somewhat better, but I was still scared. The kids came home and I went downstairs to help them with homework. Evan ran out to the store and when he returned, we all piled in the car and went to the Fuji steakhouse. My mind was in another world. Dinner was amazing, as usual. The chef dazzled us with his funny jokes and a few tricks. He rolled an egg on the griddle, calling it an "egg roll," and then he set fire to a tower of raw onion rings. When the smoke rolled out of the top, he scooted it across the grill like a train and made a 'choo-choo' sound. Each time it was the same tricks, but the kids were fascinated and loved every minute of it. I watched their eyes light up when they laughed, and suddenly, I couldn't catch my breath. I got up and ran to the bath- room. The worry and fear of the unknown took over and I felt sick, scared to death that I would leave them behind, parentless. I

splashed some cold water on my face and got hold of myself, and then went back to the table. Evan looked at me with worry in his eyes and I smiled at him.

We drove home. I put the kids to bed then went back down- stairs to talk to Evan.

"What's going on mom, and don't say nothing. I know when you're covering up," he said.

"Oh Evan, you are too smart for your own good sometimes. But you have to promise me not to say anything to the kids or anyone else, for that matter."

"Mom, what is it? Just tell me."

"I had a routine female exam last week and my mammogram showed some spots on one of my breasts. It's possible that the spots could be…cancer." I took a deep breath, and continued. "That's what I was doing today at the doctor; they did a biopsy. I won't know the results for a few days. And even if it is, the doctor said we've caught it in the early stages and I have a really good chance of beating it with some treatment. So there's no need to worry yet, okay?" I stayed composed for once, not giving in to my emotions. Evan was quiet and didn't react to my words at first.

"What does that mean exactly? Is it serious? Tell me the truth, Mom."

"Honestly, I don't know yet. I don't think so. At least, I hope not." I looked down at the floor.

"And what if…what if it is cancer? What then? Who will be here to help you?" His voice rose and he was starting to worry, to think about things.

"Evan, it's going to be all right. I know it. You just have to think positive! I'm not worried and I can't think about the 'what ifs' right now. We'll deal with whatever the results are and we'll get through it, just like we always do." He dropped his head; his sad face didn't lighten like I had hoped.

"I…I won't leave tomorrow. I'll drop out and stay here to help you with the kids. I can reenroll later. I just need to…" His lips

started to quiver and then he dropped his head into my lap and began to cry.

I couldn't allow him to take that on – not again. He gave up so much for us after his dad died trying to take care of us. I stroked his hair like I did when he was little, not saying a word. He needed to get it out. A few minutes later, he lifted his head and threw his arms around me in a tight hug.

"You will not drop out of college, you hear me? You are going to leave tomorrow, just as planned, go back to school, and graduate with honors! And, I will be there to see you graduate, is that clear? I am going to beat this, Evan. Between Laura, Teri, Lena, and Gayle, I have no doubt that they will be by my side the entire time. Your job right now is to be a kid, enjoy college, and live your life. I couldn't live with myself if you put that on hold because of me. I promise to keep you informed and if I need you, I will send for you. Deal?" I waited for his rebuttal, but it didn't come.

"Deal," he said in a hushed voice.

"Good. Now go to bed and get some rest. Please try not to worry. I'll see you off in the morning before you leave." We stood up and I hugged him again, then lifted myself to my tippy-toes and kissed his forehead. "Good night, sweetie. I love you."

"I love you, mom. Please don't leave," he whispered in my ear as we hugged.

I went upstairs and got ready for bed. I had a missed call from Mitch on my phone, but it was too late to call him back. I would call him in the morning.

Tuesday

The next morning, I was up early to fix Evan breakfast. He came down around six thirty to eat and we visited for a few minutes as if nothing was any different, but it was different and he couldn't ignore it.

"Have you told Mitch?" he asked.

"No, but I will when I know more." I smiled at him, knowing full well that I had no intention of telling Mitch anything about my situation.

Minutes later, Todd, Emma, and Travis were up and came running downstairs to say goodbye to their big brother. They exchanged hugs and goodbyes. Emma ran back upstairs crying, already missing him. The doorbell rang and I walked him to the door to say goodbye.

"I'll call you as soon as I know something, okay? Now go and have a good week. I love you." I hugged his neck quickly, trying to keep the mood light. He smiled at me, kissed my cheek, and then left as quickly as he arrived. The kids and I left shortly after that. It was another normal day, until the text messages began...

<Hey darlin', miss you! Call me – I need to hear your voice. I love you, Mitch.>

<Sorry sweetie, I'm sick. Hurts to talk. Will call when I can. I love you too! Yours, Laci.>

<Any results today? If not, don't dwell on it. Stay busy. I'm here if you need to talk. Love you, Laura>

<Nothing today. I'm scared. I can't tell Mitch. Love you too, Laci>

Wednesday

More messages came…

<Nothing today. Can't focus on anything! Scared to death. Laci>

<I know sweetie. Be patient. I've been there. Praying for you daily! Love you, Laura>

<Are you feeling any better?

Do you need me to come out there? I'm worried about you, darlin'.

Call me soon. Love you, Mitch>

<Bad migraines. No need to worry. I'm fine. Will call tomorrow. Love Laci>

I would have to let him go.

Thursday

Mitch called and left me a voicemail. He was worried sick. I would have to tell him something soon, but what?

<Any news? Love you girl! Laura>

<No. Love you too. Laci>

<Please answer my calls, Laci.
What's wrong? I'm worried about you! Mitch>

<Can't talk. Head still hurts too bad. Will call you tomorrow. L>

plans change

It's already been three days...three long days with no news. It felt more like three years! It took everything in me to keep quiet at work, but the girls knew something wasn't right. I haven't been my normal, happy, bouncy self. Mitch called every day and sent dozens of texts, but I couldn't bring myself to answer or call him back. I had sent him a few messages to let him know that I was still suffering from migraines, hoping that would satisfy the communication requirement. By now, I was sure he'd grown tired of that excuse, but I needed more time to figure out how and what to tell him. My refusal to return his phone calls and emails was how I pushed him away, anticipating bad news.

Fridays were normally the best day around the office, full of laughter and excitement of the coming weekend, but not today. Although it had been a busy day and small tasks kept my mind occupied, it was still a minute-by-minute chore to be here. After I returned to my office from the second meeting of the morning, I noticed a missed call on my phone; it was from Dr. Walker's office. It was time. I didn't want to call and hear the results, but I had to. My hands started to sweat. I got up, closed my door then called her office.

"Dr. Walker, please. This is Laci Kramer returning her

call." The receptionist put me on hold; my hands were shaking.

"Good morning, Laci. How are you doing?" Dr. Walker said politely. I threw out a half laugh to fend off my uneasiness.

"I guess that all depends on what you tell me doc. How am I doing?"

"Well, I'd like you to come in to the office to talk about the results in person. How soon can you get here?"

"I'll be there in fifteen minutes." I hung up the phone and looked out my window, enjoying the view of a water fountain in the distance. Tears welled up in my eyes but I fought them back and picked up my purse. I walked out of my office and poked my head into Sandy's office.

"Hey Sandy, sorry to bother you, but I need to leave for a short while to take care of a personal matter. I'll be back soon though," I said politely.

"Of course, go. Is everything all right?"

"I'm not sure yet. I'll explain when I get back." I turned around and walked out.

On the drive to the office, I mostly talked to myself. Then I sang a few songs to keep from talking to myself so much, but it didn't work. I went right back to talking to myself again. Maybe it wouldn't be cancer…maybe I'll be clear and Mitch and I would be able to move on and be together…forever. I desperately wanted him in my life! But if it *was* cancer, I knew he wouldn't be able to stay in my life. I'd have to find some way to tell him… to let him go. Then what? What if the treatment did work and the cancer went away…what then? If I pushed him away now, then the chances of getting him back were probably lost forever. Is that what I really wanted? No, of course it wasn't, but I didn't have a choice! Because the other alternative was that it *was* cancer and if the treatment doesn't work, I would get sick, and I…I could leave. Oh just say the word, Laci. Die. I could *die*!

That was all it took, and the grief washed over me like an ocean wave. At one point, I had trouble seeing the road through the tears. I rolled down the window and let the cold air blow through the car to help dry my tears and calm me down. Then one of my favorite dance songs came on the radio and I cranked it up loud and even opened the sunroof. Of course I had to crank up the heat too, but it helped nonetheless. Deep breaths mixed with loud singing cured me of my short-term anxiety, just in time too since the office was up ahead.

I checked in at the reception window and didn't even have to wait. They called me right back to her office. A few minutes later, she walked in, sat down in the empty chair next to me, and reached over to take my hand. I looked into her eyes and she didn't say anything. That was my answer. No words were exchanged. I simply folded over and rested my head on my knees. The emotions and tears poured out. She reached over with one hand and picked up a box of tissues from her desk, handing me one from the box. After a few minutes, I lifted my head, blew my nose, and took a deep breath to regain what little composure I could. Dr. Walker stood up and picked up her tablet and a few brochures, then sat back down and started talking.

"I'm so sorry, Dr. Walker. I couldn't hold it in," I said, apologetically.

"Laci, if you hadn't reacted this way, I would probably be more worried. You have nothing to apologize for. This isn't an easy road to walk."

Her lips kept moving, but I couldn't comprehend anything she was saying. She was speaking in a late 70s cartoon language, 'Charlie Brown's teacher to be specific.

All I heard was, 'mwa mwa wa, whup wa wa, mwa wa wa'...

Eventually I came out of the fog and joined the conversation. "Well, where do we go from here?"

"The first thing I need you to understand is that we caught this early so you have a few more options for treatment. You have Stage 2 breast cancer. The tiny areas that we located are between two and five centimeters. The good news is they haven't spread to your lymph nodes, so I don't think you'll need chemotherapy at this point. I suggest one of three things: a mastectomy of just the left breast, removing it completely and virtually eliminating any chance that the cancer will return; a bilateral mastectomy, removing both breasts and any chance that it will spread to the other one; or a lumpectomy that will preserve both your breasts and only remove the cancerous area and the tissue surrounding it. Then we'll follow up with radiation." She paused and gave me a minute to let it sink in, then continued. "The choice is yours and you should think it through carefully. We'll talk again tomorrow. For now, you should go home and process everything. It will take time, so call a friend or family member and share it with them. Don't keep this to yourself, Laci. You'll need a good support group around you during this process. You should also tell your kids so they can begin to understand. Give them time though and try not to worry, although I know that's impossible. I truly believe you have a great chance of recovery with treatment. You're a strong, healthy woman and that will work in your favor. Do you have any questions so far?" She waited for a response.

A million questions swirled around inside my head, 'How long did I have to live?', 'Would I lose my hair?', 'Who would take care of my kids?', 'Who'll do the dishes?', but I didn't ask them out loud.

"Not yet, but I'm sure I will later. Thank you, Dr. Walker." "All right then. Please call me if you need to talk. You may be more tired than normal, but you should continue to work and stay busy if you can. I'm writing you a different prescription for your migraines; they may worsen with the new stress of your situation. I want to see you tomorrow afternoon and we'll talk about your decision, and then go from there." She stood up and gave me a hug, then handed me a prescription.

I walked out feeling scared and overwhelmed, wishing I had my mom there to lean on. I didn't return to work. Instead, I sent Sandy a text to let her know I had received some news and needed to go home to sort things out but would be in Monday

to tell her everything. Once I got home, I went inside and closed the door behind me. I stood still and listened to the quiet of the house. I made my way over to the living room, dragging my body one step at a time, as if it were filled with heavy rock or sand. I dropped down on the couch, closed my eyes, took a deep breath—and screamed as loud as I could until all the air left my lungs. I wanted to cry, but I couldn't. Instead, I got mad! And when I get mad, I clean.

So, I went upstairs, changed into my grubby work clothes, and then pulled out every cleaning solution from the closet that I could find. I went back downstairs, grabbed the broom and mop from the garage, took out the vacuum, and started in on cleaning the house. I dusted, vacuumed the carpet, and washed the dishes, scrubbing one pan so hard that I nearly took off the stick-free coating. When I got to the kitchen floor, I swept it first, and then took out the wood cleaner and a soft rag. On my hands and knees, I began to clean and buff. I started in the corner of the kitchen and buffed every inch until I could see my reflection in the shine. But I didn't get very far. The snack bar was now directly above my head and I stopped. All I could see was Mitch. It was the very spot where he kissed me for the first time, where we cleaned up my spilled wine together on our first date.

And I yelled. Why me, God! Why now? Why would you do this to me? You took away my husband and left me to raise four kids on my own, wasn't that enough? I know I haven't been the best mom. I admit that there were a few times that I forgot to bathe them…probably fed then way too much cereal for dinner, but other than that I've been pretty good, haven't I? And now I've met a wonderful, amazing man and you allowed me to fall in love with him! What's up with that? What kind of twisted, sick joke was this anyway? Now I have cancer…breast cancer! Am I to die too? Was this your grand plan for my life, Lord? Because if it is…I have to be completely honest here…it SUCKS!

After I had ranted and raved, blaming God for my misfortune and current condition, I spilled over with sadness, feeling sorry for myself and anticipating only the worst—that my life would end soon despite the doctor's hope that I could beat it. I cried for what seemed like hours. All I could think about was my kids, how to tell them and where we would go from there. My cell phone rang and it made me jump. I took a deep breath and dried my tears, thinking it would be the doctor or Laura. I stood up and picked up my phone; it was Mitch. I couldn't tell him! Not then, not ever. I loved him too much to let him go through that again. So I let it ring and ring. A few minutes later, a voicemail message alert appeared and I ignored it too.

Instead of listening to his voicemail, I decided to follow the doctor's orders and tell my friends. Telling my family would have to wait until I knew more. I didn't want them to worry. So, I called Laura since she'd waited so patiently to hear my results. She was amazing. She never broke down, but simply told me to never lose hope and that even though she was far away, she would pray for me daily, without ceasing.

After that, I called Lena and Teri. I told them I had received some bad news today from my doctor and asked if they could both stop by the house after work. They must have talked to each other right after I called because neither one waited until the end of the day. Within an hour, they were at my door. Luckily, the kids weren't home yet so we were able to talk freely about my diagnosis. We cried together, and then talked about my options and what they thought I should do. We even managed to laugh a little as they tried to lift my spirits. After everything was said, Teri got up and rummaged around in my refrigerator, finding stuff to cook for the kids' dinner.

"You look exhausted, sweetie. Why don't you go up and rest?

Teri and I will take care of dinner.

"That sounds good. I did work pretty hard today." I smiled and walked upstairs, crawled into bed and covered up. Lena followed me upstairs to make sure I followed through on the whole "getting rest" thing. She sat down on the bed next to me.

"After we get dinner started, I'm going to run home and grab some things. I'll be back later, okay? I'm staying here tonight and don't try to talk me out of it, woman. After you get some rest, we'll tell the kids tonight, together. If you want to, that is." She smiled, tears in her eyes.

"I would like that very much. Thank you, Lena. I love you." "I love you too, girl. And speaking of love, have you talked to

Mitch yet?" she asked with a smile. I looked away and pretended to ignore her question.

"*La-ci?*" she prodded, sounding a lot like my mother. "You need to tell him. He needs to know."

"I can't tell him, Lena. I can't put him through that again. He lost his first wife to this disease; he won't lose me too. He has a son to think about and a winery to run. I think it's best for every- one if I just…break it off…completely."

"What? You can't do that! He loves you, Laci Jean! You know he would want to be here, helping you through this," she said, scolding me for my decision to shut him out.

"I know he would. That's why I can't tell him! I'm not changing my mind, so you might as well go and let me rest."

"Fine, I'll go. But we're not finished with this, girlfriend." And she got up and walked out, closing the door behind her. I rolled over and soaked my pillow as I cried myself to sleep.

———⁓⁓∘◠◟◝◠◠◝◟◞◠∘◠⁓⁓———

A few hours later, I woke up and looked out my window. It was already dark outside, the clock read 6:30 in big, red numbers. I could smell food in the air and decided it was time to face my kids. I walked downstairs; Lena was sitting at the table with the kids already eating. Travis and Emma ran over to me and wrapped their arms around my waist, giving me a big belly hug.

"Hi mommy, are you feeling better?" Travis asked and he looked at me with his big blue eyes. I smiled and kissed the top of his head.

"You know what? I am feeling a little better. What's for dinner?" "Teri fixed Mexican meatloaf and macaroni and cheese! It's really good." Emma said. "Sounds good to me."

I sat down and Lena fixed me a plate. Although I wasn't hungry, I ate for nourishment and to keep up my strength. After we finished, I helped Lena with the dishes, then joined the kids in the living room. I turned off the TV.

"Mom! We were watching that!" they moaned.

"I know, I'm sorry guys, but I need to talk to you for a minute. Can you come over and sit by me?" Todd was sitting in the chair next to me, checking the latest social status of his friends. He closed his laptop. Travis hopped in my lap and Emma sat next to me. Lena was on the other side of Emma. I wasn't sure how to begin, but I would take it slow and use simple terms that they could understand. It was cancer after all; it was everywhere. It didn't discriminate. It was talked about on TV, in music lyrics, in books, in school. They knew the word, but they had never known anyone with the actual disease. I knew it would be most difficult for Emma and Travis, but they needed to know.

"So I got some news today from my doctor that I need to tell you about. And before I begin, I need you to listen to the whole thing before you ask any questions, okay?" They all nodded yes.

"Last week I went to the doctor for a checkup, the same day that Mitch and Caleb visited. Do you remember that?" Again, they nodded their heads that they remembered. "Well, they ran some tests on me that day to find out if I had an illness. And today, the doctor called me in to her office and told me that the tests did say that I am sick. You've probably heard the name before, but I don't want it to scare you, okay?" I took a deep breath, pausing before I said the word. "I...I have cancer. Breast cancer.

It's what my friend Laura had a long time ago, do you remember Laura?" None of them would look at me. "Well, the good thing is that they caught my illness early so the doctor said that if I have surgery and take some special medicine, that it will get much better and hopefully go away very soon."

They didn't say anything at first; they just listened. Todd knew exactly what it all meant. He wouldn't look at me, and I could see the tears welling in his eyes. I kept going.

"The medicine they give me could make me sick, but even if it does, I need you to remember that it's making me better, okay?" I said with confidence, trying to convince myself at the same time. "But you don't look sick, mom," Travis commented, his lower lip quivering. I kissed the top of his head and smiled. A few tears escaped my eyes and rolled onto his hair, so I brushed them away. "You're right, I don't. The cancer is on the inside of my body, underneath where we can't see. And other than headaches and being tired, I probably won't look sick. Not yet, anyway," I said with a smile to encourage him. "It's going to be okay, kids. I promise. And we'll have lots of people here to help us through it, okay?" I looked down at Travis and he was crying; little high-pitched sighs were coming from his mouth as he breathed.

Lena chimed in to help lighten the mood. "And you know I'll be here to help. I'll stop by after work to help with dinner and homework after your mom starts her medicine, okay?" Emma got up and ran upstairs to her room without a word. She needed time to let it sink in. Travis was just scared. I think he was more scared of the word, of the things he had heard on TV and from other people.

"Can I turn the TV back on now, mom?" he asked, still sniffing. I couldn't help but laugh at his request, glad that he would be distracted for a little while by his favorite cartoon.

"Yes, go ahead." I squeezed him tight before he crawled off my lap and turned on the TV.

Todd still wouldn't look at me. I could tell his cheeks were red and his eyes watered. He reopened his laptop and started surfing, trying to pretend like nothing had changed. I looked over at Lena and she winked at me. It would take time for them to understand everything, and I would have to be patient.

"Okay, Travis, give your mom a hug. She needs to rest. You've got an hour of TV and then it's time to get ready for bed," Lena announced. I stood up and Travis jumped up to hug me and squeezed me so hard I thought I would snap in two. He wouldn't let go of me. I could feel his little tummy shake as he cried. I said goodnight, put him down, and he ran to the couch and covered his head with a blanket.

"He'll be okay, Laci. I'll set up with him for a while. Go on to bed." Lena said and hugged me to say goodnight.

As I walked past Todd, I messed with his hair and kept moving. I didn't want to push him too soon, so I headed upstairs to read for a little while before bed. I wasn't the least bit tired thanks to my earlier nap. The pile of books on my nightstand had grown in height, but I always kept one special book on top, the book that Mitch gave me that day we met. My chest felt heavy as I thought about giving up on a future with him, a future that I was so sure about just days ago. I chose another book to take my mind off of the inevitable. A few minutes later, my bedroom door cracked open and I saw Emma's little blonde head poke through.

"Can I come in, mom?" she asked softly.

"Of course, sweetie." I tapped the bed in hopes she would climb up next to me. She did, and I curled my arm around her, both of us sinking down into the pillows.

"Are you doing okay, Emma? I want you to ask me anything, okay sweetie? Don't ever be afraid to talk to me."

"Are you going to die, mom?" she asked, her voice quivering. And there it was, the one question I had hoped to avoid for a little while longer, but how could they not ask? My stomach churned, but I knew that my answer would need to give her a sense of hope – to help her believe that I would get better.

"You know, someday I will. We all will. But I think God still wants me around a little longer. He knows that you and your brothers need me now that Daddy is gone. So, I am going to pray every day that he will take the cancer away, okay? I need you to pray for that too. And if we do that and believe with all our hearts that I will get better…" I took a big breath and swallowed hard, fighting back the tears. "Then hopefully I will." She remained quiet for a minute, and that was when I heard the rain clicking against my bedroom window. "Do you hear that?" I whispered.

"Yeah, it's raining. I know you think that's a good thing mom, but I don't like rain."

"Oh Emma, don't you see that there is hope in that rain? That's your answer. It might seem hard to believe, but God is using that rain to wash away all this yucky stuff going on right now. It might last for days, or even weeks, but eventually it will end and the sun will come out. We might even see a rainbow." She didn't answer me, but when I looked down at her, there were small tears rolling down her cheeks, leaving their wet tracks behind.

"You will get better, mom. You have to. I can't lose you too!" And she buried her face in my side, sobbing.

I let her cry. Within minutes, she was asleep and Lena came in to check on me and say goodnight. She saw Emma at my side and smiled, then turned off my light. The peace and quiet was nice, but I was still wide awake. So, I took advantage of the time to think about the decision that lay ahead of me. What treatment option would I choose? I slowly reached my arm over to the night stand, picked up my cell phone, opened the internet browser and began to research the various treatment options. The glowing light didn't seem to bother Emma, so I kept going.

First, the mastectomy, then bi-lateral mastectomy, then a lumpectomy. I read the clinical descriptions of each one, the first two made my stomach do flip-flops. I couldn't imagine not having breasts...even as much as I have hated them at times. I was the girl in 6th grade, developed farther than any other girl my age. I remembered being teased at an early age because they were so much larger than the other girls'. My mom didn't think I needed a training bra that early, so I ran over to my neighbor's house and borrowed one from her. I would stuff it in my backpack, then go straight to the bathroom when I got to school to put it on. I was cool, oh yeah. High school was no different. They definitely got the boys' attention. But after I fell in love and got married to Andrew, they were a source of joy for him. They weren't mine anymore. He used to call them 'the girls', although I never figured out why. Still...I liked it. I wanted to keep them! If Mitch and I ever...well...I would want them, that's all. I want to be whole for our first time. If I had a mastectomy, there would be scars. How would he feel about those? Every time he looked at me, would they remind him of his wife and how she died? But why would that be an issue? It's not like we have a future, right? His mom made that all but clear to me even before this new 'development'.

I'm not telling him. He couldn't know about the cancer. I had to end things with him now so he wouldn't suffer again. I would tell him tomorrow – I was ready. Or was I? How could I break up with the man who stole my heart the minute I saw him? The man with whom I wanted to spend the rest of my life? How could I be so cruel as to do it over the phone? I needed a plan, some way to end things that made sense. *Hi Mitch, this is Laci. I'm madly in love with you and want us to be together forever, but I think we need to break up. Have a nice life.'* Somehow I didn't think that would work. What then? *Ugh!* His mother would probably do it for me…ah! That's it—his family! I would just blame it on Brad and his mother…it was obvious that they didn't like me anyway. And Evan, he wasn't real hip on me getting serious about anyone yet, I'll throw him in there too. Was I seriously feeling giddy about figuring out how to break up with the second greatest love of my life? How twisted was that? Tomorrow then. I would call him in the morning.

Now back to the treatment decision. Even if I couldn't be with Mitch, I hoped to love again one day if I made it through this and stuck around a few years. For that man, whoever he was, I would choose to keep them if I could. So…it was settled. The lumpectomy now, and hope for the future.

I yawned. All that thinking had worn me out! I put the phone back on the night stand and closed my eyes. A few minutes later, I saw it light up and it started to vibrate. It was Mitch calling again. I ignored it, but I knew I needed to check in, so I sent him a text.

<In bed. Feeling a little better. I promise I will call tomorrow. L.>

He never replied.

———————

Mitch arrived at the winery early on Saturday, hoping to get a jump start on the day's activities. He managed to beat Brad in, which was not a normal occurrence. While he was working on the inventory, he heard Brad come in, grumbling about having to fix the coffee and yawning like a bear. He walked into the office, a bit startled by Mitch's presence.

"Well, look who's here! Either something is wrong with your alarm clock little brother or I missed that daylight savings thing again." Brad said, and laughed at his own comment.

"Very funny. I couldn't sleep so I figured I might as well work." "Oh, let me guess. Girl trouble?"

"Go get your coffee, Brad. I don't really want to talk about it right now," Mitch replied, frustrated that he had been right about his lack of sleep.

"Aw come on, I'm just kidding. What's up, seriously?"

"That's just it, I don't know. It's Laci, she says she's sick. I've received four text messages from her since I left. No calls, no emails. It's not like her. Something is wrong, I can feel it. I've even tried calling the house and no one will answer. I called her work, but she wasn't there either."

"Well, she won't be at work if she's sick, first of all. And although I'm rather shocked at myself for defending your little Airplane Girl, I'm sure she'll call you when she's better. Besides, she has three kids at home to take care of remember? Stop worrying about it and let's get to work; that will take your mind off of her."

For once, Brad made sense, and his usual not-so-compassionate tone wasn't there. On some small scale, Mitch knew he was right.

"You're probably right. Let's get to work. But remind me when it's two o'clock. I have an appointment with the jeweler today," Mitch said.

"What for?" Brad now sounded a bit ticked off.

"To pick out Laci's ring. I told you that I was going to pro- pose. I've decided to ask her when she and the kids come down, on Thanksgiving."

"What? You're kidding right? You didn't tell me it was going to happen on Thanksgiving! I figured you would put the ring on some twelve-month layaway plan and ask her sometime next year! I'm telling you, Mitch; it's just too soon!"

"Butt out, Brad. This is none of your business. I love her and I need her in my life. I don't want to wait any longer; life is too short. You of all people should know that."

Mitch just looked at Brad with anger in his eyes and stormed out of the office, retreating to the wedding barn to do some work. He felt closer to Laci there.

Around noon, he tried to call Laci again. It was almost nine in the morning her time and if she felt better, he knew she would be up and around.

Please answer, Laci, please.

a storm is brewing

My original plans included sleeping late that day, but I hadn't factored in the early morning sun pouring through my bedroom window. By eight o'clock, I was wide-awake and I felt pretty good. I lay there for another ten minutes, just because I could. Emma was still sound asleep, so I quietly slid out of bed and threw on my sweats and sweatshirt. It was a cold, November morning. I thought about the two things in November that I loved: my birthday, coming up in another week, and a big Thanksgiving dinner. Oh boy...Thanksgiving. Thanksgiving with Mitch and his family! I had almost forgotten that he'd asked us to come down there! I would definitely have to call him today...break things off before the surgery, before I got sick. Before he got his hopes up that we would be coming out for the holiday.

I walked downstairs, flipped on the fireplace, and turned on the TV to a satellite radio station called Sounds of the Season. Christmas music was my favorite and always put me in a good mood. That day was no different, despite the circumstances. I didn't care if it was more than a month before the holiday. It made me remember being back home, and as I sang along with the music, I felt like cooking for the first time in days. I decided to fix Emma's favorite breakfast. I brewed myself a cup of coffee and proceeded to stir up a batch of my homemade buttermilk pancake batter. I put some bacon in the oven, and then turned on the stove to heat the griddle. In the middle of flipping the pancakes, the "Little Drummer Boy" came on and I started to tear up. All I could think about was not being there to fix them breakfast anymore, not being there to take care of my kids. My heart was breaking, but I couldn't do anything about it. I didn't want to be this way! I wasn't a helpless child…I'm a strong, independent woman. Depending on others was not my strong suit. I would have to be strong for my kids from now on. No tears today, Laci. No more tears. Stick to the plan.

I was cooking and singing away, lost in my own little world, when my phone rang. "Creepy Stalker Guy" flashed across the screen and I smiled thinking about the day he added it to my contact list. Stick to the plan. I had to let him go…for his own good. I turned off the griddle so I wouldn't burn the pancakes, and then answered the phone.

"Good morning," I said in my sweetest voice, easing into the conversation.

"Laci! Thank God you answered! I have been so worried about you, darlin'!" he ranted, making me feel guilty for not calling him over the last few days. But his voice was so sweet and warm. I had missed him more than I realized. I could hear his love for me coming through the phone and it felt good and safe, and then I began to doubt my ability to stick to the plan. I took a deep breath and exhaled slowly, preparing myself for what was ahead. "I'm…fine, mostly. I'm so sorry I haven't called. But at least I was communicating in a small way. You did get my text messages, didn't you? That's all I could do. My head hurt so badly when I spoke. Migraines really take their toll on me."

"I know they do. But you're okay right? Headache is gone and you're back to normal?" he asked.

I paused and wondered if my plan was really the best way. But I couldn't back down now! An emergency session of the itty-bitty-committee began…naturally God piped up right away with option one, encouraging me to tell him about the cancer because he loved me and would support me and help me through it. 'You *know* he will', God said. The devil's advocate gave me option two: tell him about the cancer and he'll probably walk away… why would he stick around for this knowing how it ended the first time? And option three was mine…don't tell him a darn thing about the cancer. Just break up with him and let him down gently. I couldn't let him carry this burden again, I loved him too much. Stick to the plan, Laci. Blame it on the family, the distance – both very sound reasons. It would be clean and easy that way. And for the first time in history, I chose option three…*my* way.

"Yes, much better, thank you. No more headache, but… umm…we need to talk, Mitch. Do you have some time?"

"Of course I do! I couldn't agree more; we haven't talked in days! I miss you, Laci. I think I'll come out there in a few weeks and fly back here with you and the kids for Thanksgiving. I could help you with all the luggage and—"

I couldn't listen to him go on and on anymore.

"Mitch, please, just stop for a second and listen." I interrupted him and let out a deep breath. "We need to talk about us." My tone didn't lend itself to a positive conversation ahead and he didn't reply back right away. It was quiet for a minute.

"Okay, what about us? What's going on, Laci?"

I closed my eyes, breathing consciously so I wouldn't pass out in the middle of it, then I let the words come out one at a time.

"I…I think it would be best if we…took some time off from our relationship. I'm not sure it's going to work out like we'd hoped. You see, while I was sick, I had a lot of time to think about things, about us and these last few months together. When you walked into my life, I wasn't looking for a relationship, but there you were. And the more we talked and got to know each other, the more it seemed like God was literally telling me to fall in love with you, to go forward with my life and leave the pain behind me once and for all. And I did. I bought it hook, line, and sinker. I fell for you the minute I saw you in that airport. But lately, I've noticed that it's become more and more difficult for us to be together. The trips are farther apart. I can't even afford to come and see you, which means you're bearing all the weight of this relationship. Every time you visit, it gets harder on me and the kids. You blow in for a few days and then you're gone. They're growing quite attached to you, Mitch and I don't want them to end up getting hurt."

"Wait a minute…wait just a minute, darlin'! Did I understand you right? Are you actually saying what I think you're saying? Because it sounds an awful lot like you don't want to be together anymore? Where is this coming from, Laci? I was just up there six days ago and everything was fine, more than fine! And how am I going to hurt the kids? I love your kids like my own, and you know that! Did I do or say anything to hurt you or cause you to feel this way?" he asked. His voice was tense, shocked, and sad all at the same time.

I had to remind myself to stick to the plan and not give in, no matter how much I wanted to. "No! You haven't done anything wrong, please believe me. You are the same, wonderful man I fell in love with. It's…it's just better this way. I've been neglecting my kids and even my job has suffered since all this started. It's gone too far and it's my fault. I am trying to be realistic about this, that's all. Maybe for the first time since we met, I'm actually seeing this for what it is: a long-distance relationship that wasn't meant to last."

"It will last! Why wouldn't it? I love you and I know you love me! And I don't mind being the one that travels all the time, I'm used to it. Caleb doesn't mind, trust me. He adores you! I want to be there more often, but Brad and the winery need me too." Mitch's tone grew more intense, as he became desperate to make me believe his words. I closed my eyes, picturing his sweet face in my mind, and quiet tears fell from my eyes. It took everything in me to keep from sobbing.

"I know. You need to run your business and support your brother. I understand that, I do. That's what I mean, you're spread too thin and…well, let's be honest, your brother doesn't really like me and I don't want your relationship with him to be strained because you're coming up here all the time."

"Brad is a big baby and he'll eventually come around. I'm not worried about him and I don't care what he thinks. And the winery is doing fine too, so you shouldn't worry about either of them." "It's not just your brother. I'm pretty sure your mom isn't too fond of me either. You are bouncing back and forth, exhausted all the time and not able to give one hundred percent to Caleb, the winery, or me for that matter. It's not fair to any of us. I love you too much to come between you and your family, Mitch." Silent tears continued to fall and I looked up at the ceiling, begging

God to help me through it.

"My family doesn't get a vote in this! This is about you and me…us. We are meant to be together; I know it with every fiber in me, Laci Kramer! Don't deny it; you know it too. I don't know what spurred all of this, but I'm not going to lose you."

"If we were meant to be together, it wouldn't be this hard. And just to get it out on the table, we can't come down for Thanksgiving now. I...I need to move on and so do you." I exhaled slowly.

I felt a bit dizzy so I walked over to the kitchen table and sat down. But he didn't say anything. The phone was silent at the other end and for a second, I wondered if I had just bro- ken up with my phone rather than Mitch. But then he laughed a short laugh, and I knew he had heard every word. Why was he laughing?

"You're just messing with me right? You can't be serious after all that we've been through, after the way we met and how God brought us together. You can't be ending what we have. I love you, Laci! I thought you loved me too. What's really going on?" he pleaded, not wanting my words to be real in any way.

"I'm not messing with you. I wouldn't do that. I can't keep this up anymore, the back and forth. It's too much! I don't know how else to explain it, Mitch. I love you, but where is this going, really? It's just like your mother said, your life is there and my life is here. It will never work out. It's better that we realize that now before..." My voice quivered, and the reality of what I was doing had finally hit. Was I really doing this? Letting go of the man I love, the one who turned my entire world right side up in such a short time? I truly believed he was my soul mate, if there really was such a thing! The one I wanted to love for the rest of my life. But how long would that life be? I may not see my next birthday for all I knew. I wouldn't let him suffer that. I was doing the right thing. *Stick to the plan...* And I talked myself off the ledge, believing I had spared him another heartache that I couldn't allow him to endure. Not again.

"What do you mean, 'like my mother said'? What did she say to you, Laci?" he asked, frustration overflowing from his voice.

"It was nothing, don't worry about it. But she was right. Eventually one of us will have to choose to give up our life for the other. So this is me, choosing to end this relationship now so neither one of us have to give up anything."

"That's it then. I don't get a say in this? Don't you realize that I would give up everything for you? Please, Laci. What has changed in the last six days? Please tell me. We can fix this. You are my whole world and I can't lose you like this, darlin'. I don't care what my mother said! Tell me how to fix this..." he said softly, his voice genuinely sad and unbelieving.

"Let me go, Mitch. It's for the best. You deserve to be with someone that your family likes and who can be there to support you. I can't give you that. But please know one thing: I do love you, with all the love my heart can hold. I don't want to hurt you like this, but it's the only way. I'll always love you even though we can't be together. I know you don't understand now, but I hope you will someday and will be able to forgive me somehow. I want

you to move on and find love again. Can you do that for me? Please?" I closed my eyes, tears falling to the floor.

"No. I can't do that! I won't move on like this never happened because it did happen. It happened to you and me. I love you, Laci Kramer and this isn't over. I'm getting on a plane and coming out there!"

"No, Mitch. Don't. I don't want you here! I'll move if I have to, I swear! It's over. And it won't do you any good to send me emails or keep calling me. I just can't do this anymore. I'm sorry. I've got to go; my bacon is burning and I need to finish cooking breakfast for the kids. Please forgive me." My voice cracked and I began to cry harder, barely getting out the last few words. "I love you." I hung up before he could reply or keep fighting me. It was better that I didn't drag it out, better for him. I set the phone down on the table and slid off the chair and onto the floor, sobbing and heaving long cries filled with the pain of letting him go. My stomach ached from crying so hard. The floor squeaked and startled me. When I looked up, I saw Lena standing over me. She joined me on the floor and took my hands.

"Oh sweetie, I couldn't help but overhear the end of your call. I'm so sorry." She covered her arms around me, holding me tight as I cried on her shoulder. I could barely breathe. I just gave up the love of my life to protect him. I did what I had to do! I stuck with the plan. So why do I feel like such a fool?

"It's over, Lena. I ended it. He's out of my life forever." Still whimpering, I tried to catch my breath. "I told him not to come up or call, that I didn't want him here. I know he's confused, but I didn't know what else to do! I couldn't stand by and allow him to suffer while he watches me die the way his wife did. He deserves so much better," I said, continuing to convince myself that I did the right thing.

"I know, sweetie. I know. I support your decision and you've got to do what you think is right, but I just have one question: why are you so certain you're going to die? I know you, girlfriend, and I don't believe you're going to give up without a fight! That's not the Laci I know and love. So, what happens when you kick this cancer's butt and survive? Where does he fit in then?"

"Whatever possessed you to ask such hard questions this early in the morning?" I laughed. "I haven't even had my breakfast yet!"

"So you're going to avoid my question altogether?"

"No, not all of it anyway. I'm not certain that I will die, but I know there are no guarantees in this life. I have to prepare myself for the worst scenario so I can deal with this on my own terms. I have to know that the people I love will be taken care of after I'm gone. If I have spared him heartache by letting him go, then that's me, taking care of him. If I can't do that, then I won't be able to live with myself, no pun intended." I started to giggle. My giggling caused Lena to laugh too and pretty soon, we were laughing so hard we were beating our hands on the floor. This time, tears of laughter rolled down my cheeks. We stopped laughing and looked at each other, still smiling.

"I need you to promise me that he won't find out about me, not from anyone. The kids, work, no one can tell him. I'll tell the kids that we broke up and to keep it quiet about the cancer because it would upset him."

"How do you think the kids will react to this—you and Mitch?

They're awfully fond of him, you know. Especially Emma." "Oh, she'll be mad, no doubt about it. She'll just have to get

over it; they all will. And in comparison to what lies ahead, breaking up with Mitch is the least of my worries."

We helped each other up off the floor and finished cooking breakfast. My bacon was a bit overdone, but not horrible. Besides, bacon was one of my 'happy foods'. Even burnt, I could still eat my weight in the stuff. With all the talking, crying, and laughing, Lena hadn't even noticed the music playing in the background until the kitchen quieted a bit.

"Is this Christmas music?" she asked.

"Yes it is! It makes me happy," I replied, smiling at her.

"Works for me, girlfriend!" Even *she* knew that it would help push out the sadness that still lingered in the air.

"Speaking of what's ahead, have you made a decision on what to do about your treatment?"

"I have. After Emma fell asleep last night, I couldn't sleep so I Googled each one of them. It wasn't easy, but I settled on the lumpectomy and radiation. It's the one that makes the most sense for me right now. I just couldn't wrap my head around a mastectomy yet. I guess I'm thankful to have the choice. Some women don't get that luxury. I wouldn't hesitate though if things get worse or if the lumpectomy doesn't work. I have an appointment today to let her know my decision."

"If that's what feels right to you, then it's the right decision. And I'll be here all day, so don't worry about the kids. Why don't you go to a movie or something after your appointment, get your mind off everything?"

"I would like that, thank you. And Lena, I know I'll never be able to repay you or thank you enough for everything you're doing, but thank you anyway. You and Teri are the closest thing to family that I have up here and I..." I pushed on through the tears. "I love you so much. I don't know what I would do with- out you."

"Then it's a good thing you'll never have to find out! I'm here for the long haul, sister. There's no need to thank me because there isn't anywhere else I'd rather be than here with you and the kids. Now go get everyone up so we can eat, I'm starving!" She hugged me.

After breakfast, I got ready to face the day. First on the list was telling my family, a task which I had been avoiding, but it was time—past time. I spent the better part of the morning on the phone telling my parents, my brother, and even my sweet grandma. They were devastated at first, but I managed to convince them it wasn't that serious. I didn't think they bought it, but they didn't really have a choice. My mom and dad offered to come up, but I assured them I had lots of help and that I would keep them updated. My brother and his wife wanted to come up too, but he had so much work that he couldn't possibly get away. There was a chance my sister-in-law Tonya would come up after the surgery if she could. I missed my family so much! It was the worst part about living on the other side of the country; it might as well be the other side of the planet.

I finished up the phone calls and left for my appointment with Dr. Walker. Once I got there, it went rather fast. I shared my decision with her about the treatment and she explained how things would work from there on out. She had already referred me to the oncology department for treatment and recommended a surgery date within the next two weeks. She said to expect a call from my new doctor next week to get things started. Time was of the essence, and it was ticking away. I missed Mitch every second that passed. I left her office and followed Lena's advice. I went to a movie, and then visited the bookstore to lose myself in the latest work of fiction about angels, demon hunters, and vampires. On my way home, my phone buzzed. Mitch again, the third call since I broke things off that morning. I thought about blocking his number, but I couldn't do it. Even though I didn't want to talk to him, I still wanted to see his name pop up on my phone. I couldn't go back; what was done was done.

Mitch hung up the phone and stood there, staring at the ground in disbelief of what had just transpired. Brad was standing at the edge of the barn and he had heard the end of Mitch's conversation by accident. He walked inside and saw the look on his face. "You don't look so good, little brother," Brad said. "Are you okay?"

"It's over," Mitch said softly. "That was Laci. She wants to… break up. No wait, I believe she just broke up with me." Mitch looked up, ran his hand through his hair, then started pacing around the barn.

"Come again?"

"It's over, I said. She ended it. She broke up, dumped me. Do you need any more clarification?"

"Umm…no, no. That about covers it," Brad said. He paused for a minute, then in his usual smug manner, he added, "Is this where I say, 'I told you so' or should I save that for later?" Brad asked, trying to be funny.

Mitch looked up at Brad, tears in his eyes. Brad could see the hurt on his face, but he didn't really know how to help. Selfishly, he was glad Laci was finally out of the picture. Now they could finally get on with the winery and focus on business. Still, he hadn't seen his brother hurt like that in a long time.

"Hey, Mitch. I'm sorry little brother. I didn't mean that. Did she tell you why she was breaking up?" Brad actually showed remorse for his comments and walked over to Mitch to give him a consoling pat on the shoulder.

"Yeah, sort of. It just doesn't make any sense, none of it. Six days ago, we were right as rain. She didn't even want me to leave. Now, supposedly the distance is making it too hard and her kids are being affected. She even said that my mother told her that one of us would eventually have to give up their life to make it work. She ended it so neither of us would have to give that up. My own mother helped push her out! And you didn't help either. She could tell you didn't like her. Thanks for that!"

"I liked her…sort of. This isn't my fault, Mitch, so don't blame me! But maybe she's right about one thing. It has been hard on the rest of us whether you want to admit it or not. I've been trying to hold things together here while you go back and forth to see her, but it hasn't been easy. Have you ever considered the possibility that it wasn't meant to be?"

"No. I won't consider it. She's the one; I know it. I feel it with everything in me. Something is wrong and I have to get to the bottom of it. I'm going to go see her."

"You can't leave now! Our new vendor is coming in town this week to see the winery and you need to be here. You're the schmoozer, remember? I can't do that alone and you know it."

"Ugh! You're right. I'll stay until after their visit, but then I'm leaving. I have to see her, work this out face to face."

"Mitch, I know I'm not the best person to take advice from on relationships, but maybe you should give her some space. Don't rush right up there just yet. Give her some time to think about things, put some distance between you two. Maybe she'll come around?" Brad said, giving Mitch a gentle pat on the shoulder.

"Yeah, maybe. I guess it can't hurt to give her some time. But I can't shake this feeling, Brad. Something isn't right about all this. I just wish I knew what it was."

Mitch's face was sullen; all the light in his eyes had faded, and for the first time, Brad realized how much he had felt for Laci.

"Not to be the bearer of more bad news, but you might want to call the jeweler, dude." Brad's lack of tact still floored Mitch after all these years, thought he wasn't sure why.

"Right. The jeweler," he said with a laugh. "I bet this whole thing just made your day, didn't it, Brad?" Mitch asked in spite.

"No. It didn't. I'm sorry this is happening to you, I really am! I want you to be happy and...well, I'm sorry I didn't support you and Laci. If I could take it back, I would."

Mitch took a deep breath and let it out, "I know. I'm sorry, this isn't your fault. I'll call the jeweler and then meet you inside. I need a minute."

"Yeah, yeah. Take all the time you need, little brother. You'll get through this, don't worry." Brad said, and he gave Mitch a brotherly hug to comfort him in some small way.

Mitch called the jeweler, but he didn't cancel the order. He rescheduled the appointment for later. He wasn't about to change his plans. Laci was the one, *his* one. The one he was meant to be with forever. He knew it the minute he saw her on that plane and he wasn't about to stop fighting for her now.

the eye of the storm

Sunday was a blur and I was completely worthless. I moped around the house and did absolutely nothing but wallow in my own self-pity. Honestly, I was never so happy to see Monday arrive. I put the kids on the bus and headed to my favorite Starbucks for a morning caffeine fix. That day, I needed it more than ever, plus I loved seeing the coffee crew every morning; they were all so nice and they made me smile. That was the one part of my daily routine that I refused to change, for as long as possible anyway. Sandy arrived at the office shortly after I did. I said good morning and followed her into her office, then closed the door behind me.

"Uh oh, this can't be good. What's going on with you, sister? I've been worried about you, and Lena won't spill anything! You're not quitting, are you?" She asked, her forehead creased with worry lines. I sat down in the seat across her, and I couldn't help but laugh at her question, wishing that were the case in a way. At least then I'd be leaving on my own terms as opposed to the cancer that was then dictating my fate.

"No, it's a little more complicated than that." I took in a long breath, exhaled slowly, and then began to share my story. She could tell it was serious, and she immediately got up, walked around her desk, and sat down in the chair next to me.

"So, I'm sure you remember that I had my annual exam a little over a week ago, mammogram, the whole works, you know. A few days later, my doctor asked me to come back in to talk to her. My mammogram had come back abnormal and showed several spots on my left breast. I had an MRI and biopsy of the area on the same day, which is rare. Only Lena and Teri knew about it; I didn't want them to say anything to you yet." I paused to take another long breath to calm my shaky voice. "Then last Friday, my doctor called and wanted me to come in to review my results; that's when I left for some 'personal' business. And as soon as I saw my doctor's face, I knew. It's breast cancer, Sandy," I said. I remained quiet waiting for her response but I didn't have to wait long. Her mouth dropped open, her eyes turned red and started to water, tears not far behind.

"Oh, Laci. I'm so sorry sweetie. What can I do? What do you need?" she asked as she hugged me tight. I could feel her warm tears falling onto my shoulders.

"It's okay, or will be I think. They caught it in the early stages. Right now, there's really nothing to do except wait. I should hear from my oncologist today to find out when the surgeon can get me on his or her schedule. I've researched all my options and decided to have a lumpectomy. They'll only remove the cancerous area, and I'll be able to keep my breast unless it returns later. I should probably talk to HR and see how to work the time off and fill out some paperwork. My doctor said she was going to recommend that my surgery be scheduled sometime in the next week, but I'm not sure what the recovery period will look like yet. Until then, and even afterwards unless I'm sick, I want to keep working and function like everything is normal, okay? I guess I'll have to start telling people once I find out about the surgery, but let's keep it quiet for now. The last thing I need is everyone treating me like I'm going to break or something. I couldn't handle that." "All right, if that's what you want, you got it. But promise me that you won't overdo it around here; your health comes first right now. If work starts to stress you out, then you tell me. Is that clear?" She smiled at me and wiped the tears from her eyes. "Yes, yes. I promise." I smiled and rolled my eyes at her being my "mother hen," which I loved. "Thank you, Sandy. I am so grateful to you, for everything." I stood up, gave her another quick hug, and went back to my office.

It was such a relief to finally tell her, to have no more secrets. I hated keeping things from her. Even though she was my boss – and I treated her with the utmost respect, she was also a dear friend and one of the most special women in my life. I was surprised she hadn't asked about Mitch, but grateful all the same. I'm not sure I could've handled her well-meaning lecture about what I did to him right now. I was sure it would come up eventually.

Before lunch, my new oncologist from the local hospital called to introduce herself and check to see how I was doing. Her name was Dr. Amanda Conley and she was very nice, easy to talk to and very gracious to answer all my questions. I must have asked her a hundred of them in the span of ten minutes, but she didn't care. She mentioned that she'd helped cancer patients in the community for over twenty years and the ones who educated themselves seemed to have a better outlook on their whole experience. She also informed me that my surgeon, Dr. Light, had an immediate opening on her surgery schedule for this Friday. Friday…four days from today…the day before my birthday! Great timing, doc! Party you say? Why of course, what's a birthday party without a little anesthesia, bad hospital food and good pain killers? A winning combination! She encouraged me to take advantage of the early surgery date if I could. I closed my eyes to think. It was all moving so fast! Was I ready? I needed to hear Mitch's voice…but he couldn't know.

Scared, uncertain, and my stomach now in knots, I told her to put me on the schedule. She gave me a couple of websites to research about the procedure, and then made me an appointment to meet the surgeon in the morning, talk through my options again, and make sure I understood what to expect. Then we hung up. It was settled. I didn't expect it to happen so soon, but a small part of me was glad it would be done and over with.

Sandy was at a meeting, so I sent her a quick email and gave her an update about my appointment the next morning. Then it was time to tell the others. I gathered everyone around: Lena, Teri, Gail, and Sue. First, I had to share the whole story with Sue and Gail because they were still unaware of my situation. Then I gave everyone the updated version about that Friday.

"Saying all that, I wanted you all to know that I also told Sandy this morning, so she knows everything now. And I have an update about my surgery. I got a call this morning and they scheduled it for this Friday morning, a little earlier than I originally planned. The surgeon had an opening." Their faces went blank, not sure what to say at first. Sue and Gail were both in shock from hearing about the cancer in general.

"So I'm moving in on Thursday night?" Lena asked and gave me a smile and a big hug.

"That would be perfect! Thank you, Lena."

"And I'll pick you up Friday morning and take you to the hospital," Teri said as she stepped over close to me and also gave me a hug. "And I'll stay with you until they take you back to surgery." The outpouring of their friendship and love continued. I was bawling like a baby before they were done.

"I'll bring dinner for everyone on Friday night after work," Sue said and followed it with a hug.

Then Gail added her part. "And I'll be there to pick you up from the hospital and take you home. But just so you know, I'm bringing a big bouquet of pink balloons that look like gigantic boobs!" Gail's effort to lighten the mood worked perfectly. We laughed hysterically and before long, the tears were gone.

"You guys, I don't know what to say. If I didn't have you, I don't know what I'd do. Thank you, all of you. I love you all so much!" I smiled and the group hug ensued.

"I just want to know one thing. Where is Mitch? Why isn't he up here helping you? You haven't mentioned him in days!" Sue asked, and rightly so. I hadn't mentioned him or the breakup. Lena was giving Sue the evil-eye. She dragged her pointer finger from one side of her throat to the other, like she would take her out if she didn't drop the subject. It totally cracked me up.

"It's okay, Lena, I need to say it out loud." I looked down at the floor to avoid the reactions that I knew would follow. "After I received the news about my cancer, I realized that I couldn't let him suffer again like he did with his first wife. So I didn't tell him. He doesn't know about the cancer and he won't find out. It was best to just break up and blame it on the distance and the fact that his family doesn't like me anyway. I won't let him go through it again." Gail's eyes flew open in disbelief and her words of wisdom began spilling out with intense passion.

"You're kidding right? Please tell me you're joking! I've never seen any two people meant for each other more than you and Mitch; you can't just turn that off girl! He loves you and you love him. You need him right now!" I knew she was right, of course. Everything was all wrong without him, but I did what I had to do.

"Look, I know none of you agree with what I did. I can't change it now, but trust me, it's better this way. He'll be able to move on and find someone else that won't remind him of how he lost his wife. He'll be happier, eventually. I…I did what was best for him because I love him. I can't let him suffer again. I'm sorry, but that's the end of this discussion." They all knew it too. I wasn't going to change my mind. Nothing would.

For the rest of the day, I simply enjoyed my job, crossing things off my to-do list. I didn't want to leave any loose ends for Sandy to worry about after I was gone. In between work, the girls and I enjoyed laughing and goofing off together as if there were no cancer, no surgery, and no love lost. No drama.

The next morning, I met with my surgeon, Dr. Light. She was a very nice woman, attractive, probably not much older than me, and she had a sweet demeanor that made me feel comfort- able asking questions. She was highly educated and confident, but she spoke to me in layman terms with genuine concern and compassion. After we talked about all my options, she made sure I understood everything about the treatment I had chosen. I felt a strong connection to her on some level, as if we had known each other for years. But maybe it was because I was putting my life in her hands soon.

Over the next few days, my goal was to drown myself in the normality of life. I got caught up on laundry, cleaned house, washed every dish, vegged out on the couch with the kids watching our favorite TV shows, stocked up on groceries, and paid bills. The worst part was that Mitch still called once a day despite me telling him not to. He wouldn't give up! Every time I saw his name on the phone it felt like I was being punched in the gut.

Thursday was both the best and worst day. I woke up, sad that it would be my last day at work for a while, but glad that I was about to move forward with treating my cancer. I arrived at work and walked into an office filled with an array of pink and white balloons, pink ribbons draped around every ledge and corner and a table full of food, everything from sweet to savory. Birthday cards and presents overflowed on my desk and before nine o'clock, I was bawling like a baby. Lena and Sandy had planned it with a "Good luck, happy birthday" theme and had outdone themselves. I was, once again, overwhelmed by the depths of their friendship. "You guys are too much!" I said as I took in the colorful display, smiling from ear to ear.

"Well don't get used to it, sister! This is just a bribe to make sure you come back healthy and happy. I'm not accepting this whole cancer thing as an excuse for you to slack off," Sandy said, laughing.

My jaw dropped open and I burst out laughing. The rest of them started cracking jokes on the cancer too, making light of it in a way that wasn't mean or disrespectful, but real. They made me feel like it was just a roadblock and that I would get through it. In some way, it gave me power over it and helped put it into a new perspective. I didn't want my cancer to own me or define me! God would define the outcome, whatever that might be. Obviously, I was pulling for the 'let's *beat* this thing' route. The morning was a complete bust as far as work, as none of us got anything done. It was a day to cheer me up, make me laugh, and give me hope. I did manage to get a few last-minute items completed, and around two o'clock, Sandy told me to go home and enjoy the rest of the day with my kids. I collected my gifts and cleared my desk, then said my goodbyes. As I left, I was showered with hugs and kisses.

"I love you guys!" I shouted as I walked out the door, followed by their loud "we love you too" in unison.

I picked up the kids from school, and we all went to a late afternoon movie then grabbed an early dinner since I couldn't have food after a certain hour. By the time we got home, it was after seven and Lena had already arrived to settle in. We all stayed up extra late playing Uno and hanging out.

"All right guys, it's after ten. Time for bed; you've got school tomorrow and I've got a hot date with a surgeon. Lena will want you up early to make sure everyone has time to eat breakfast." They started groaning. "I'll be up soon to say good night, don't worry, and I'll peek in to say goodbye before I leave in the morning too. I might even beat you home from school tomorrow, but remember that I may be sleeping okay? I'll need lots of rest over the next few days." I reminded them.

"Are the doctors going to take the cancer out tomorrow, mom?" Travis asked, his eyes sad with worry.

"They sure are, sweetie. Then next week they'll give me some medicine to keep it away." I smiled to keep the mood light.

"Why hasn't Mitch called or come up here, mom?" Emma asked. I looked at Lena and knew it was time to break the news to them.

"You know, guys, Mitch and I realized that even though we really liked each other, it was becoming harder to be together. We're not really together anymore. It's sort of complicated. He just lives too far away and his family and the winery depend on him to be there. They are really important to him." It was a terrible explanation and I knew it, but I couldn't tell them the real reason I let him go.

"More important than you or us?"

"Well, yes. They are his family and we're not. I know he will always care about us and he misses us so much, but sometimes things just don't work out like we want them to."

"Great, first dad, now Mitch! Everyone we love just leaves!" And she ran off to her room, crying. Travis gave me a hug and he followed Emma upstairs, his shoulders drooping as he walked away.

"It will be all right, Laci. Kids are resilient; they'll come around," Lena added. "I'm off to bed girl. Don't worry about any- thing here, okay? Just relax and focus on getting better, nothing else. I love you, girlfriend!" she said as she squeezed me in one of her bear hugs.

"Good night, Lena. I love you too. Thank you," I whispered, and she quickly turned around and walked away to hide the tears in her eyes.

I picked up the game, wrote the kids an "I love you" note on the whiteboard that clung to the fridge, then turned off the lights and headed up to my room. I needed to relax. I couldn't have slept even if I tried.

I drew myself a hot bubble-bath, turned on some soft music, lit a couple of candles, got undressed, then turned out the lights and lowered myself through the hot steam into the water. The house was quiet and still, not counting the music. As I lay there,

I tried to take my mind off all the other "stuff "—the cancer, the surgery, the unknown. Unfortunately there was one thing that I couldn't turn off: my heart. It still ached and yearned for Mitch—his touch, his voice, his love. I closed my eyes and found him in my thoughts, waiting for me with open arms. For a minute, I could almost feel his warm hands holding my face as we kissed, his soft lips pressed against mine. I remembered his warm embrace, his eyes, and his sweet, southern voice that could set off every nerve in my body, especially when he called me darlin'. Every time he said it, it literally took my breath away and unraveled me from the inside out. I wanted to stay in that moment forever, with my one.

———⁓⁓∙⊙⟶⊙⟵∙⁓⁓———

Mitch had spent the last five days in a state of denial, still holding out that Laci would pick up the phone and want him back. He couldn't sleep. Nights were spent tossing and turning. Eventually he got up and worked on winery business to keep his mind busy. His appetite was also gone; he nibbled on soup and crackers when he couldn't tolerate the grumbling any longer. He went to the winery every day, doing what was needed and not talking much. He saw his mother on Monday but didn't say much to her. What little he did wasn't very pleasant. He was still furious at her for causing Laci to have doubts about their future. When he declined her invitation to their weekly dinner, she began to suspect that something was wrong but didn't press him.

"I'm headed home, Brad. I'll see you in the morning," Mitch said, calling it a day at the winery.

"Sounds good, little brother. If you don't mind me asking, did you…have any luck today?" Brad asked, trying to be supportive.

"No. No answer."

Mitch tried several times a day to call Laci, and she refused to answer his calls. He kept trying though, hoping she would give up and answer and let him tell her that he could make things right. Let him have a chance to be the man she needed. But there had been no word from her, the kids, or her friends since she had ended things over the phone. Not one word.

"Look, I know you have no desire to hear my advice on the subject, but can I make one suggestion?"

"Sure, Brad! I'm sure it can't be any worse than the advice you offered Laci when you told her to leave me alone. What great advice do you have for me, oh wise one?"

"I admit, I screwed up and I'm sorry about that! But trust me when I say that you need to leave her alone. Stop calling her, Mitch. You're going to mess around and push her farther away by bugging her. My advice? My advice is to give her some space; let her think. Let her breath a little and have a chance to miss you. Maybe then she'll come around?"

Mitch didn't say a word. He was kind of hacked off that Brad actually made sense. He was standing next to one of the bar stools that his uncle had carved for the winery, remembering how much Laci had loved them. He felt sick to his stomach at the idea of giving up. He longed for her in every way possible.

"Fine. I'll stop calling. Maybe you're right; maybe she just needs time to figure things out. Maybe I scared her when I asked her to come down for the holiday. I sometimes forget that it's only been a few months since we met. But she was so excited about it; it still doesn't make sense! I *know* something is wrong, I can feel it, Brad!" Mitch was frustrated and he couldn't help but voice it.

"Well, if there is, then you'll have to wait until she's ready to let you in and tell you about it on her own terms. Trust me." Brad spoke as if he had experience unbeknownst to Mitch. From what Mitch remembered, Brad's past with women had been a colorful one to say the least. He had never been very forthcoming about his relationships, and to some extent, Mitch was glad. To his knowledge, Brad never even had a steady girlfriend, had never been engaged, nor had he ever married. But Mitch got the sense that there was one in his past—one that got away.

It was almost midnight and he was working in the office when he heard Caleb come in from his date. Caleb saw him and he poked his head in, as was his routine.

"Hey, Dad, you okay? You've been putting in a lot of hours lately—late ones."

"Ah, just trying to stay on top of things. Grand opening will be here before you know it," he said, trying not to worry him. He hadn't exactly told him about the breakup yet. In Mitch's mind, it wasn't real.

"I don't believe you, Dad. I also haven't seen you smile in days or mention Laci; neither one is normal for you. So what's really going on?" Caleb asked, pressing him to open up. Mitch filled him in on the events that transpired over the weekend and surprisingly, Caleb was more upset by his news than he anticipated, but it felt good to tell him and not carry it alone.

"Dad, I'm so sorry about Laci. That really sucks. But you're right, it doesn't make any sense. I'm sure she'll come around after she works through whatever she has going on. I do know she loves you. Any idiot could see that when she looked at you," he said, smiling. Caleb gave his dad a hug and went up to bed.

Mitch sat there thinking about everything he wanted to say to Laci, and then decided that if she wouldn't talk to him, then maybe she might read his words. She always said how much she loved his emails, especially the ones that were waiting in her inbox first thing in the morning. She would even check her phone before she got out bed, read it, and get up wearing a smile. Well this time, he had a few things to get off his chest. He pulled up his email and started typing.

Like all good things, my relaxing bath had ended too soon. The water was cold and I was freezing. I got out, dried off and put on my pj's, then crawled into bed. Before I turned off the light, I pulled out my tablet to check email one last time. I knew that I wouldn't get much opportunity the next day.

Ten new messages. Junk...more junk...Laura saying she loves me...and...Mitch. What? Oh this wasn't good. Why did he have to send me an email? I slammed the tablet lid down and set it down beside me, then turned off the light. I wasn't going to read it! No way! A little later, I checked the clock to see that an hour had passed and I wasn't any closer to sleep than I was before. I looked over at my tablet as if it were a person. I'm not reading you so forget it! I closed my eyes. The clock beckoned to me again, thirty minutes later. Finally, after another thirty minute check to make sure the clock was still working, I gave in and opened my tablet. What would be the harm in reading it? But what if he hated me and told me off? What if he has already moved on? I know...it's only been five days so that's unlikely. He'd better not have moved on– I'd be so mad! What if...oh fine! I'll read it already! I clicked on the email.

The subject simply read "Words."

My dearest Laci,

I've tried to reach you for days and you refuse to answer my calls. I hope you will at least read these words and let them penetrate your heart.

Your reasons for ending what we had don't add up, darlin'. It's as if someone else put you up to it or convinced you that what we had wouldn't work, but I know you don't believe that! I could hear your love for me in your voice, through your words.

The spoken word is filled with so many emotions, layer upon layer, with the most pure of them at the bottom, hidden away where no one can see, also making them the hardest to reach. But not yours, not from me anyway. They were evident the last time we spoke and I know something is wrong! Please tell me, Laci. We can get through it, whatever it is. I thought I would never find love again after Karin, but I thought wrong. I've replayed the day we met over and over in my head and I know we were brought together for a reason. You do too! You can't deny that.

I won't call anymore if that's what you want, but I'm not giving up. If I could get away and come see you, I would, but I'm not sure you would open your door and I fear I would push you farther away. Besides, the winery is only a few months away from opening and there is much to do, more every day.

There is nothing that I wouldn't do to get you back in my life, Laci. All I need is a chance to show you. I have never been as deeply connected to another as I am to you, not even Karin, as much as that pains me to say. You, my dear, are one of two reasons that I still get up and breathe every day. The other being Caleb, of course. He misses you. I pray that God will show you that our love is meant to be and that there is still hope for us. Maybe you'll find it...in the rain.

P.S. Happy Birthday, darlin'. I love you.

Always yours, Mitch, your CSG

Tears poured down my cheeks as I closed the tablet. Why did he have to call me darlin'? And he even remembered my birth- day! I read it several times, wishing I could change things, wishing I could call him and tell him everything. But I couldn't. What was done was done. I closed my eyes, exhausted and ready to sleep, but I opened my eyes for one last second to ask the ceiling a question. What was CSG? And then it hit me: Creepy Stalker Guy. I smiled.

healing rain

Teri was at my house by 5 a.m. to pick me up. I snuck into the kids' rooms, quietly said goodbye, and gave them a kiss, and then we were off to the hospital. On the way there, I called Evan to say hello and tell him I loved him but he didn't answer. He was probably in class already. Then I called my mom to let her know about the surgery. Not the best way to tell her probably, but at least by waiting until the last minute, I knew she wouldn't try and fly up here. It was too much for her or my dad right now. I kept the conversation short to minimize the stress and keep my blood pressure in check, but inside, I wished she was there to hold me tight and tell me everything was going to be okay. After we arrived, I checked in and things moved pretty fast from there. "Well girl, good luck this morning; everything will be fine, don't worry. Gail will be here when you get out of surgery to take you home and the hospital has all of our phone numbers in case you need us for anything. I love you sweetie. See you soon." Teri gave me a big hug before they took me back. "Thanks, Teri. I love you too."

The prep for surgery went slow, which was fairly normal I guess. Then my surgeon came in to the holding area to talk to me and I knew it was almost time.

"Good morning, Laci. How are you feeling this morning?" Dr. Light asked politely.

Hi, Dr. Light. I'm good, thanks."

"I hear it's your birthday tomorrow. Happy birthday! I'm sorry you'll have to spend it lying at home recovering, but hopefully this procedure will help ensure that you have many more birth- days to come," she said, smiling.

"Thanks. I hope so too."

"Okay, I think we're all set for you back there. Do you have any questions for me before we start?"

"No, I think I'm good. I just want to get it over with. How long will it take?"

"You'll be in surgery about an hour, and then you'll be here a few more hours afterward so we can monitor you. As I said the other day, I'll be inserting a catheter in your left breast after I perform the lumpectomy to remove the cancer. This will allow you to receive the MammoSite radiation treatments. We'll start those on Monday after your incisions have had some time to heal. I'll also be removing your lymph nodes under your left arm to prevent anything from spreading to that area, so you'll have three different incision points. You'll be a little sore afterwards. Are you up for it?" she asked, smiling.

"Oh sure, bring it on!" I said with a nervous laugh.

A few minutes later, I was lying on the table under a bright light watching several people wearing blue coats and little blue caps walk around me.

"I'll see you in a few hours, Laci. Let's get that cancer out, shall we?" Dr. Light said, and then asked me to count backwards. Ten, nine, I love you Mitch…eight, sev…

Mitch's morning had been pretty uneventful, boring even. He needed some fresh air and he decided to take a walk. All morning he kept seeing the image of her face in his mind. He couldn't shake the feeling that something was different that day, something wasn't right. He walked onto the truss bridge that Laci loved and stopped in the middle, staring at the babbling creek below.

He closed his eyes, and remembered the way she looked, her laugh, her sweet face, her love of rain. Then he looked up and he asked God to keep her safe, then made his plea. *Show me what to do, Lord! I need her. How do I get her back? Give me a sign or something!*

He waited around for a few more minutes, as if the answer would arrive via pigeon courier, but nothing came. Frustrated and feeling hopeless, he walked back to the winery and thought about the gift he had sent for her birthday. *Has she received it yet? Would she open it?* It was a just small piece to a larger gift that he still hoped to give her someday, but it was enough, for now.

———ฟฟ๐๐๏๒๙๐๏๏๒฿๐๐ฟฟ———

The nurse must have thought I was deaf because she kept yelling in my ear. "Wake up, Laci. We need to check your blood pressure." My eyes opened and closed again.

I just wanted to be left alone so I could sleep. I shivered as a rush of cold air blew above my head, my teeth now chattering. I turned my head to look at her.

"Hi Laci, my name is Victoria and I'll be your nurse today. Are you in any pain?" she asked. I desperately wanted to say 'duh', but felt that would be a tad inappropriate since she was just doing her job.

"Yes, it's th-throbbing…here," I mumbled as I lifted my right arm. It wobbled it over to my left side; I was trying to point in the direction of the pain but it never made it there. It just fell back down on top of me.

"That's okay, Laci. I will order you some pain meds. They should be here soon. For now, I'm just going to check your vitals." I couldn't help but wonder why she hadn't already ordered me the pain meds, knowing I would probably have *some* level of pain after that procedure, but then my thoughts drifted to my old dog, Cookie. She used to sleep with me when I got sick. I wished she were there now, lying at my feet to comfort me. The fog in my head had begun to clear and I grew more alert by the minute, the pain grew too. After I had completely woken and was responding to the pain meds, my nurse wheeled me to an observation room. I spent the next few hours watching TV and eating ice chips, feeling pretty good overall. Nurse Victoria came back in to check my vitals again and see how I was doing.

"Your vitals look good so you can probably go home in a couple of hours. Oh, and your visitors are waiting outside. I'll send them in," she commented as she left my room.

Gail came in first, carrying a large bouquet of pink balloons just as she promised, but right behind her followed Teri, Lena, Sue, and even Sandy. The whole crew! I was never so happy to see them.

"So I'm a pretty good excuse to skip work, huh?" I said, smiling. "You know it, sister! And we thought you might want this,"

Lena pulled out a small box addressed to me, return addressed stamped "Crystal Creek, NC." It was from Mitch!

"What is this?" I could feel my brow furrow as I looked at the box, fearing that someone had told him about my situation.

"We don't know! That's why we brought it; open it up!" Lena laughed. "Oh, come on, you know you want to!"

"Fine. But whatever it is, I don't want it."

I opened the box to find a tiny, round, silver, bead-like charm with crystal blue raindrops all around it. My jaw fell open as I stared at it. It looked like it would fit on one of those fancy charm bracelets that you only found in really nice jewelry stores. Where did he find a raindrop charm? Why would he even send it to me after what I had done?

"Oh it's beautiful, Laci!" Lena exploded with excitement, jumping up and down.

"Shh, keep it down girl! There are other patients in here, you know." She cracked me up so I couldn't help but laugh at her.

"Read the card, read the card!" Sandy urged.

Inside the box was a little card with my name on the front. I opened it and read it out loud to the group.

Dearest Laci,

I was hoping to give you this in person and wish you a happy birthday, but just know that I am thinking of you. I hope you like the charm. It reminded me of you…and your rain.

All my love,

Mitch

Large teardrops sat on the edge of my eyes, waiting to fall. His gift just made things even worse. As if I wasn't feeling guilty enough already for dumping him, he went out and bought me jewelry!

"Wow, that's sweet." Sandy said in a quiet voice. "Oh Laci, can't you see that he misses you and still loves you? You need to tell him what's going on. Get him back!" She continued. The others chimed in and started to sound like a gaggle of mother hens. "That's not going to happen, so let it go ladies, please?" I pleaded, tears now streaming down my cheeks. I wrapped up the charm and put it back in the box with the card. "Why did he get me a charm anyway? I don't even have a charm bracelet to put it on!" I was frustrated, sore, and tired and I just wanted to go home. They dropped the subject, feeling a little uncomfortable.

"Well, sweetie, we'll get out of here. It sounds like you're going home soon and we just wanted to see you and tell you we love you," Teri said.

"I love you guys too, I do. Thank you for coming; it really meant a lot to me. It's just been a long morning. Sorry if I sound crabby." "Laci, you've just had breast cancer surgery; you have a right to be a little crabby and out of sorts. All of us coming at once was probably a bit overwhelming. So, get some rest and make Lena do everything for you!" Sandy said laughing, looking at Lena.

"And I gave her the afternoon off so she could take you home and help you get settled in."

"Thank you, all of you. I'll keep in touch and will be back in the office soon, I promise," I said, a weary smile on my face.

They all walked out and Lena went to grab some coffee. I just sat there and cried, now hurting on the outside and the inside. Why did life have to be so hard at times? I dried my tears as the nurse entered the room. She had my release paperwork in her hand and she told me I was free to go home. Lena came in a few minutes later and I told her to go get the car. The nurse helped me out of bed and into my clothes, and then wheeled me down to the exit. The first part was over.

After we got home, I went straight to bed and slept the rest of the day, not even waking for dinner. I never heard the kids come home from school, nor did I stir until the wee hours of the morning only to use the restroom.

I spent most of Saturday in bed or on the couch feeling sorry for myself. Yep, it was my best birthday *ever*...I was living the dream. Lena had taken the kids to the mall to give me some peace and quiet. They have all been so amazing with this whole situation so far. The kids were so respectful, always caring for my every need. And Lena has been the ultimate, sacrificial friend. She cooked, cleaned, and even did my laundry – I was humbled by her unending love for me and my family.

On the bright side, I finally had some time to read. Lately I had been so busy with work that I rarely picked up a book any- more. I decided to try out a new author that I hadn't read before and was pleasantly surprised. It was a shame that it took cancer to slow me down and show me what I was missing. I was so caught up in my job, and all along, had ignored what mattered most... my kids, my friends, and the simple pleasures of reading or planting flowers in the garden. Now I just hoped I would get through this – make up for lost time.

I had read nearly half the book when I heard the garage door go up. A few minutes later, there was whispering outside my door. Lena peeked her head in to see if I was awake and seeing that I was, they all burst into my room and shouted "Happy birthday!" throwing confetti over my bed. Lena went back into the hallway and brought in a cake. There were so many candles burning on top, it could have created its own aurora borealis, thus signifying my most mature life. They sang "Happy Birthday" to me and gave me their presents. It was the sweetest surprise and it made my day. The kids showered me with hugs, we enjoyed our cake, and we laughed together talking about random things. It felt good and I was so blessed by their sweet gesture, but they could tell I was exhausted, so they cleaned up the mess and let me go to bed.

———∿∿o◝◟◜◞◝◟◜◞o∿∿———

Sunday started off better, at first. Every few hours, Travis asked me if I was feeling better and I always answered yes just to see his sweet smile. Honestly, I felt horrible. Everything from the waist up was throbbing, including my head. I loaded up on the pain meds and stuck to the couch most of the day, reading and sleeping. It was dusk outside the next time I woke up, and I found myself alone. The kids and Lena were all upstairs doing something. I could hear the rain outside, beating against the windows in a steady rhythm. I peered through the blinds above the couch and just watched it, wishing I could just run through it and feel it against my skin. I was sure it was freezing outside, being a mid-November evening, but somehow that didn't seem to factor into my decision. I stood up slowly, a little wobbly from lying around most of the day, and walked straight toward the front door. Quietly, I opened the door and stepped outside. I walked down the front steps and onto the front lawn, then looked up at the sky and let the rain pour down over my entire body, drenching me from head to toe. I started to shiver, but I stayed, spinning around and around with my arms open wide, just like when I was little. Only this time, I pretended that it was a "healing rain," removing the bad stuff from both the outside and the inside, as it soaked through and touched every inch of my skin. But as I stood there, feeling the pain of unfulfilled dreams, all I could do was cry harder and harder, inconsolable as I thought about the uncertain future in front of me. My tears mingled with the rain, no one could tell them apart. I shouted up into the sky, calling out for my one, hoping he would hear me somehow. "I love you Mitch! I'm so sorry I let you go. I'm sorry I didn't tell you! I love you! Please come back! I need you!" Everything hurt worse now and I felt nauseous. I heard a high-pitched ring in my ears and the sound of the rain grew weak, then my vision went dark.

Emma had run downstairs to get a drink and noticed the front door open. She looked out through the glass of the storm door and saw her mom standing there in the yard, yelling, but then she stopped and started to stumble around. Emma wasn't sure what was happening; she just watched her mom crumple over and col- lapse into the grass below, like a movie running in slow motion. Emma screamed.

"Lena! Lena! Come quick, it's my mom. She fell outside! She's not getting up, Lena!" Emma yelled. Lena came running down the stairs and flew outside; Todd followed behind her. Emma stood there crying and scared as she watched through the window. She knew there was only one person who could help and she had to tell him; she had to tell Mitch. She ran to her mom's purse and dug out her cell phone, but she couldn't find his name anywhere. She looked through every name again, and then one caught her eye. She remembered him joking with her mom about being her creepy stalker guy, so she dialed the number, hoping it was him.

It was getting late and despite the fact that he wouldn't be able to sleep, Mitch decided to go to bed anyway. He turned out the lights and walked to the kitchen to get a glass of water when his cell phone rang. Expecting it to be Brad or Caleb, he didn't hurry to pick it up. On the third ring, he picked up his phone from the counter behind him and his eyes flew wide-open, shocked that he was seeing her name appear on the screen. He fumbled to find the green "answer" button, a smile on his face as big as Texas.

"Laci, I can't believe it's you! I'm so glad you called, darlin'! How are you?" He was more than anxious awaiting her reply, but instead of Laci's voice, he heard a little girl's small whimper as she cried softly into the phone.

"Emma? Sweetie, is that you?" he asked, worried that some- thing had happened and his nerves instantly on edge.

"Ye-yes. My mom fell outside, Mitch. She isn't moving! I think she might be dying from her cancer. I…I'm scared, Mitch. Can you come? Please come!" Emma burst out in a loud cry, crying so hard he could barely make out her words. Mitch was confused and completely shocked by what she said, unsure of what was going on.

"Emma, tell me what's wrong. What cancer? What's happening?" he asked, panic laced through his words.

"My mom, she's outside lying on the grass. She was outside in the rain and I watched her fall over. Lena and Todd went out- side to bring her back inside, but she's not moving. Her surgery was supposed to take the cancer out of her, but I don't think it worked. Can you help, Mitch? Can you come here?"

"Sweetie, what cancer? What's wrong with your mom? What are you talking about?"

"She has breast cancer. She didn't want to tell you because it would hurt you too much. That's why she broke up with you. I heard her tell Lena that one day. She had surgery a couple days ago and they took it out, the cancer. She was really tired today, but I thought she was better," she explained, sobbing and taking big breaths in between words to catch her breath.

It all made sense now, why she turned him away and shut him out. *She was protecting me.* Mitch stared down at the counter, stunned by the news and not sure how to respond.

"Mitch, are you there? Can you come, Mitch? She needs you." Emma's voice was so fragile and her hopes were pinned on him now.

"I'm here, Emma. I'll…umm…I'll call you back okay, sweetie? I need to check a few things here first, but I'll be there soon, I promise," he said. He regretted saying the words as soon as they left his mouth, but she needed reassurance. Mitch hung up the phone and walked over to the kitchen table and sat down, staring into the black night outside. He looked over and stared at the chair Laci had sat in, picturing her there, laughing about her new Crawdad hat, and his head fell forward onto the table, resting on his arms. Quiet sobs came flowing from beneath his arms; the house was empty so they echoed all around him. The second love of his life shut him out because once again, the same awful disease that took his wife was now taking her too. Mitch knew exactly why she had pushed him away and he didn't blame her. His mind raced, full of questions. *Would I have stayed if she had told me? Could I go through that again, feeling the heartache of watching her wither right in front of my eyes, just like Karin did? Could I put Caleb through that again? How could you do this, God? Why? I'm scared to go! I won't be enough for her right now – she needs more than I can give her!*

Mitch ran out on the front porch, the air inside stifling. He couldn't catch his breath. He threw himself against the porch railing and yelled into the night sky. "What now, huh? Are you going to take her from me too? How can I do this again? What do you expect from me, God?" he cried out. Then out of nowhere, a lightning bolt shot down from the sky and hit a power box down the road, sending sparks flying all around. The power in his house went out and everything was now black and quiet. A few seconds later, a clap of thunder boomed in the south and rolled for what seemed like an eternity. He felt the porch rail vibrate beneath his hands and he pushed himself back, watching the spectacle unfold. The rain started slow, but within seconds, it had gained power and speed, pouring down in front of him—sheets so white and thick that he could no longer see his driveway just a few feet away. He walked off the porch and into the rain, feeling it beat against his skin, and he yelled at the top of his lungs. When he stopped yelling, another clap of thunder sounded over him and he thought he heard Laci's voice calling out to him. Now he knew he was crazy and he shook his head, but he still heard her voice. *This is my answer; this is Laci's rain! I love her so much! I can't let her do this alone. I have to be there, no matter what happens.*

Mitch ran back inside the dark house and found his cell on the table. He called Caleb and Brad to give them the news, and then called Laci's number hoping Emma would answer.

"Hello?" Emma said, her voice still shaky.

"Emma, this is Mitch, darlin'. I'm getting on a plane in just a couple of hours and I'll see you in the morning, okay? But can you do me a favor?"

"Yes, yes! What is it?" she asked, already a happier tone to her voice, more hopeful.

"Don't tell your mom that you called me, all right? I want to surprise her and if you tell her, it might upset her more. You can tell Lena if you want, but keep it a secret between just you two, okay? Can you do that?"

"Oh yes! I am the best at keeping secrets!" She laughed. Mitch laughed right along with her. They said goodbye and hung up.

He had one more call to make even though it was late, but it was one call that would change everything.

silver lining

Lena and Todd pulled Laci up off the ground and carried her inside, water dripping off of them and forming puddles on the floor. They laid her down. She was breathing but completely unconscious. Lena kept yelling at her, "Laci, wake up. Laci!"

"Todd, call 911!"

Todd called and described his mom's situation to the operator, fairly calm despite the chaos that had just taken place. After a few minutes passed, Laci's head started to move back and forth and she was trying to talk. Travis watched from the stairs above, crying and scared, afraid he had lost his mom. Emma walked down the stairs, sat down beside him, and wrapped her arm around his shoulder. She whispered in his ear, "It's going to be okay. Help is on the way." She gave him a hug, smiling as she kept her secret.

"Laci, this is Lena. Are you hurt anywhere, sweetie?" Lena asked her in a loud voice. Laci mumbled something about the rain, and then called out his name. "Oh, thank God!" Lena exclaimed.

Lena looked up, "Your mom is okay, kids. She's going to be just fine, all right?"

"Mitch, gotta tell Mitch...I...I love him," Laci mumbled in a breathless voice that was barely audible. The ambulance pulled up into the driveway. The EMT came inside and evaluated Laci, checked her stitches and her catheter, then determined that she had gone into some sort of shock, either from the cold or stress from the surgery, and decided it was best to take her in for observation.

"Todd, I'm going to follow them to the hospital and make sure she's okay. I'll call as soon as I know more. I'm sure they'll keep her overnight, but I'll be back once she's in good hands. Can you get the kids some dinner and help calm them down? If they don't want to go to bed until I get back, that's fine," Lena said.

"Yeah, sure…go." Todd's sullen response worried Lena, afraid he might not be up for the task.

"Are you sure you're okay, Todd? Do you want me to call Teri?" Lena thought that sending reinforcements might be a good plan at that point.

"Do you think she'd come? I don't really want to be here alone right now," he said.

"I'll call her right now."

Lena dialed Teri's number and told her what had just happened. Teri didn't hesitate and was already on her way over to be with the kids. Lena picked up her purse, about to walk out the door, when Emma pulled at her from behind. Lena turned around.

"What is it Emma? Are you all right?" Lena asked her.

"I have to tell you something, but it's a secret." Emma replied, and stood up on her toes to whisper in Lena's ear. "I called Mitch and he's coming. But don't tell mom. It's a secret between you and me," she whispered. Lena quickly stood upright.

"What? How did you…"

"I used mom's cell phone when you were outside; I had to tell him, Lena! I was so scared! I'm sorry! Did I do something wrong?" Emma was worried her actions would get her in trouble. "Oh no, sweetie. You did just right. And I won't say a word, okay? It will be our secret, I promise," she said, smiling. She gave

Emma a hug goodbye and then left for the hospital.

Upon her arrival, Lena parked the car and then took a deep breath. It had all happened so fast and she couldn't keep it in; the stress of the weekend hit her like a ton of bricks so she took a

moment to let it all out and get herself together. Afterwards, she thought it might be a good idea to contact Mitch and fill in the gaps that Emma might have created. She pulled out a small card from her wallet and dialed his number, which she had kept for a "rainy day."

"Hello?" Mitch answered.

"Mitch? This is Lena, Laci's friend. I hear you're going to pay us a visit soon?" she asked.

"Lena, Hi! Of course. I…uh…Emma called me earlier and told me what happened. Is everything okay? I'm on my way to the airport now, but please don't tell Laci. I have to be there with her," he pleaded.

"Mitch, you have my complete and total blessing, sweetie. I never wanted her to leave you out of this, but she thought it was best and I couldn't change her mind. So please, get here as fast as you can! She could use a silver lining right now. And, she's been calling your name since I pulled her in out of the rain."

"She has? She was really calling for me? Are you absolutely sure?"

"I was standing right beside her. Trust me, yours was the only name coming from her lips. Why?"

"Oh, it's nothing. Just surprised, that's all." Mitch couldn't help but remember what he had heard in the storm, wondering how it could even be possible. "Lena, would you mind telling me what happened today? And, tell me how bad it is…the cancer, I mean. What's her diagnosis? And the surgery…did they remove…?" He couldn't finish his sentence, afraid of the answer. "It's okay,

Mitch. As far as what happened today, they think her body just went into shock while she was standing out there. Between the pain from her surgery and the meds she's taking, combined with staying outside in the cold rain too long like a crazy woman, her body just gave out. She was an accident waiting to happen. That girl and her rain! But before the paramedics left, they said she would be just fine. And they caught her breast cancer in the early stage so she has a great chance of beating it from what the doctor said. It's isolated in her left breast, and no, they didn't have to remove anything except the cancer itself. No mastectomy. She didn't want it." Lena said, happy to share the good news.

"Hallelujah! That's the best news I've heard all day! Please send me text updates when you can. I'll let you know when I land and get directions to the hospital from you then. And Lena, thank you, for taking such good care of her for me."

"She's our girl; it's my job! And I love her too," she said, sniffing quietly. "Well, I'm at the hospital now so I'd better get in there. I'm glad you're coming, Mitch."

"You and me both!" he said excitedly, then hung up.

Lena found her way over to the reception desk and asked for Laci's room. They escorted her up to the main hospital floor, and as she suspected, they had already admitted her. When she got to her room, Laci was sound asleep and the nurse in was checking her IV.

"Hi, I'm Lena…uh…Laci's sister," she said, lying through her teeth, but she wasn't about to be kicked out just because she wasn't related. It wasn't a big stretch; they were sisters, just not by blood.

"Hello. I'll be out of your way soon. She's doing much bet- ter. They've got her on some good pain meds and an antibiotic to make sure her incisions don't become infected, but she'll be fine after she gets some rest. The doctor will be in soon to check on her."

"Thank you, that's what I was hoping to hear."

Lena pulled up a chair and watched her, smiling as she thought about the surprise that awaited her. She sent Mitch a text with a short update. It wasn't long before Laci stirred and saw Lena sitting there.

"Lena...what...what's going on?" she asked, unable to recall the events of the evening.

"Well, apparently you got some harebrained notion to go out- side and play in the rain! Then you got cold and passed out; your body went into shock I guess. What were you thinking, girl?" Lena asked her in a stern voice. Then she laughed.

"I...I just wanted to feel it one more time, you know? I hadn't played in the rain in so long and I couldn't help myself. I pre- tended it was healing me," Laci said softly. A little laugh followed. "Hopefully it healed your brain. You could have died out there

if we hadn't found you when we did!"

"I know, I know...it wasn't one of my finer decisions in life now that I think about it. I was trying to come back inside, but then everything went black. That's all I remember."

"It's all right, you're going to be fine. The doctor will be in soon to check on you. I'll wait until she leaves, then I'll head back home with the kids. And yes, they're fine; a little shook up, but I've already called them and they know you're resting. I'll bring them in tomorrow to visit."

Dr. Light walked into my room, and needless to say, she gave me the third degree for my crazy stunt.

"Good evening, Laci. I must admit I didn't expect to see you in here for something quite like this. A little old to be playing in the rain, aren't you?" she asked with a smile.

"Sorry, Dr. Light. I don't know what came over me. I love the rain, what can I say? I promise it won't happen again."

"You are doing fine. I'm giving you an antibiotic to prevent any infection, but your stitches look fine and the catheter is functioning, so that's good. So, if you are still doing well in the morning, we'll get you started on your first round of MammoSite some- time tomorrow. You should be able to go home tomorrow night if all goes well, but I'll be back to check on you in the morning. Any questions?" she asked politely.

"Nope, I think I'm good. Thanks, Dr. Light, and I'm so sorry for all the trouble."

"It was no trouble. I'm just glad you're all right, and I hope it was fun while it lasted." She smiled and left the room.

"Well, girl, now that I know you're healthy and on the road to recovery, I'm going to get back to the house. I'm sure the kids are still a little freaked out." Lena said.

"Thanks, Lena. I'm so sorry, really. I never meant to scare you or the kids. It was a stupid idea going out there. Forgive me?"

"Girl, don't worry about it; just get well and get home. I understand, sort of. Regardless, I love you, and that's really all the matters," she said as she hugged me goodbye. "I'll be back in the morning with the kids; they may want to see you before I take them to school."

"I would like that, thanks. Love you too sweetie. See you tomorrow," I said as she walked out, then I broke down and cried, feeling stupid for my actions and completely exhausted. I lay there and tried to sleep, but the beeping from my monitor kept me awake. I buzzed for the nurse to come in and turn it off, but she never came. I rolled over and stared at the wall, wishing I could get a do-over of the whole thing. If I could, I would tell Mitch everything and take my chances on what his reaction would be. At least the choice would have been his to make and not mine to take.

Mitch prepared himself for a long flight and layover ahead. He was set to arrive in Seattle around ten Monday morning, about eleven hours from then, but it was the only option and he wasn't about to miss it. Lena had just sent him a text update after she left the hospital and all was well with Laci. Knowing that, he felt good getting on board and he could hardly wait to see her again and hold her in his arms. The one thing he didn't know was how she would react. She had gone to extreme lengths to keep it from him. How would she feel now that he knew? Would she be angry and turn him away? These questions, and more, occupied his mind during his flight. Sleeping was nearly impossible at that point, for him anyway. Most of the passengers around him were sleeping fine. Mitch was consumed with worry for Laci, her journey ahead, and what their future looked like, or if there would be one at all. He just wanted to get there and hold her in his arms, stroke her hair, dry her tears, and make sure she knew how much he loved her.

He pulled out a small box tucked inside of his carry-on bag and opened it, then he stared down at the one thing that would change their lives forever, if she accepted it. The stones gleamed in the dim light of the cabin. It was a platinum ring with heir- loom diamonds and blue sapphires surrounding the one carat round stone in the center. Mitch knew that Laci wouldn't want a ring that was over-the-top. She would want a simple but elegant one, something that her grandmother might have worn back in the day. So Mitch had contacted Tim, his jeweler and family friend, and together they created something extraordinary. The sapphires were added to represent the rain that Laci loved so much. But even after everything ended, he couldn't bring himself to cancel the order. And during the storm, he realized why he hadn't. After making his flight arrangements, Mitch had called Tim to explain the circumstances and made arrangements to pick it up on his way out of town. He smiled as he pictured Laci's face after seeing the ring and he asked her for her hand in marriage. His stomach suddenly flipped; he felt nervous about how he would ask her, and where. The moment would surely present itself, so he put it out of his mind for the time being.

Only a few more hours until she would be mine forever, he thought to himself. How long their forever would last he wasn't sure, but who really did?

His flight landed earlier than expected so he called Lena to let her know. She sent him a text with the hospital address and he plugged it in to his phone navigation app. He picked up his rental car, and in no time, he was on his way to Laci. His *one.*

stubborn love

Lena read Mitch's text and couldn't stop smiling, knowing he was only an hour away. She knew it was the best thing for Laci, for both of them. *They would need each other more now than ever,* she thought.

"Okay kids, let's move it! Just because you're skipping school this morning doesn't mean we can skip all day, so go get dressed! We're stopping to get your mom some coffee so we need to hurry." Lena told them. She had called the school earlier to let them know the kids would be visiting their mom at the hospital first and then be back to school by lunch. She was also hoping that Mitch would arrive around the same time and that the kids' presence would cushion the blow of his surprise arrival. Lena had a good feeling she wasn't going to be too happy about how he found out, but that was life.

"Are you sure we're not going to get sick when we visit her, Lena?" Travis asked, honestly concerned about being in the hospital. He worried about those things more often than a person of his age should for some reason.

"Yes, buddy. You'll be just fine; I promise." She laughed and gave him a big hug, picking him up off the ground and swinging him around to make him laugh. It worked.

I woke up early, barely having slept the night before. The TV was on but there was no sound; I was just watching a silent movie, numb to everything going on around me. I was still sore from my little adventure yesterday, but mostly I couldn't stop thinking about the treatment scheduled for later today. I was so nervous that I would get sick afterwards, or worse, while it was actually happening. I didn't have much time to dwell on it though because I heard the kids' voices echo down the hall in their excitement. Lena walked in and the kids followed right behind her. They squealed my name and jumped up into my bed, squishing me with their hugs.

"Mom! We missed you!" Emma and Travis shouted as they climbed up into my bed. Todd didn't say much, he just stood in the back with his arms crossed.

"Hi guys!" I said, holding them tight. "I missed you too! I'm so sorry I scared you yesterday, but I'm fine, really. You don't need to worry, okay?" I tried to assure them, but I wasn't too sure myself. "Hi Todd, how are you?" I asked. He looked at me and I could see tears in his eyes.

"I'm fine." But he never looked at me. I knew the events of last night had scared him pretty good. Why had I been so stupid going outside like that? That's the last thing those kids needed was another reason to worry about me.

"I'm so glad you're feeling better, mom," Emma said softly as she hugged me.

"All right you two, get off of your mom so she can breathe." Lena lifted her hand and offered me a beautiful white and green cup. It was warm and soothing to the touch. "I brought you a little something to drink; thought you could use it," she said with a big smile on her face.

"You are an angel, flat out. I love you!" I exclaimed with a smile, sipping my black and white mocha.

"I know you do. And you'll love me even more because I brought you some clean clothes, your makeup, hair stuff, the works. I thought you might like to freshen up."

"Yep, you are the "rock star of the month," woman! What would I do without you?" I asked, smiling at her. Lena's ability to put others' needs before her own never waned – she just kept giving and giving. She was amazing, and I grew more thankful every day that God had it in his plan for our paths to cross when they did. I looked over at the kids, who were already engrossed in a cartoon on my TV. Todd was texting someone on his phone. I turned up the TV volume and Lena moved closer to me so we could talk.

"You would be lost without me, no doubt. But seriously, are you feeling better?"

"Yes, a lot better, honest. I'm a little nervous about today's treatment, but other than that I'm back to normal, or whatever normal is for me," I answered, laughing at my current state.

"Well, being nervous sounds pretty normal to me. But I'm sure it will go fine. I'm just sorry I can't be here with you. I can still ask Sandy for the day off if you want."

"No, no. I'll be fine. Dr. Light said it is a long, boring six hours and I can't have anyone in the room anyway. I will need a ride home, however."

"Your chariot will be ready and waiting, your highness," Lena replied, laughing and bowed in front of me like a goofball. I laughed at her as Nurse Victoria came in my room to check my vitals again, as if they had changed in the last hour. For fun, I thought about holding my breath to freak her out, but I refrained. I had caused enough trouble for one day.

"Is it okay if I change into some real clothes, Victoria?" I asked. Even though my thin backless gown was the latest rage in fashion around there, I had worn it long enough. I missed wearing real clothes.

"I think that would be fine. I'll get you unhooked from your IV and you'll be all set. I heard the doctor say she was going to release you to the oncology department in a little while so they can get you prepped for your first treatment."

"Oh…that's…good, I guess." I wasn't enthused at all with the news, but I knew it would be coming sooner or later. She unhooked me from all the wires and tubes and I got up to go change.

While Laci was in the bathroom changing, Lena received a text from Mitch saying he had arrived at the hospital and was on his way up. She held her breath, excited that he was there, but wondered how things were going to transpire. Lena whispered the news in Emma's ear, and Emma started jumping up and down.

"Where is he?" she asked Lena in a soft whisper, and then she quickly went silent as they heard Laci coming out of the bathroom.

After a quick change of clothes and a splash of makeup, I felt more like myself again, and probably appeared a little less scary. I looked over at Lena and Emma, both acting suspicious, like they were up to no good.

"What are you two talking about over there?" I asked. "Nothing; I was just telling Lena about my new friend that is going to sit by me at lunch today," Emma said, trying to throw her mom off, smiling from ear to ear.

"*Okay*, that's nice." Not believing a word of it, I climbed back into bed and finished my mocha.

Victoria came back in to reconnect my wires and tubes, and on her way out she looked at me and said, "I'll send your gentle- man visitor in now; he's been waiting outside your door for some reason." She winked at me and gave me a thumbs-up. "He's a looker, girl! No wonder you wanted to get dressed!" she said with a smile, and she walked out.

"Umm…wait, Victoria…I don't have any…" But she was gone. I didn't know any gentleman that would be visiting me… not anymore. And certainly none that I would have considered a *looker*.

I looked at Lena and she was smiling, as if she knew some- thing, but I simply turned to watch the door for the mysterious visitor. At first all I saw were flowers as he walked in, but then he turned toward me and lowered the vase. His beautiful eyes stared at me and he smiled. It was *him*! He was there, standing in front of me as big as life— my Mitch.

"Hey, darlin'," he said softly, then he walked closer to me and set the vase down on the table next to me. My eyes grew to twice their normal size, my mouth fell open, and my heart started racing so fast it set off the dang heart monitor. I gasped for air, and gasped again, and again. Apparently I took in a little too much. I saw Victoria rush in, then everything went black and I felt myself falling backward into my bed.

"Laci, wake up sweetie. You had a panic attack. Can you hear me?" Victoria yelled in my ear. My Mitch…I saw him! Or, I thought I did. Was it really him or was I dreaming?

"Yes, I can...hear you," I said as I opened my eyes and looked around the room, but Mitch was nowhere in sight. I was dreaming! That figures... What was I saying – thank goodness I was dreaming!

"I...I thought I saw someone. I'm fine, Victoria. It's nothing." "Oh you saw something all right! That delicious piece of *man* candy is standing outside waiting for you to come around. He feels just awful about causing you to faint," Victoria replied. Having spent the last twenty-four hours with Victoria, I had already determined that she wasn't one to beat around the bush – she was blunt, a matter-of-fact kind of gal, and I respected her for that.

"He's here? He's really here?" I looked at Lena, my hands were shaking and I started to cry. She was nodding her head up and down, confirming my statement. Slowly, my face turned from a "shocked and awed" look to the "mad and angry" look, knowing that someone in the room had some explaining to do as to why he was there and standing outside my room! I wiped the tears from my face and grabbed a few tissues from the box in a fury of rage. Victoria walked out and I looked directly at Lena. The kids were standing next to her and Emma was crying.

"Spill it girl! What's he doing here? How does he even know I'm here, Lena?" I said in an angry, yet subdued voice.

"It's a long story, and I'll tell you everything, but right now—" She was cut off as Mitch slowly walked back into the room and right up to my bed. He was close enough to touch, and smell, and...kiss. *Ugh!* No, I was mad, darn it! I couldn't let myself give in to him! Mitch took my hand and looked straight in my eyes. "Let me start this again. Hi, darlin'." He leaned down and tried to give me a kiss, but I turned my head away from him and he pulled away. I could see him smiling in my peripheral vision which infuriated me, so I turned to face him again.

"Don't you 'hi, darlin'" me. What are you doing here? How did you know I was here? I want answers." I looked at Lena, not happy with the turn of events.

"I missed you," he said softly.

"Oh, stop it! I don't want you here, Mitch!" I said, in as mean a tone as I could muster. I reminded myself again that I was mad. Well, not mad, but I was definitely upset...sort of. Oh who was I trying to fool? All I really wanted to do was grab ahold of him and never let go!

"Yes, you do, and you know it, so stop faking being mad at us." He said, still holding a smug smile on his face.

I threw my head back against my pillow, trying to throw a hissy fit. Dang it! Why did he always have to be right? I did want him there! I just didn't know whether to be mad, happy, sad or plum hacked off that someone told him about all of this. Mitch sat down on the edge of my bed and took my hand into his; it was so warm and soft. Tears started to roll down my cheeks as I looked at him, not able to hold them in any longer.

"Don't be mad," he said as he wiped the tears from my cheeks. "When you fell outside, Emma called me. She was so scared, Laci. And she asked me to come. I called Lena to have her fill in the blanks. So yes, I know everything. And actually, I'm rather upset with *you*! How dare you purposely break up with me to spare my feelings? That should have been my choice, Laci. I love you!" His eyes said it all. He did love me, all of me, even the parts I didn't think he could love. He smiled at me, then he lifted my hand and kissed it in that familiar, sweet way of his. For a moment, I thought I might faint again and almost pressed the nurse's call button!

"I can't let you go through this again, Mitch. It's too much to ask." I pleaded my case, hoping he would understand.

"Since when do you get to decide what's too much for me and what's not? Last I checked, I still have a say in what I do with my life and with whom I choose to spend it."

"I…I'm sorry! I thought I was doing what was best for you. I didn't want you to suffer through this all over again, the hospital, the treatments, losing me to the same disease as Karin. I couldn't live with myself knowing the pain that I would cause you to endure."

"You are exasperatingly stubborn, Ms. Kramer. And I love you! You of all people should know that nothing in this life is guaranteed. When Karin got sick, I had months to prepare for her death. I knew it was coming and the diagnosis wasn't good even from the beginning. But you lost Andrew in the blink of an eye—unexpectedly, with no notice, no sickness; he was just… gone. We both lost someone, but right up until the very end, we loved. I want that with you, darlin'. I choose you! I want to love you forever, whatever that looks like. You can't protect everyone you love from every bad thing, Laci. I love you, and I want to be with you from this moment until our very last." He paused for a moment but he never took his eyes away from me. Then I watched as he reached into his pocket and pulled out a small, blue velvet box. He opened it slowly and took out the most amazing, exquisite ring I had ever seen. The lights above my head shone down and illuminated every stone. Tiny rainbows danced above each one. My hands shook even more and I looked at him in disbelief as the tears started to pour from my eyes. I could feel them roll down my cheeks, totally ruining my fresh makeup job. All that work for nothing!

"I know this probably isn't the most romantic of places, nor is it the way I originally had this planned. It's not a candle-lit room with music playing or some grandstanding gesture in the middle of a huge crowd, but I know in my heart that this is exactly the right time and place. I need you to know that I love you, cancer or no cancer. I don't care what the future holds as long as I am sharing it with you, the good and the bad. You are my future, Laci, and you're the only one I want to love for the rest of my life and yours." His smile grew even bigger as he stood up, then bent down on one knee on the floor next to my bed, took my hand in his, and looked up at me with tears in his eyes. I could barely breathe. This was really happening! The man who strolled into that airport gate and stole my heart now knelt before me, in my hospital bed. I didn't deserve him or his love, but oh how I wanted them both.

"Ms. Laci Kramer, my unexpected surprise, my Airplane Girl, my girl who has hope in the rain, hope in her God above, who changed my life and brought out the man I had buried but always wanted to become, who makes me want to believe that nothing is impossible, who gave me a reason to keep living, will you marry me and allow me to take care of you, to love you, and to keep you safe and happy for the rest of your life?" He slid the ring over my left ring finger and held my hand tight inside his, then paused to wait for my answer.

I had trouble catching my breath and the tears flowed down, but I knew my answer and I wasn't about to make him wait any longer.

"Say yes, mom! What are you waiting for?" Emma screamed out, impatient and beside herself with excitement. Her outburst was impossible to ignore and we all laughed out loud, which broke the tension in the room. My heart raced and I still felt faint, but I stayed locked on his gaze and as my nose dropped and lips quivered, I smiled and answered his question.

"Yes! Yes, of course I'll marry you, my creepy stalker Crawdad fan! I love you!" I shouted, and I quickly climbed off the bed to meet him on the floor. I sobbed and threw my arms around him, holding him tight.

Lena started clapping like she did every time she got all happy and excited and the kids cheered, causing quite a ruckus in the room. We started laughing and helped each other up off the floor, and then he gently picked me up and sat me back on the bed. He moved in closer to me, his body in between my legs that now dangled off the bed and his arms wrapped around me. I rested my head against his chest and held him tight. The familiar sound of his heartbeat put a smile on my face, and I had a sense of peace come over me that I hadn't felt since that roller coaster ride began. Then he brought his warm hands up and cupped them around the sides of my face and kissed me with his soft, tender lips.

I could hear Lena crying, as Travis and Emma both ran up to us and hugged our legs, happier than I ever imagined they would be by that latest development. I couldn't stop smiling. Even in the midst of turmoil and uncertainty, it was the happiest I had felt in years. Mitch pulled away and gave the kids a big hug then lifted them both up onto the bed with me.

"Yeah! Mommy and Mr. Mitch are together again!" Travis said in a happy voice.

"Well, congratulations you two! It's about darn time!" Lena said, sniffing.

"Thank you, Lena. I couldn't have done this without your help. And thank you for being honest with me and not keeping her secret," Mitch said, laughing.

"That's what family is for, right?" Lena said, then she laughed and walked over to give us both a hug. "I'm going to take off and get the kids to school; you two need some private time. Come on, kids, time to go! Give your mom and Mitch a hug."

Todd walked over and gave me a hug, hanging on tightly and crying softly. He lifted his head. "I love you, mom. I'm glad you're okay," he said.

Mitch watched them and then he walked up behind Todd and put a hand on his shoulder to comfort him. He was worried that Todd might be upset by his proposal to his mom.

"Hey Todd, I'm sorry I didn't talk to you about all this first, but I want you to be okay with this, your mom and me getting married. Do we have your blessing?" Mitch asked him. Todd turned around and smiled.

"Me? Oh sure. I'm just glad you're back. I hate being the only man around the house," Todd replied, smiling. His random comment made us laugh. They shook hands, and then Mitch yanked on Todd's arm and pulled him into a manly bear hug. I think it freaked Todd out a little, but it made him smile.

"So about that ride home, your highness?" Lena asked. I looked at Mitch first and started to answer, but he interrupted.

"I'll make sure she gets home safe, Lena," Mitch answered as he stared into my eyes. Never even looking in Lena's direction, he bent down and kissed me. I heard the kids snicker, and then they walked out the door.

He was mine again…and this time it would be forever!

the royal treatment

Alone, finally…in my hospital room. The smell of chlorine bleach and alcohol hung in the air…oh yeah, this was romantic! We sat facing each other on my bed and I spent the next several minutes trying to explain everything to him, the cancer, the rea- son I did what I did, and my recent excursion playing in the rain that had landed me in the hospital. But all I could do was stare at my ring. He had invested so much love in it and taken such care to find it, picking out the sapphires to represent my rain. It was simple and had a charming, old-fashioned character to it, but at the same time it was incredibly beautiful and perfect in every way. It was exactly what I had hoped for someday. I was amazed that in such a short time, he had come to know me so well, better than I knew myself at times. My heart overflowed with joy, realizing that he would soon be mine forever. Part of me still couldn't understand why he chose this, why he wanted me like this – a walking basket of cracked eggs. But hopefully they would make for a good omelet someday. And all that really mattered now was that he *did* want me.

He loved me, cracked eggs and all. My gaze wandered and I got quiet for a minute, lost in my thoughts.

"What are you thinking?" Mitch asked. "Ha! I am thinking so many things right now it's not even possible to put them into words, but mostly about you and how lucky I am that you never gave up on us being together." I smiled and took his soft hands in mine, running my fingers over his, and then pretended to put a ring on his left ring finger.

"I told you before you hung up that day, I wasn't about to give up and that we weren't over. I will admit that Brad told me to stop calling though and give you some space."

"Brad, huh? Your brother Brad, with no relationship experience to speak of at all, actually gave you advice about us?" I had to laugh at that one.

"I know it seems hard to believe, but he did. And, it actually made sense in some weird way."

"Hmm, well, he was right. Every time you would call and I saw your name pop up on my phone, I became even more frustrated and the guilt of what I did magnified. You don't know how bad I wanted to answer, to talk to you and tell you everything, to hear your sweet voice tell me that everything was going to be okay. But I couldn't. I couldn't hurt you even more."

"There is one thing I haven't told you yet about what happened after Emma called, the night I made my decision to come here." Mitch's face grew puzzled, as if he still couldn't understand the event himself.

"What happened?"

"It was a gulley washer, Laci, in the middle of November. I was standing on the porch, trying to wrap my head around what Emma had just told me. I was mad, scared, and felt completely alone and helpless so I just started yelling. I yelled at God from the top of my lungs and the deepest pit of my soul, trying to understand why he would do this to me again. Why he would do this to you! All I could think about was him taking you from me, just like Karin. It scared me to death. That's when the thunder started. It rumbled so loud I felt the vibrations through the porch. Then a lightning bolt came down and hit the power box down the street. You should have seen the sparks fly! I stood there in complete darkness. Then the rain started to fall so hard I couldn't even see the trees in the yard. All I wanted to do was stand in it, so I walked out into the rain and yelled some more. And in that moment, I knew. It was *your* rain. I felt you right there with me and—you'll think I'm crazy—but I could've sworn I heard you calling my name, Laci. I know it was probably my mind playing tricks on me, but it's the truth. I knew you needed me and I needed you too."

"Whoa. That is definitely goose bump–worthy. Lena, she told me I kept calling out for you. I was kind of 'out-of-it' so I really don't remember, but I do remember yelling your name when I was outside, playing in the rain. I wanted so badly for you to hear me." Then I felt my head start to spin a little. That story, along with others like how our spouses had died the same year and how he wasn't even supposed to be on that flight with me, made me realize that all these things happened to bring us to that very moment in time, that perfect moment.

"Well, I heard you." He smiled at me, then leaned over and gave me a kiss. The nurse cleared her through throat as she walked in my room and we sat up and smiled at each other.

"I hear congratulations are in order?" Victoria asked with a pink blush in her cheeks as she smiled.

"Yes, ma'am. She said yes!" Mitch replied.

"Well, congratulations to both of you! You've had quite a morning, Laci!" she giggled, then continued. "And I have release papers for you."

"That's good, but I'm not heading home just yet, am I?" I asked, but already knew the answer.

"Nope. They want me to escort you down to oncology to start your treatment. It says here you'll have two treatments today," she said, reading the paperwork. "After the first one, you'll have a six-hour wait in between. Providing they get started on time, you should be home by seven or so tonight. It's going to be a long day, so prepare yourself."

As she reviewed the upcoming events of the day, the reality of what lay ahead was now upon us. I was nervous thinking about it and wondered if it would hurt or what the treatment would do to me, if I would get sick or have any side effects. But there was no sense dwelling on it. I would do what I had to do, and hope for the best. And now that Mitch was here by my side, I knew I could handle anything.

We made our way to the oncology department, Mitch on foot behind me and my wheelchair escort. Dr. Conley, my oncologist, was waiting in the reception area. I got up out of the chair and introduced her to my fiancé. She walked us through the procedure, explained how everything would work, and then introduced me to Iris, my technician for the day. Iris was a very pretty lady, beautiful brown complexion, most likely of Middle Eastern descent. I loved her accent. I could tell she had a kind heart and was quite patient with us as we asked her several questions. Through our short conversation, I learned she had a PhD and was highly technical, but she gave me every confidence that she knew what she was doing.

"I'm afraid there is no one else allowed in the treatment room, however. Your fiancé will have to wait in a designated room around the corner. The prep and treatment should take about an hour all together," Iris commented and she looked over at Mitch, then smiled. When I heard her say the word fiancé, I couldn't help but smile. I loved hearing it – I loved saying it.

Mitch turned to face me and pulled me into his arms. "Well, I'd better give you a good luck kiss now, huh?" he asked, and he kissed me gently.

"Hmm, maybe one more, my fiancé…just for good measure." He laughed and kissed me again, then gave me a hug and whispered in my ear, "I'll be right here when you get back, darlin'.

I love you."

I walked away with Iris, then turned to see his sweet face just before we rounded the corner ahead. He was still watching and blew me a kiss.

The treatment room was quiet and secluded. I sat in a chair while she plugged in the IV drip and took my vitals, and then she walked me over to a tall bed on wheels. She helped me up and I tried to get comfortable, but it was like laying on a slab of cold concrete. Once there, she connected my catheter to what she referred to as "the juice." I had to laugh at her terminology. She would mention juice…my stomach was growling. Why didn't I eat? Well, that's easy – because I would have hurled it all up the minute treatment started that's why. And I was too busy get- ting engaged!

Thirty minutes later, I was hooked-up, prepped-up, and already fed-up thinking about going through that ordeal twice a day over the next four days. There wasn't much pain during the prep process—a few sticks and pokes, but overall not bad. So far, the best part was the hot blankets Iris kept covering me with to keep me warm in this Arctic tundra of a room. I couldn't help but wonder what Mitch was thinking as he sat in the waiting room. Was he thinking about us and our upcoming wedding? Ah! I'm going to be Mrs. Mitchell Young! Or…was he remembering Karin and her ordeal? I still don't think he realizes how hard this was going to be, the pain of losing Karin could start all over again and I would be the source of that pain. But, maybe I didn't give him enough credit. He's probably stronger than I realized…

⁓⁓⁓

After Laci left his sight, Mitch bent over and took a few deep breaths, trying to calm his nerves. He walked around pacing the floors, then decided to grab the closest magazine and sat down. He flipped through it in a matter of seconds, then got up and started pacing again. He was a bundle of nerves and his mind was in a million different places—the past, the present, and everywhere in between. He thought it best if he stayed out of the past. Still, he couldn't help but recall all the waiting he had done when Karin came in for her chemo treatments and how he watched as it slowly took its toll on her body until she couldn't fight it any- more. And then it hit him: that maybe God had allowed him to walk down that path with Karin, even losing her to the disease, to prepare him and make him stronger for his future, for Laci. And he was stronger now. He knew what to expect and knew he could encourage her even when she felt like giving up.

Once again, he sat down. This time, he closed his eyes and just thought about Laci—how she looked the day they met, her laugh, how she made fun of his Crawdads, her love of coffee, or rather her obsession with coffee, and how her face had lit up when he proposed. Those images brought an immediate smile to his face and he knew without a doubt that he was exactly where he belonged—there with her.

He decided to call Caleb and his mom to give them an update about Laci's health, and then shared the good news that she was now his fiancé. They were both thrilled and passed along their blessing and prayers for her. Brad, however, would be a different conversation entirely and Mitch would have to find the right time to tell him.

———∿∿○◠◡◠◡◠◡○◠∿∿———

"All right Laci, we're almost ready to begin. Would you like me to put some music on in the background during your treatment?" Iris asked.

"That would be nice, thank you, Iris. Will you be around if I need anything?" I asked, nervous about being in there alone.

"Oh yes. I'll be in that booth right up there and we'll be able to communicate through this intercom," she said, pointing to a little box on the table next to my bed. "Just push this button if you need to talk to me, okay? Everything will be just fine," she assured me and gently patted my arm in consolation. "Are you ready?" she asked.

"As I'll ever be, I suppose," I replied, reluctant of course, but ready to get it over with.

The treatment only lasted about twenty minutes. The "juice" felt cold going in, but the sensation didn't last long, and eventually I didn't feel anything. Naturally, the heat had long left the blankets that covered me. So to keep my mind off of being cold, I closed my eyes, listened to the music, and prayed, mostly asking God for healing. It was the longest twenty minutes I had ever experienced, my mind racing with one thought after another. I walked through the last twenty-four hours, playing in the rain, falling, how Emma even thought to call Mitch afterwards, him standing in the rain and hearing me call his name, his coming here and, in spite of everything, proposing to me knowing full well my diagnosis and the uncertainty of the journey still ahead. I was so thankful for everything I had in my life right then, my kids, Mitch, my friends, the privilege of being blessed with so much when I deserved so little. Whatever happened next, I would always be grateful to God for the life I was given. And I closed my eyes to rest.

After my treatment was over, Iris came in and unhooked me from the juice, gave me some water, drew some blood, and thirty minutes later, I was being wheeled over to the waiting area. We turned the corner and my eyes lit up the minute I saw Mitch's face; he was waiting for me just like he promised. He came over and bent down next to me, brushed the hair from my eyes, kissed me on the forehead then helped me up out of the chair. I could tell he was worried about me, and maybe even a little nervous, but it was sweet. And I was just glad to have him here by my side. "I'll see you back here in six hours, Laci. You are both welcome to stay here and wait, but you may want to go home and get some rest. You'll be feeling the effects of the treatment soon if you haven't already." Iris said and she walked out, leaving me in Mitch's care.

"Are you okay? How did it go?" he asked.

"Um, it was fine. It didn't hurt and I didn't get sick, so I con- sider it a success." I smiled, spilling out a yawn.

"That's what I like to hear." He wrapped his arms around me. "There are some nice snacks over here, are you hungry?" He walked me over to the buffet of finger foods on a small table.

It was the only waiting room on the floor where patients didn't have to rely on a vending machine to get nourishment. Iris said that church groups and various organizations around town donated items every day for cancer patients. I was not only grateful for the snacks, seeing as that I was starving, but also for the people who brought them. I vowed to myself that someday, I would be part of this effort to support those that came after me. It seemed like such a small thing, but to me, it was huge. I enjoyed a snack and some coffee with Mitch, and then we headed home. I fell asleep the minute we started driving. It was only a fifteen-minute drive, but I couldn't stay awake. After we arrived, he helped me inside, flipped on the fireplace, closed the blinds, and we curled up on the couch. My head was in his lap and he just held me close while we talked.

"It's kind of weird being here. I didn't think I would ever see you, the kids, or this house again," he said and I felt horrible as I relived the pain I caused him.

"I'm sorry, Mitch. I wish I could take back what I did. I was so stupid to push you away." I looked away to avoid his gaze, embarrassed by my actions.

He turned my face toward him. "I'm not. You did what you did because you loved me. I always knew you did." He smiled.

"I do, and always will, Mr. Young," I said. My heart overflowed as I reached up and pulled his face down toward me, drinking in his sweet, warm lips.

We sat and enjoyed each other's company for as long as possible, but Iris was right. The effects of the treatment had already begun and all I wanted to do was sleep. I couldn't keep my eyes open. Mitch walked me upstairs and tucked me into bed, then he pulled a chair over next to me, refusing to leave my side. He simply watched TV and read while I lay there and slept.

Five hours later, Mitch woke me to get ready. I got up slowly and started to climb off the bed, and that was when I noticed the drastic difference—my energy and bodily strength had virtually disappeared and I struggled to stand. Mitch had to help me off the bed and basically carried me down the stairs. It was a strange feeling, as if my body was moving through water. The harder I pushed myself, the more resistance I felt. The kids were home and Lena was cooking dinner, so we said a quick goodbye and left for round two.

Iris met us in the foyer, and she walked me back. She noticed the change in my energy level right away as she prepped me for the treatment. Then right before it began, Dr. Conley came in to check on me and ask how things were going.

"How are you doing, Laci? Are you feeling sick or experiencing any pain since the first treatment?"

"No pain to speak of, but I feel heavy and very tired. Does that make sense?"

"Yes, and it's a typical reaction to the MammoSite treatment. You're basically receiving a concentrated dose of medicine to treat the cancer. Typically, in other patients, this same dosage would be administered over a period of two to three days. It will definitely take a toll on your energy level, so be prepared to sleep a lot this week and in the weeks to come after the treatment is over," she stated.

"I like sleep. Sleep is good. I don't think I'll have any trouble following that prescription," I replied, smiling. And round two began.

Once we were back home, I could barely sit for even a few minutes without falling asleep, so I said good night to everyone and called it a night. Lena followed me up and helped me change into my PJ's, and then I crawled into bed.

"I love you, girl. I know Mitch is here now, but you yell if you need anything, even if it's in the middle of the night," she said and she gave me a hug.

"I will. Thank you, sweetie. I love you too." She left the room and Mitch came in right behind her and sat down on the bed next to me.

"I'm going to hang out downstairs with Lena and the kids for a little while if that's okay. And, I know this isn't my normal practice, but I'd like to sleep here tonight. I'll just crash on your couch, but I want to be here, in case you need me," Mitch said softly. His sweet southern voice made my heart flutter. I reached up and laid my hand on his cheek as he hovered over me.

"No," I whispered. "Not downstairs. I want you in here, with me." And I patted the empty place next to me in the bed. "Please? I promise I won't compromise your virtue in any way." I smiled at him and he laughed softly.

"Okay, if you're sure that's what you want."

"The closer I can be to you right now, the better," I replied, and he leaned down and kissed me good night then turned out my light. I didn't remember him leaving the room.

Mitch went downstairs and visited with the kids for a while, helping Emma with her homework and playing a game on the Xbox with Travis. After they went off to bed, he spent some time talking with Lena.

"So, how's our girl doing?" Lena asked.

"She's exhausted. Today was only day one and she's already spent. It's going to be a long week. She's definitely not our happy, fun-loving Laci right now, but it's to be expected."

"Well, you just worry about her. I'll take care of the kids this week and fix all the meals. She's going to need you now more than ever, my dear."

"I know. This is where I'm meant to be; it's where I was always meant to be, with her. Why couldn't she see that?" he asked Lena, looking for answers to help make sense of everything.

"I don't know. She was too scared, I guess. The day she called you and ended things, she changed, like a switch just flipped off inside of her. She was doing what she had to do. But that's all over now. It's a new beginning for both of you, and after her treatment and recovery, we have a wedding to plan!"

"We certainly do." Mitch answered.

"But you have another long day ahead of you, so you'd better get some rest, my friend."

"Yeah, guess you're right. About that, I don't know if this bothers you or not, but I'll be sleeping in Laci's room."

"Mitch, why on earth would that bother me? It makes me feel better knowing you'll be close to her. Besides, I don't think she'll be in any mood for 'hanky-panky.'" Lena said and she laughed quietly.

"You actually used the words 'hanky-panky'? Seriously?" Mitch couldn't help but laugh.

"Oh, you know what I mean."

"Yes, I do, and on that note, I'll say good night, Lena."

"Good night, *lover boy*," she said in a silly tone and she continued to laugh all the way up to her room.

Mitch just shook his head back and forth, amazed by Lena's good heart and sense of humor. It was refreshing and he was so glad that she was part of Laci's life. Before he went to bed, he decided to take a few minutes to relax and enjoy the quiet of the house. He turned off most all the lights except for a small lamp and sat down on the couch. He was exhausted, almost too exhausted to sleep. Instead, he reviewed the events of the last twenty-four hours in his head and smiled. That day, he felt a tremendous weight had been lifted from him now that he had Laci back in his life and she had agreed to marry him. That weight however was replaced by another—her cancer. But, even as worried as he was, it felt different; he could feel it. God had given him an indescribable peace about everything, despite the unknown.

"She's going to be all right, I know it," he said into the void. He certainly didn't see it as a perfect start to their new life together, but it was a start and that was all the mattered. She didn't ask for it, nor did anyone, but getting her through it was his one and only concern. He knew his role was one of support and love, but also to remain upbeat and put her needs first, and keep that beautiful smile on her face. They were all things he was more than happy to do, both now and for the rest of her life.

Mitch looked at his watch and yawned. It was late, but he decided to call Brad and give him an update. Out of anyone back home, he would surely still be awake.

"H-Hello?" Brad mumbled.

"Are you asleep?" Mitch asked, surprised.

"It's after midnight here, remember little brother? Or do you forget that too when you're in the 'Laci time zone'?"

"Sorry, dude. I just wanted to give you the news. Are you coherent or should I call back tomorrow?"

"No, no, I'm awake now…please continue!" Brad yawned; he was obviously none too thrilled by the late-night call.

"Well, first off, Laci is better for the most part. She's out of the hospital and started treatment today, but it wiped her out. It will be a long week for her to say the least. Second, and my favorite news of the day—she said yes, Brad. Laci and I are getting married!" Mitch's voice picked up volume a little in his excitement.

"You proposed, already? For crying out loud, you just got there! I thought you were going to wait a few days to make sure…you know, make sure it was the right decision?"

"Brad, she broke up because of the cancer, not because she didn't love me anymore. She loved me so much she was willing to let me go so I wouldn't have to go through this again. Haven't you ever loved anyone that much? Honestly?"

"Honestly? It's too late at night to even answer that question. And honestly, I think she was doing you a favor. I happen to agree with her decision to let you go. You shouldn't have to go through this again; it's not like she was already your wife or anything. You're not obligated to her! And besides, when you lost Karin, I lost you too, remember? I can't lose you again, Mitch. I just got you back, man."

Underneath Brad's words, Mitch could hear his pain. It was then that he knew that it wasn't Laci at all; it was the fear of losing him to Laci. Still, he could feel his heart race and he felt the urge to reach through the phone and strangle some sense into his brother, once and for all.

"You are so selfish at times! Don't you realize that Laci *is* the reason you got me back! I'm not going to lose her; I know it. And you won't lose me either, but I can't let her go through this alone. From the first minute I ever laid eyes on her…" Mitch sighed and paused for a moment to calm his nerves. "I knew. We were meant to be together, Brad, from the very beginning. I love her, brother." "I know. I guess I've always known; I just didn't want to you to leave. I want you to be happy, Mitch. I really do." Brad said, resigned to his brother's decision. He now realized he had been selfish. The truth was that Brad had always known that Laci was the reason for his brother's happiness. He wasn't just worried that Mitch would leave though; he was jealous. He wanted it for himself—love.

"I am, and thank you. Are we good?" Mitch asked.

"We're good, I promise. So any idea when you'll be home? No rush, just curious."

"Would you mind if I stayed through Thanksgiving? I just want to get her through treatment and make sure she's strong enough to be on her own before I leave."

"Works for me, and tell her I said hi and that I hope she feels better soon. I mean it."

"Thanks Brad. I'll tell her. I love you, brother."

"Love you too; now stop calling me in the middle of the night, will ya?" They laughed and said goodbye.

Upstairs, he threw on his sweats and a T-shirt, then he crawled into bed next to Laci and covered up. She was facing him and all he could do was stare at her, feeling a little awkward at first, but she was so beautiful, peaceful, and serene. In that perfect moment, he couldn't imagine being anywhere else but right there, next to his bride-to-be.

hope returns

The two-a-day treatments took every ounce of energy I had. Thursday was the worst. I couldn't sleep, but I wanted to more than anything. Mitch and I sat up in my room for hours that night and talked about the holidays ahead, his family, my family, and the wedding.

"Laci, I've been thinking. I know it's not your home yet, but what would you think about getting married in Crystal Creek… at the Young Vines Winery…in the wedding barn? We could be the very first couple to marry there; sort of 'christen' it for other couples to come."

The very thought of getting married in that barn made my heart rate go up as I remembered the day he had showed it to me for the first time. Ever since then, that was exactly what I had dreamt when I thought about the possibility of marrying him. He didn't know that of course. My cheeks were flushed and I felt a few tears escape—tears of joy.

"Wait a minute, back up! You named the winery and you're just now sharing it with me?"

"Well, I thought it would be more of a surprise this way. We named it Young Vines to represent the three Young men – a tribute to our family legacy. Our logo shows three grape vines winding around the label, twisted together – one for each of us; Brad, Caleb, and me. Caleb actually came up with the logo. It looks
 pretty cool. Now, are you going to answer the important question too or just comment on the name of the winery?"

I laughed. "I would be honored to marry you at your winery, Mr. Young!"

"Really? Are you sure, Laci? Because you know I'll marry you here if that's what you want; this is your home."

"Again, I know I'm a woman and can frequently change my mind, but I'm fairly certain that was a yes! Besides, my home is wherever you are. You live in Crystal Creek, and your business is there too, so that's where I want to be. Young Vines Winery, I love the name, Mitch!" I smiled and he pulled me over and hugged me where I sat, squeezing the air right out of my lungs. I was so drained though that I could barely revel in the joy of the moment. "Ouch!" I winced. "Watch the juice tube there. I still have one treatment to go yet."

"Oh, sorry, darlin'. I'll be so glad when this is over for you." "I know, me too. But back to those plans, what did you mean earlier when you said 'it's not your home yet'?" I asked. A quirky smile appeared on my face.

He grinned and said, "Well, I was hoping you and the kids would move to North Carolina, build a new life there with me. Would you want that? After you are strong enough, of course. And I'm not above bribery either. To sweeten the deal, I'd like to offer you a job."

Just to mess with him, using my best fake southern accent, I said, "Well, gracious me, sweetie, once we're married you won't have to pay for those services; they'll be free with a signed marriage contract!" I batted my eyelashes at him, then got so tickled at my own lame humor that my incisions started to hurt and throb a little. He laughed at me too, of course.

"Haha, very funny, Ms. Kramer," he said, laughing. "I meant your real job. You would be the new marketing and events director for the winery." I could tell he was very proud of the title he'd created for me. "Seriously though, what do you think, about moving?" he asked, gently moving the hair out of my eyes like he always did.

"I wouldn't want to be anywhere else, Mitch. Job or no job. You have a winery to run and I want to be a part of it, help you get it off the ground," I said softly and I took his hands. "I'll need to talk to the kids, of course, but only as a formality. And they'll no doubt put up a good defense, but in the long run, they'll just have to understand that this is what's best for all of us. And it's what I want more than anything. I love you." I pulled him close and kissed his sweet lips.

He leaned up and put my chin in his hands, holding it between his thumb and forefinger, so close I could still feel his breath on my face, and said "I love you, too. I don't know what I did to deserve you, darlin', but whatever it was, I'll spend the rest of my life to make sure I don't lose you." He smiled and pulled me close, holding me in his arms. Then I heard him whisper in my ear, "Even if that means taking you to countless Crawdad games," he said with a chuckle.

"You can 'take me out to the ballgame' anytime handsome," I replied, and smiled, but as I pulled away, tears filled my eyes. I had finally reached that point of complete and total exhaustion, and it was evident to Mitch as well.

As we sat on my bed, he took me by the hand and closed his eyes. I watched his mouth move but no words were heard, just a soft prayer going up on my behalf. I stared at him, amazed by his strength and unending faith, and I smiled and closed my eyes to join him. My eyes grew heavy and the last thing I remember was Mitch kissing me good night.

I woke up the next morning with him lying by my side, having slept the entire night without waking once, which hadn't happened in over a week. That was some prayer! Now, head-on, I faced my last day of the "royal treatment," but hopefully the beginning of a cancer-free life.

———⟡———

t had been a week since my radiation treatments ended. Those five long days of two treatments a day seemed to last forever and took its toll on me in every way possible. The complete exhaustion I felt was unrivaled by anything I had ever experienced before and all I could do was sleep. But since then, I've slowly started to gain my strength back, taking it one day at a time.

It was Thanksgiving Day and I woke up to the sound of the Macy's Day Parade on the television and the smell of coffee in the air. I had so much to be thankful for and I didn't even know where to begin. I immediately thought of one thing, and that was my very special surprise of Evan and Caleb. They had both flown in to spend the holiday weekend with us. My new family was all together again and it felt good.

"Good morning, darlin'. How are you feeling on this fine, Thanksgiving day?" he asked as I walked into the kitchen, his arms outstretched and inviting me in for a warm hug. I didn't waste any time and walked right into his embrace.

"Morning! I feel pretty good, actually. Not much pain at all." I was surprised that I hadn't noticed that earlier. My catheter was removed after the treatment was over and that incision, as well as the incision under my left arm, had both caused me a lot of pain over the last several days. Neither one had healed as fast as they should have, but they looked much better that day.

"That's definitely something to be thankful for, as are you," he said and he gave me a quick kiss. He then smiled at me, but he had that *look* on his face.

"What's wrong?" I asked.

"Oh, it's nothing really. It's just…today was the day I had planned on proposing to you, during dinner, if you and the kids had come down. I had it all planned out."

"Aww, Mitch. I'm so sorry it didn't go according to your plan, but I'm not sorry about how it worked out." I pulled him close. "I'm sure that a proposal in front of your family would have been very sweet, but think of it like this: not only did you get a two-week jump on being engaged to me, you also got to sleep in my bed before our wedding night!" I laughed, then kissed him on the cheek.

"That's a *big* emphasis on *sleeping*." He laughed. "And no, not exactly what I had planned, but I agree, it was definitely bet- ter." He smiled then let me go so he could stir his grits; that, along with homemade biscuits and jam, was apparently a Young family tradition on Thanksgiving morning. I, for one, couldn't stand grits. I wondered if his tradition would become our first fight once I broke the news to him. Nah… I just laughed at him, poured myself a cup of coffee, then sat down on the couch with the kids and watched the parade.

The day flew by and I cherished every moment as we shared our first Thanksgiving together. I looked around the table at each face: Todd, Emma, Travis, Evan, Caleb, and my husband-to-be. Never had I been so thankful for what God had given me—my kids, Mitch, the breath in my lungs, the days I had yet to come, our upcoming wedding, and our future. It was more than I could bear and I felt the tears well up inside.

"Ah, Mom, don't cry. It's time to carve the turkey!" Evan said, trying to lighten the moment. I laughed at his corny voice.

"I'm sorry. I can't help it. I'm thankful for each of you and love you all so much." I blubbered, reaching for a napkin to wipe my tears. At different intervals, they all chimed in with various forms of 'I love you too' and Emma, now crying with me, got up from her chair and came over to give me a hug.

"Well, I would like to propose a toast," Mitch said as he held up a wine glass in his left hand and his right hand held mine. The kids picked up their water glasses and followed his example. Although they were not too familiar with the practice, they thought it was cool, for sure. "To Laci, for finding the strength to face your cancer with a smile on your face and fierce optimism in your heart, for being a loving mother, and for loving me and agreeing to be my wife. I love you, darlin'. I'm truly thankful to have you in my life." And they all lifted their glasses to me and drank.

"Speaking of weddings, have you two set a date yet?" Evan asked. I looked at Mitch and we both smiled, waiting for just the right moment to tell them.

"Well, yes we have," I replied.

"I think you should get married during spring break, on the beach in Florida or something so we can surf while we're there," Caleb spouted out and everyone cracked up at his suggestion.

"Oh yeah, Mom and Mitch getting married right alongside a few hundred drunk college kids; that's romantic," Todd interjected. "Your mom and I are getting married on April third in North Carolina—at the winery. Two weeks before the grand opening. We'll be the first couple to get married in the new wedding barn," he said, smiling from ear to ear as his gaze locked on mine.

"Really?" Emma exclaimed in surprise. "Why there? Why not up here? My friends won't get to come now." She pouted at the thought.

"Well, it's easier for both of our families to have it there, and it's where we want to get married. It's not really up for debate. Plus, it's warm and sunny there, perfect for an outdoor wedding." I said.

"Should we tell them the other part?" Mitch asked.

"What other part?" Evan asked with a curious smile.

"Might as well." And I looked around the table, took a deep breath, and announced, "Mitch has asked us to move to North Carolina and live with him, probably in March after I've had time to heal and get back to normal. I want to be there to help plan the wedding. And he even offered me a job doing all the marketing and event planning for the winery—weddings, parties, and everything in between. Mitch is going to look for a house for us when he goes back home." I exhaled and waited for the outpouring of opinions and disapproval. To my delight however, it didn't come right away.

"Wow, that's awesome!" Evan said, and gave Caleb a high five, obviously happy with the upcoming change of scenery.

"You're the least affected by this; why are you so excited?" I asked, laughing.

"Because of all the hot southern chicks I'll get to meet! Caleb said they're all over the place down there!"

"Oh, he did, did he?" Mitch asked, giving Caleb a 'look' of disapproval. But then he just started laughing and said, "He's right; they're everywhere."

"Mitch!" I yelled, and I punched him playfully in the side of the arm. That was when I caught a glimpse of Emma and saw the tears in her eyes. Oh boy, there it comes. I knew this wasn't going to be easy, but this may be more than I could take right now. She wouldn't come right out and speak her mind, so I nudged Mitch's knee under the table so he would look at her and help me deal with it.

"Are you getting fresh with me at the Thanksgiving dinner table, darlin'?" he asked with a quirky smile and moved a little closer to me to have some fun. I gave him my 'are-you-serious' look and nodded my head in Emma's direction. Besides, as my new husband, he needed to learn what 'the look' was right?

"I'll take that as a no then—" When he saw Emma, he realized what was going on, nodding his head at me that he'd figured it out. I was impressed he'd learned that so quickly. He was definitely a keeper!

"Hey Emma, how do you feel about moving sweetie? Be honest okay?" Mitch asked her sweetly.

She looked at him with pouty eyes. "This is the only home I've ever known; all my friends are here. I...I don't want to move. I want you and Mom to be happy, but why can't you move here?" "Well, we talked about that, Emma, but it's just too hard with the winery. I have a business to run there, and even though your mom has a job here, she can do her job anywhere and I can't. Do you understand? I know it's not easy to move, trust me. I moved around a lot as a kid too, but after I was settled into a new place, I made new friends and life went on. It will just take time to get used to it." Mitch got up from the table and went around and kneeled on the floor next to her and took her by the hand. "I love you, Em. I love all of you, and I promise to do whatever I can to make it a good place for you to live." Mitch explained, trying to convey how much she meant to him. It was like watching a baby eat chocolate cake for the first time...she just devoured every piece of it right from his hand. This southern charm thing was really starting to hack me off now...

"I know you will." And she gave him a big hug and her tears were dry within minutes. "When we move, do I get my own room?" she asked, and we all started laughing. She got over that quick! My daughter...the 10-year-old tidal wave of drama, and I wouldn't have her any other way.

"I'm sure we can work something out," he answered, smiling at her.

He laughed some more, and we enjoyed our turkey and dressing and pumpkin pie, then talked about the upcoming move and the wedding for what seemed like hours. Finally, after lots of good debate, we had everyone's approval to begin a new adventure.

The day after Thanksgiving was traditionally set aside for deco- rating and putting up the Christmas tree, but I was so tired I could barely hang the stockings. So, with my Christmas music playing to set the mood, Mitch and the kids did everything. He brought in all the totes from the garage, and with one decoration after another, they adorned my house with the Christmas spirit. Although I missed being part of it, the joy I felt as I watched them laugh together and have fun being a family was beyond measure.

The funniest part was watching Todd, Caleb, and Evan bond as they untangled the strings of lights then hung the garland on the tree—crooked. Mitch helped Emma climb a small ladder to put the angel on the tree and then we turned off all the big lights in the room, sat back, and admired their work. The glow of the holiday season filled the room with a warmth that only came with that time of year. I made homemade hot cocoa with marshmallows, and we spent the rest of the night watching one Christmas movie after another on the Hallmark channel. It was my favorite holiday pastime, next to baking cookies with Emma, which I would have to save for another day.

Mitch went upstairs for a few minutes then came back down holding a small box, wrapped in Christmas paper and a small red ribbon. I looked at him with a spark of curiosity, wondering when he'd had time to shop during the madness of those recent weeks. He sat down next to me and handed me the box.

"What's this? It's not Christmas yet!"

"I know. It was originally your birthday gift, but with every- thing going on, I forgot about it. I came across it in my suitcase when I was packing and thought it would be more fun to make it your first Christmas present. Open it," he said, smiling. I untied the ribbon and unwrapped my present like a lion devouring its prey. Inside was a familiar hinged box, just like to the one I had received in the hospital, only longer. I opened the box and inside was a dainty, silver Pandora bracelet adorned with two more little round charms like the one he had sent before. One charm had a small engagement ring on the outside, and the other just said "Forever." He helped me put it around my wrist and I climbed into his lap, wrapped my arms around his neck, and looked into his sweet face.

"Oh, Mitch, it's beautiful! Thank you!"

"You're welcome. Now you have a place for your raindrop charm. Merry early Christmas, Laci. I love you," he whispered. He wrapped his arms around me. His lips found mine and I felt every ounce of his love, longing for the day when we would love each other as man and wife.

Mitch and Caleb returned home and within a week, I had received a dozen emails from him with pictures of houses for sale, none of which really grabbed my attention yet, but it was fun to shop nonetheless.

It had been a month since my surgery. I grew tired easily, but I improved with each passing day. I still had to be extra careful with my left arm. Since they had removed my lymph nodes from that arm, even the smallest cut or scrape could cause an infection and make me really sick. The best part was that I felt well enough to have my parents come up and spend a couple weeks with us at Christmas – it was so nice to see them again. Mitch mailed us a ton of presents since he couldn't be here and the kids were now even bigger fans than before. As if that was even possible…he had all of them wrapped around his little finger. My mom and I took a day and went shopping for a wedding dress and I finally settled on one from a local dress shop in town. It was amazing and I could hardly wait to wear it! Thanks to my parents, it was a wonderful, relaxing holiday. I was sad to see them go, but it was nice to have things back to normal…or at least the new *'post- cancer'* normal.

I returned to work for half days and slept the other half to maintain my energy as best I could. While at the office, I had lots of help with the remaining wedding plans. Between the girls at work and my church family, the kids and I had meals brought out at least twice a week. I couldn't have managed without them. Well, that wasn't true. I could have managed, but I'm sure my kids would have grown tired of cocoa crunch cereal every night. By February, I was back to work full time and getting things ready for the person that would take over my position. I held the fantastical notion that no one could ever take my place, but I was sure Sandy would eventually need someone so I had to get over that pretty quick.

———∿∾◦◖◈◗◦∾∿———

Time moved on, faster every day. That day would be no exception. It was my last day at the bank and my stomach already felt sick at the thought of leaving them behind. They've been with me through everything…from losing Andrew, kid problems, picking the wrong men, meeting strange men on an airplane, to facing cancer, my greatest challenge ever. They showed me the true depth of their friendship during that time and stood by me through it all. I tried to hold back the tears as I fixed my hair and re-did my makeup for the third time now, but it didn't work.

Mitch knocked on the bathroom door and I told him to come in.

"It's time to go, darlin'," he said. He had flown in a few days before to help me finish packing, ship my car, and fly with us to our new home. He was the only way I would get through the day. "I know. I'm ready, I guess, physically anyway," I said in a gloomy tone.

We dropped the kids off at school and stopped in at my Starbucks for my last work morning black-and-white mocha. Peggy made my drink; she calls it the "Laci special" as I've been ordering that same drink every morning for over a year. I said my goodbyes to the whole crew and went on my way, crying again as we drove off. Mitch dropped me off at the bank and gave me a good-luck kiss.

"Have a good day, darlin'. It will be all right, I promise. Just call when you're ready," he said in his sweet voice.

We spent the day goofing off, eating too much junk food, crying, laughing, doing minimal work unless we couldn't avoid it, and just enjoying each other. But it was time to say goodbye and I couldn't put it off any longer. Everyone stood around just waiting for someone to say something. So I did.

"For the last five years, you have all been my friends and my family. You were never just coworkers. I will miss you more than

you know. I love you guys." That was all I could manage to get out before the tears overwhelmed me.

One by one, they said goodbye and they gave me hugs, crying right along with me.

"You and Mitch have an amazing love, you know. Finding each other the way you did after everything you two had lost, it's so obvious that he was always meant to find you. I've never seen you happier and I know it will last forever," Sandy said, wiping the tears from her eyes.

"If we have a love even close to what you and John have together, I will consider myself very blessed indeed. Thank you, Sandy, for everything. I love you," I said, and I cried even harder as I hugged her goodbye.

Lena, Teri, and Gail walked me outside to meet Mitch, and we said our last goodbyes at the car. They waved as we drove off, and once we turned the corner, I never looked back. It was hard to think about my life in Washington coming to a close after everything I had been through there, but my new life with Mitch awaited and I could hardly wait.

wedding, wine, and a chance of rain

I stood staring out the window of the upstairs office in the winery, which had been temporarily transformed into a bridal dressing room, and watched as the wind picked up pink dogwood blossoms and tossed them through the air. Spring in North Carolina had finally arrived, and just in time too. It was my wedding day after all!

The sun was already shining bright and I couldn't stop smiling. I could see the activity below as the flowers arrived and chairs were set up. And much to my surprise, Lena and Sandy had flown down to see me get hitched to my Airplane Man. I could already hear Lena laughing. It was poetic that they would be there since they had watched it unfold from the very beginning. Evan, Caleb and Todd were all helping set up chairs and goofing off; they were soon to be brothers.

My most special gift arrived yesterday, however: Laura and her husband David. Laura has been my best friend for the past seventeen years; with me in spirit every step of the way during my cancer just like I was through hers. She had agreed to be my matron-of-honor, so we spent most of that day shopping for her dress and sharing some good girlfriend time together. It was a long, grueling day of fun, laughing, wine tasting, and more laughing as we created some new memories together – exactly what I needed before my big day. After the kids and I had arrived a few weeks ago, we moved into Mitch's house since it wasn't sold yet, and he moved in with Brad. He didn't want us living together until after everything was "official." Such a romantic!

Due to a sad turn of events, however, we didn't even have to buy a house. Mitch's uncle had passed away from severe pneumonia not long after Mitch returned home from visiting me in Washington. In the will, he'd left his three-thousand-square-foot house to Mitch and "his new family." It was a gorgeous, two-story log home with every modern convenience inside. Most of the woodwork had been crafted by his uncle's own hand and we were honored to call it our home. Although we missed him dearly, we were thankful that God had prepared a place for us long before we ever knew that we'd need it. Actually, once I thought about it, I realized that God had prepared the way for us since the very beginning. Why did it take me so long to see that?

The entire family had worked countless hours to get the winery ready to open and the wedding barn ready for that night's inaugural ceremony. When we weren't working on that, Mitch and I were working on our new house, trying to make it our own. My mom and Mitch's mom, Maggie, were both fussing over my hair and makeup. During which time, they also tried to get to know each other. As endearing as it was, if I had heard them compare one more *old-fashioned* recipe and debate about whose was better, I would have screamed. My mom walked away to get something to drink and I took the opportunity to rest. I sat in my chair and just stared into the mirror to check things over, then closed my eyes for a second and took a few deep breaths.

"How are you feeling, Laci sweetheart?" Maggie asked in her sweet voice, still standing next to me.

"Oh, you know, nervous, excited, freaking out, a little tired, but overall pretty good," I replied as I tapped my foot rapidly on the floor with my heel.

"Well, you just take it easy for a bit. We've got a couple hours yet until things get started. Can I get you anything?"

"No, I'm fine. But thank you." She started to walk off, but she hesitated and turned back toward me, deep thoughts evident on her face.

"Laci, I never said anything before, and I know we didn't have the smoothest of starts, but I've always known you were the one." She smiled and picked up the brush next to my hand then slowly began to brush my hair, then continued. "The minute I saw Mitch's face that night he came to dinner, after meeting you that weekend, I knew something special had happened to him. The smile on his sweet face was one I hadn't seen in years and you put it there. I never meant to imply that you couldn't make it work when you came to visit. On the contrary, I said that to spur you to go after what you wanted—to choose his love despite the obstacles. I'm sorry if it didn't come across that way, but I'm glad you found your way back to each other. So thank you for loving him. I'm proud to have you as my daughter-in-law." She kissed the top of my head, gently laid the brush back down, and took a tissue from the box, wiping her tears as she walked away.

Her honesty and love for her son brought me to tears and I reached for a tissue to stop the incoming makeup destruction. I was amazed by her story and grateful she had shared it. Naturally, the butterflies in my stomach also got worse.

"I'm the one who should be thanking you," I said out loud to myself.

The music started to play and that meant the ceremony would begin soon, so Laura came in to help me into my dress. She unzipped the bag and pulled out my floor-length gown in the palest shade of soft pink. Her mouth dropped to the floor and she just looked at me with a huge smile on her face.

"It's pink! Where on earth did you find a pink dress? It's… it's amazing, Laci, just gorgeous. I can't wait to see it on you!" she said with tears in her eyes.

"Mom and I found it when she came up for Christmas. She didn't think I should get pink, so I didn't buy it that day, but when I went back it was still there and I knew that was the one. I didn't want white or even off-white. I wanted something representative of me, of my journey. Everywhere we go, there are pink ribbon pins and stickers, necklaces, shirts, and more—available for anyone who wants to identify with breast cancer. Maybe it's to support research, or identify themselves as a survivor or one who is still on the journey. But pink isn't just a color for little girls anymore; it's for those who have endured cancer, either firsthand or through their loved ones. Pink is powerful and beautiful, as are the women who have suffered, lived, and died from this horrible disease. I wanted to wear my pink dress in honor of them, of you and your mom, and me." I hugged her and we stood there holding each other, trying not to cry, but it didn't work.

Laura was only fourteen when she lost her mother to breast cancer. It drastically changed her future, but it also shaped and molded her into the beautiful woman she had become. It probably gave her even more resolve to beat her own cancer when she faced it a few years ago. And because of those experiences, she was able to help me, as she will continue to help and love others that cross her path on a daily basis. She would celebrate four years being cancer-free that year, and I was so thankful to God that we were both still there to celebrate that day together. I couldn't imagine my life without her friendship. She was my soul-sister, and the most amazing one I could have ever asked for. I stepped into the dress; the satin and silk material was soft on my skin. The bodice was tight, adorned with tiny sparkling rhinestones and pearls from my waist up. The same beading also decorated the shear straps that widened as they went up and over my shoulder. The sweetheart neck line dipped just slightly to show off the beautiful floating pearl necklace that my mom had brought for me to wear. But the gown was my favorite part. It was the same smooth satin, fitting close to my body and going all the way to the floor. On top, there was a loose, flowing layer of shear tool that trailed behind me to create a small train. The small appliqués sewn on the tool added a touch of elegance and old-fashioned charm that I loved. It was beautiful, and I loved wearing it, but I couldn't hardly wait until I would finally be able to take it off! I smiled at my inside thought and soaked in every moment.

"Laci, you look simply amazing," Laura said, tears sliding down her cheek.

There was a knock at the door, and then I heard his sweet voice. "Laci, it's Mitch. I need to talk to you darlin', before we go out there," he said in a serious tone and I looked at Laura with a look of fear in my face. That doesn't sound good. What could he want? Surely he wasn't having second thoughts…oh God please, not that – anything but that. Laura walked out the door and closed it behind her to give us some privacy. I walked over to the door so we could talk. Of course, we had to talk *through* the door, otherwise it would be considered bad luck if he saw me, violating all the traditional rules.

"Hey, handsome," I said in a chipper voice, masking my apprehension. "What's going on? Everything's okay, right?" I heard him giggle softly.

"Yeah, everything's all right. I...I just needed to hear your voice before everything starts. Things will be a little chaotic later, so I wanted you to know that I love you and I can't wait to be your husband. So, that's it I guess. I'll be the one waiting for you at the end of the aisle in the white tux. See you soon, Miss Kramer." He walked away. I rested my head against the door and smiled. I was even more anxious after our chat! Could we get on with the ceremony? Please?

I opened the door and looked around. "Dad! Where are you? It's time to go!" And he came around the corner, looking all "dad- like" in his dashingly handsome tux. I gave him a kiss on the cheek and we walked downstairs. My stomach jumped; I was filled with joy and excitement, but a little nervous too. Laura fluffed my hair and handed me my bouquet of pink and white tulips mixed with lavender and greenery, all tied together in pink satin ribbon that hung down in front of my dress. Emma walked up to me wearing her sweet, pink flower girl dress, and Travis stood tall and proud in his little tux, carrying his ring pillow and scratching his neck. I bent down and gave them a kiss, but I noticed that Travis was now scratching his arms and his legs too, and at closer examination, I realized he was covered with hives! Hives...of *all* the days and hours, he had to get hives *then!*

"Uh...Dad! You need to stall. We've got a little boy with bigger issues here."

My dad walked out and whispered in my mom's ear, then she spread the news to the others and we raced around to find Travis some medicine. Naturally my mom had a pharmacy in her purse and she carried antihistamines for every occasion. We cut one in half to simulate a child-sized dose and kept our fingers crossed that it would get better. Seeing as how he was still functional and not in pain, we made the decision to move forward with the ceremony. The music began again, and Emma and Travis walked out one at a time, going up the aisle and taking their place at the front of the barn. And then it was my turn!

I hooked my arm around my dad's and we started our journey. As I walked down the aisle, my favorite Lady Antebellum song was playing in the background: "Heart of the World." It seemed appropriate since it was about a wedding, wine, coffee—all our favorites, but mostly how she'll never *not* be his girl. That was me. I would be his girl forever…from this day forward.

We were inside the barn now. It was dusk out so the lights that lined the barn twinkled a little brighter. The most beautiful white and pink flowers had been placed all around on hay bales and a few hung from the chandeliers. White tulle was draped all around the ceiling, adding just the right touch of softness and elegance. It was what I had envisioned since the day he first brought me there and it was beautiful. White chairs were on both sides of me and I looked around to see our friends and family; some were crying, some were smiling, but all were watching me. My eyes, however, were now fixed on Mitch; his gaze was also locked on me. In that moment, he was the only one that mattered. His warm brown eyes sparkled under the lights as he watched me walk toward him and my heart sped up at the sight of him. He was so incredibly handsome standing there in his white tux. And although I couldn't stop by knees from shaking, I was anxious to be his in every way, so I picked up the pace as we walked down the aisle.

I stopped next to Mitch and my dad kissed me on the cheek, then sat down. I handed my bouquet to Laura. Brad was standing behind Mitch, smiling, and for once he looked truly happy for us. Mitch never took his eyes off of me though, and he took my hands in his and squeezed them tight. His eyes watered and he leaned over and whispered in my ear, "You look amazing, darlin'. Simply beautiful." I smiled and felt the heat rise in my cheeks. It was time for our vows.

"Laci Jean Kramer, we both boarded a plane to Phoenix not long ago. It was pouring down rain outside as I recall. You were the surprise of a lifetime and you stole my heart the minute I saw you in the seat next to mine. But I knew you were the one when you made fun of my Crawdads." And he smiled and laughed at the memory. "Today, I am the luckiest man alive because I get to put this ring on your finger and love you for the rest of your life. Nothing can separate us from the love we have—a love that was set in motion the day we met. Even cancer couldn't keep us apart, and although you tried pretty darn hard to let it, I always knew we would be together. It will be my honor to be your husband and love you through the good, the bad, and the beautiful days yet to come. I love you with all my heart, darlin'."

The tears poured down as I tried to find my voice to share mine. "Luke Mitchell Young," I said, as I choked back the tears, "you are my handsome Airplane Man, my creepy stalker Crawdad fan, my tall, sweet southern glass of iced tea, and I spotted you first!" I laughed, and the guests laughed along with me. "You had me blushing before you ever boarded that plane and you've been my 'one' ever since. It did rain that day, and on our first date, and I hope it will rain on us for years to come so we can enjoy what comes after the rain. Sometimes it will be sun, or maybe we'll see a rainbow, or it might just be a new way to look at our life, but it will always bring joy. It brought me you, and I thank God for you every day. I would be honored to be your wife, to love you and hold you all the days of my life. To give you strength when you have none, to lift you up when you are down, to make sweet wine with you, and laugh with you as we grow old together. I love you so much it hurts to spend even a few minutes away from you, and I hope that never changes as long as we live." I slid his ring over his left ring finger and held it tight as I shook nervously. He squeezed my hand and pulled me closer. The pastor quoted a few verses and began to pray, but I never heard one word of it. Instead, I heard the rumbling of thunder in the distance and I immediately lifted my head and looked at Mitch, my eyes as big as half dollars. He too was staring at me, about to laugh.

Within minutes, the thunder grew louder, and the rain poured down, straight and hard. Luckily it wasn't blowing so no one got wet, but Mitch and I couldn't help but laugh. The pastor obviously figured out what was going on and ended his prayer. In his loudest voice, he announced, "Ladies and gentleman, it is my pleasure to introduce you to Mr. and Mrs. Mitchell Young! You may kiss your bride, Mr. Young," the pastor said with a smile.

And with those words, he was mine. I was Mrs. Mitch Young! Finally! His arms wrapped around me and his sweet lips found mine. A passionate and fierce fire ignited between us and our guests were now clapping and hollering in the background as the rain kept pouring down. I wanted more, but I knew it was time we got inside the winery to greet our guests and enjoy the festivities yet to come.

We ran down the aisle and out of the barn, and then Mitch just stopped! He stood there staring at me in the rain and he grabbed my face, pulling me close and kissing me again. Guests followed us and cheered as we stood there – my dress, my hair, and my face all sopping wet. I didn't care; it was our rain.

After we got inside, I went up to change into my "after" dress, dried my hair, and freshened up. Mitch did the same and then we came down to join the party. Hugs, kisses, dancing, laughter, and lots of good wine filled the room inside the winery. The music was blaring and everyone was having a great time. It was a day I would never forget.

"So, Mrs. Young," Mitch said, pulling me into his arms on the dance floor. "What do you say we get out of here and go have a little party of our own?" he asked, a coy smile spread across his face.

"Why, Mr. Young...I do declare...are you propositioning me?" I asked in my fake southern belle voice.

"As I recall, I'm requesting those free services that come with a signed marriage license," he replied.

"Now *that* is a romantic offer, indeed. How could I refuse?" I laughed and kissed him, then whispered in his ear. "What's mine...is now yours." And I smiled.

We went upstairs to grab our bags, then came down to say goodbye.

"Well, little brother, you did it. I'm happy for you," Brad said. "Thanks, Brad, for everything."

"Now, get out of here and go enjoy your wife." And Brad shook Mitch's hand and hugged him tight.

The girls gathered around me and we said our goodbyes, sharing a few more tears together. Then it was time to say goodbye to the kids. We were leaving them in Maggie's care while we honeymooned; she was their new grandmother. But I was happy that they would have that time to get to know each other. She needed them as much as they needed her. We gave the kids a kiss and hug goodbye, then we walked out to our limo that escorted us into Greensboro.

Mitch's mom had given us a suite at a fancy hotel so we could enjoy our wedding night before we flew off on our honeymoon the next day. After arriving at the hotel, I went into the bathroom to get ready and looked in the mirror at the small scars made from the incisions, wondering if they would bother him. I had waited for this night for such a long time and wanted everything to be perfect, but nervous at the thought. I decided to put it out of my mind and knew that he loved me enough to overlook them. I put on my robe and walked out to find Mitch standing on our private balcony, staring into the night sky. Every star above was hanging out for us to see and the view of the city lights illuminated the ground below. He turned to look at me and stared; my robe was slightly agape to entice him back inside. He walked toward me, picked me up in his arms, and carried me to bed.

After an amazing week in Italy, mostly spent drinking more wine than I had in my lifetime and making love as often as possible, we flew home to begin our new life. Preparations for the winery's grand opening began. I had more fun setting up my new kitchen, cooking our meals, and living in our new house than I ever thought possible. My energy had waned since the honey- moon though, and it didn't seem to be getting any better.

Before I left Washington, my oncologist, Dr. Conley, had coordinated the transfer of my care to a local oncologist in Greensboro named Dr. Blythe. She wanted to make sure my follow-up care was in good hands and Dr. Blythe was the best in the area. Thankfully, my appointment was that week and we would be able to address my fatigue. She ran a few tests and told us everything I was experiencing was normal. I had just experienced an intense time of excitement and stress, albeit good stress, but my body wasn't quite ready to cope with the aftereffects yet.

We left there feeling hopeful. And, later that week, she called to let us know that my sonogram and MRI results both came back normal and showed no signs of cancer. The treatment had worked. An enormous weight lifted from my shoulders, and I felt like I had just been given the gift of life. Mitch hugged me tight and we celebrated the news by taking the kids out for dinner on the town.

"Mitch, you haven't shown me one bottle of wine yet for the grand opening. When do I get to see the label? Where are you hiding them?" I asked at the table.

"Yeah, about that. I've been sort of hiding them from you on purpose. It's a surprise," he said.

"The wine is a surprise, for me?"

"Yep, Brad and I are doing something special at the grand opening. You'll just have to wait and see."

And I waited, but I constantly bugged him throughout the week for hints—which he never gave! So aggravating at times, my new, sexy husband…and I loved saying that…husband!

———◦◦◦◦◦———

It was a warm April night, warmer than usual at nearly eighty degrees for that time of year. The grand opening of the Young Vines Winery had arrived and everything was ready to go. Almost everything, that is. I still hadn't seen our main wine labeled for sale that night. I started nosing around every nook and cranny in the winery but to no avail. He had hidden it well.

Guests started to arrive and before long, we had a full house. People were sitting at the long bar tasting wine, eating food, and shopping in the wine store that we had stocked with anything wine-related we could find. I was stationed in the wedding barn at my events table, showing off pictures of our wedding to hope- fully sell the barn's potential to anyone that might be interested. Within the first hour, I had two events booked for May. Mitch came out on the porch and with a cordless microphone in his hand, he made an announcement.

"Ladies and gentlemen, if I could get everyone to come inside the winery for a few minutes, I have a very special announcement to make," he said. What announcement? Why hadn't he told me about his announcement earlier? We're supposed to be partners in this little venture and he was already leaving me out of the loop...I could tell this was going to work out splendidly.

Everyone walked inside and gathered around. Boxes were stacked on the bar, covered with blankets to hide them from sight. I walked over next to Mitch and gave him a confused look. He just smiled and gave me a kiss, then said, "Don't worry, it's your surprise, so just relax and enjoy it." Mitch climbed up on a tall chair so he could see above the crowd, then he made his announcement.

"I'd like to thank you for coming out tonight. My wife, my brother Brad, and I are all honored to have you at our new winery. It's been an exciting time for us getting this place up and running and finding grape suppliers from across the country to make the fine wine you have tasted so far tonight. But there is one wine we wanted to save for last and it's very special to me." Mitch hopped off the chair, turned behind him, and took a bottle out of an open box behind him. He climbed back up on the chair and raised the bottle up for everyone to see.

"This is Young Vines' premier label of the year. It's called Laci's Rain, and it's a late harvest Riesling made from the finest grapes found in the state of Washington which is where my beautiful wife lived before marrying me. I've dedicated this label to her and her love of the rain." He looked down at me and smiled. I was already crying, a complete basket case. He continued.

"You see, Laci believes that the rain holds hope, that it washes away the old to bring in new joys of life, and I happen to agree. Our journey to find each other began with rain and we were married in the rain, but in the middle of our whirlwind romance, she developed breast cancer and life changed for us. She even tried to dump me." He smiled and the guests laughed softly. "She was diagnosed early thanks to her personal routine and regular checkups. Because of that early detection, her cancer was found and removed, and she is now on the road to a cancer-free life. Laci is the second love of my life and I wouldn't be standing here today if it weren't for her giving me the courage and strength I needed to believe I still had love in my future. *Her* love. You see, I lost my first wife to breast cancer too, so when I found out about Laci's diagnosis, it was a personal struggle for me as well." The crowd, now completely silent, listened intently to his story.

"This label shows a small, pink ribbon in the corner, in honor of both men and women who have struggled with this disease. And today, if you purchase a bottle of Laci's Rain, we will donate twenty-five percent of the proceeds to a local, nonprofit organization that specializes in helping patients deal with the effects of breast cancer before, during, and after diagnosis. They have full-time psycho-oncologists on staff to run their survivorship program, and it's one of the best in our state. They've already reached out to us about Laci's follow-up care and their doctors and staff are, without a doubt, all about caring for the patient and their families during this time. I want to make sure we give what- ever we can to help them keep doing their job. So, before I let you come up and taste it, I'd like to introduce my wife, Laci," he said, and he reached his hand out to me to pull me up on the chair with him, wet, makeup-stained face and all. Everyone clapped, cheered and whistled, and I was never so embarrassed in my life. I buried my head in Mitch's shoulder to hide the tears.

"Thank you so much! And without delaying the fun anymore, please come up and taste our Riesling, and take a bottle, or two, or three, home with you tonight." Everyone laughed which lightened the moment. Meanwhile, I was still crying, amazed at what the man had just done for me. I was speechless.

We climbed down off the chair and he held me in his arms, brushing my wet hair from my eyes.

"Are you surprised, darlin'?" he asked. But I just shook my head back and forth, not able to say a word. He laughed and hugged me tight. "It's okay, I do that to women, I know." He laughed.

"You are too much...I..." I gasped for air in between sobs. "Thank you, thank you so much, Mitch. I love you!" I threw my arms around him and held him tight.

The grand opening was a success, and we sold over five hundred bottles of wine that night alone. The Young Vines Winery even made the local news, and we were in the papers the next morning. My wine had also become quite popular online, selling to people all over the United States. I thought I was a marketing professional, but in my wildest dreams, I never imagined the success it would have. And the best part is that he never intended it as a marketing campaign for the winery; it was about his love for me and giving back to others that could help those like me.

And that was now my goal as well, to help others. Along with my job at the winery, I started the Treats for Treatment program and recruited hundreds of men and women to provide baked goods and snacks to the local cancer treatment center for patients and their families. Emma loved to bake so we were able to do it together, and it taught her about the joys of volunteering and helping others at a young age.

I also became a strong advocate of breast cancer awareness and early detection practices, speaking to various women's groups and organizations around the local area, and I even served on the board of a local women's cancer research foundation.

Mitch, the kids, and I had all settled into our new life here at Crystal Creek and I was happier than I had been in a long, long time, with only the best yet to come.

Fall was already upon us and the trees around the cabin had already started to change color. Mitch and I sat on our front porch, enjoying a glass of wine together after dinner and I looked over at him and smiled.

"What?"

"Nothing. Just thinking that I'm madly in love with you," I said softly.

"Hmmm…I like the sound of that, darlin'. Why don't you *show* me how madly in love you really are?" he replied, leaning over to kiss me.

I laughed out loud, and out of nowhere, it started to rain, just a light shower. I figured it was as good a time to tell him as any.

"Oh, I'll show you all right." I stood up, walked over, and stood in front of him. He wrapped his arms around my waist and I put my hands around his neck, running my fingers through his hair. Then I pulled one of his arms away from me, took hold of his hand, and gently placed it on my stomach. "In about 9 months." And I smiled.

We were all changed in some way by everything that happened that year. We were not the same people we once were before the cancer. But in the face of adversity, God never left us. Our faith in him kept it all together and gave us hope—hope in life, in love, and even a little hope…in the rain.

notes from the author

Each year, one out of every eight women will be diagnosed with breast cancer in their lifetime. It's one of the most common cancers among women in America and the second leading cause of cancer deaths in women. Fortunately, death rates have been steadily declining since 1989, believed to be the result of early detection through screening, increased awareness, and improved treatment. At this time, there are over 2.8 million breast cancer survivors in the United States![1]

My dear friend, Laura Tinnin-Lewis was diagnosed with breast cancer in 2009, only three months after her wedding day. Like many women, the disease was hereditary. She lost her mother to breast cancer in 1974, long before there were pink ribbons and 'walks for the cure'. Although Laura's experience did not require a mastectomy, it was devastating to her all the same – both emotionally and physically. After she initially received the news, she worried that her mother's death would be her own, but thankfully she has been cancer free for four years now. *Praise God!* I used Laura's real-life experience with breast cancer in this book as a way to honor her and help raise awareness to others about the importance of having an annual exam to improve the chances of early detection. It could save your life!

After seventeen years, through many life events both good and bad, we are still the best of friends. She is the most giving and kind woman I have ever known and my life has been truly blessed by her friendship and love.

To celebrate our friendship, and the completion of this book, Laura and I visited Charlotte, NC last summer and even attended a Hickory Crawdad game in Hickory, NC, donned with our pink Crawdad hats adorned with a rhinestone pink ribbon. And we look forward to celebrating her fifth cancer-free year together, at a Crawdad game!

1   Americancancersociety.com/2013 Statistics

(Pictured left to right: Laura Lewis, Joey Gallo-Hickory Crawdad player, and Sandy Sinnett, Author)

CPSIA information can be obtained
at www.ICGtesting.com
Printed in the USA
FFHW011048041219
56476150-62284FF